Too much.

Elena tasted exactly as he'd imagined—of woman and exotic spices, of sunshine and passion. Bemused, confused, more aroused than he'd ever been, he fought himself. He wouldn't—couldn't—allow this flood of sensation, of longing.

Shivering, she moaned low in her throat, and he deepened the kiss, his body reacting to the quick catch of her breath. The wolf inside him snarled, agitated. He wanted to mate, now.

Elena used her tongue against his, urgent. Hot. He craved more. He ached to bury himself inside her welcoming softness. To claim her. *Mate.*

No. Not possible. Not for him. Somehow he dredged up the strength to push away. "I'm sorry," he snarled. "I wish I could say that won't happen again, but I can't."

Books by Karen Whiddon

Silhouette Nocturne

*Cry of the Wolf #7
*Touch of the Wolf #12
*Dance of the Wolf #45

*The Pack

KAREN WHIDDON

started weaving fanciful tales for her younger brothers at the age of eleven. Amidst the Catskill Mountains of New York, then the Rocky Mountains of Colorado, she fueled her imagination with the natural beauty of the rugged peaks, and spun stories of love that captivated her family.

Karen now lives in North Texas, where she shares her life with her very own hero of a husband and three doting dogs. Also an entrepreneur, she divides her time between the business she started and writing the contemporary romantic-suspense and paranormal romances that readers enjoy. You can e-mail Karen at KWhiddon1@aol.com or write to her at P.O. Box 820807, Fort Worth, TX 76182. Fans of her writing can also check out her Web site, www.KarenWhiddon.com.

DANCE OF THE WOLF

KAREN WHIDDON

Silhouette Books

nocturne™

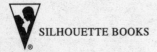

SILHOUETTE BOOKS

ISBN-13: 978-0-373-61792-0
ISBN-10:   0-373-61792-5

DANCE OF THE WOLF

www.silhouettenocturne.com

Printed in U.S.A.

Dear Reader,

Thanks to all of you who have written me to let me know you love THE PACK. I'm glad you enjoy reading the stories as much as I enjoy writing them. Since the first Pack book came out in 2004, I've had a ringside seat to view these stories unfolding around me. The men and women in these books have become special to me, and with each new book I'm able to explore different aspects of their diverse lives.

Being a shape-shifter brings the word *diversity* to a new level. In real life, there will always be those who can't look past the outside to see the real person within, just as there are those who celebrate the differences and similarities among all of us. In most of these books, I explore the dynamics of the human/shifter relationship. It always fascinates me to see how my hero or heroine reacts upon learning there is more to the world than at first the eye can see.

I hope you enjoy *Dance of the Wolf.* When I originally came up with the title, I envisioned Dr. Jared Gies, a man once crippled by a car accident, finally dancing with the love of his life, Elena Cabrera. While he doesn't actually *physically* dance, I believe his spirit does, in celebration of the freedom of the love he finally finds.

Look for my next Pack book, working title *Wild Wolf,* to be published by Silhouette Nocturne in 2009.

Until next time, happy reading!

Karen Whiddon

As always, to my wonderful husband, Lonnie,
truly the love of my life.

Chapter 1

"Missing? The show starts in fifteen minutes. What do you mean he's missing?" Elena Cabrera stared at her older sister, Joy, who worked part-time helping Elena run her nightclub. Even dressed in a black silk evening gown, per Fantasies' strict dress code, Joy managed to look nurturing rather than sexy, something that irked her to no end.

"No one can find him." Joy twisted her hands. "I even called his grandmother's apartment. His brother said he hadn't seen him since yesterday."

They both knew it was only a ten-minute walk from the apartment to Fantasies. Damien usually enjoyed the exercise.

Elena struggled to hold back panic. Ever since she'd seen a man she'd trusted change into something else, her

world had been shaky. If men could become beasts…
shuddering, she pushed away the thought. If she kept
worrying about it, soon she'd be scrutinizing everyone,
looking for signs that they were like Charles Watkins.

"I'm worried." Elena bit her lip. "This is so not like
him. Damien's reliable."

"Damien's *weird*. And now, he's disappeared," Joy
repeated. "Ever since you fired Dr. Watkins, all the employees have been restless."

"Restless?" This was the first she'd heard about that.
"What do you mean?"

Joy shrugged. "Unsettled. Uneasy. I've even heard
them mention something about discrimination."

Discrimination? Elena nearly snorted. As if one
could discriminate against a monster! Of course, her
sister didn't know about Watkins. Elena hadn't told
anyone what she'd seen. If she had, the men in white
coats would be coming for her with a straitjacket. "I
didn't fire him. After all, he didn't work for me."

"Same difference. You let him run his clinic here.
Then you two fought." Joy crossed her arms. "And he
disappeared." Leaning close, she eyed her sister. "I
know there's something you're not telling me."

Oh, was there ever. But no way could Elena ever reveal the truth. *Werewolves didn't exist.* Or…did they?

Belatedly she realized Joy's frown had deepened.
"Elena, what really happened with you two?"

"Nothing. We dated a few times. Nothing serious."
He'd only told her he loved her, and then shown her
what he could become. For a man who preferred to be
called by his last name, he'd moved into intimacy fast.

Joy knew how Elena felt about rash decisions. After all, Elena still blamed herself for their younger cousin's death years ago when they'd all been children. Though the family had told her repeatedly over the years that there'd been nothing she could have done to save him, she still carried the guilt inside her. Never mind that he'd been born with an undetected congenital heart defect— the fact that she'd been playing tag with him when he collapsed made her believe she'd inadvertently killed him.

Elena had been a solemn child, a studious teenager, determined to make no waves, cause no one pain. She'd shunned casual affairs, eschewed dating, preferring her studies instead. She'd been the first in her family to graduate from high school as valedictorian, the first to attend college.

Then her aunt had died and, to the surprise of everyone, left Fantasies to Elena. Though running a male strip club had been a far cry from the career she'd planned in medicine, Elena had felt this was another way to atone for the loss of her cousin, that same aunt's son. She'd dropped out of college and taken over Fantasies, where she strived to be a friend and/or mother figure to all her employees.

Blinking, she forced her thoughts back to the present. "We can talk about Watkins later. I'm seriously worried about Damien. Something must have happened to him." Werewolf attack? "He's never been late before."

"Maybe he went looking for Dr. Watkins."

Elena stared. "Why would he do that?"

"They were friends. A lot of the dancers liked him. Since no one's heard from him, maybe Damien thought he could find him."

Picking up the phone, Elena dialed the front desk. One of the hostesses answered. "Any sign of Damien?"

"No, Miss Elena. He hasn't checked in. I talked with Bob a couple of minutes ago and he hasn't seen him, either."

Bob was her full-time security guard. An ex-cop, he patrolled the place as if he were guarding a harem. Which he was, in a way. Did Bob know about Watkins? Was Bob *like* Watkins? She had to stop. If she kept thinking like this, she'd drive herself crazy.

"Call me if he shows," Elena ordered.

After hanging up, she fished her cell phone from her pocket and scrolled down until she saw Damien's name. This time, she let it ring twenty-two times. No answer. She knew they didn't have an answering machine. Mama DeLeon must not be near the phone.

"Damn it!" She frowned at Joy. It was Monday night, the slowest of the week, but still, the show must go on. "Tell Ryan and the rest of the guys to move up their spots to cover Damien's."

Joy nodded. "What are you going to do?" She checked her watch. "We open in fifteen minutes."

"Find him, of course. Watch things for me." Already moving, Elena snatched her sweater off the back of her chair as she headed out the door.

Because Fantasies opened at nine, the late-March sky had already turned black. The cool air felt good, so she tied the sweater around her waist. Dirty streetlights illuminated her small parking lot as she crossed the aisles, heading toward the sidewalk.

Her stilettos tapped the concrete. Her long, maroon

evening gown would have looked completely out of place, if people hadn't known who she was. But this block of downtown Dallas completely emptied after the office workers went home, and most visitors to the area were there for her club.

Elena focused on her goal. She had to find Damien. The youngest of her dancers, he was more like an adopted son than an employee.

Damien's mother had been a hard-core crack addict. His father had been in the penitentiary since before Damien's birth, and Damien lived with his grandmother, a kindhearted, elderly woman known as Mama DeLeon. Damien had been broke, afraid and strung out when he'd stumbled into the back door of her club looking for a handout.

Becoming first his friend, then a mother figure, Elena knew Damien would never skip out on her. He'd call if he couldn't make it. Something was wrong—she only hoped whatever it was wasn't as bad as her overactive imagination conjured up.

She kept seeing Watkins, his body changing, his bones becoming different shapes, his skin growing a covering of dark hair. No longer human, but wolf.

A werewolf. Watkins had been an honest-to-God werewolf. She shuddered. Damien had hung around him. She couldn't help but wonder if werewolves ate humans. For Damien's sake, she hoped not.

Damien's grandmother's apartment was four blocks from Fantasies. Though the area got rougher away from the club, she wasn't worried. Everyone around here knew her, and those who didn't soon learned the others watched out for her. Anyone noting her long-legged stride could see she had a destination, a purpose. No one would mess with her.

Intent on her goal, crossing the deserted street, she didn't notice the black Mercedes swerving around the curve. Neither she nor the car hesitated, only missing a beat at the moment of impact, the force of which flung her onto the hood of the Mercedes hard enough to crack the windshield.

Christ! Dr. Jared Gies never saw the woman, not until the instant his right front bumper caught her squarely in the hip. He slammed on his brakes but it was too late—she'd been doomed from the second she'd stepped in front of his car.

His fault. He'd been driving too fast, intent on too much else but the road—hell hounds! He was a doctor. Sworn to save and heal, not kill. If he'd killed this woman he might as well take a gun to his own head. He hadn't hit her that hard, had he? Had he?

Pulling over to the curb, he climbed from his car, grabbed his cane and rushed to her crumpled body. *Don't let her be dead, don't let her be dead* repeated over and over inside his head, a frantic litany.

Sometimes being a medical doctor had its pluses, even if he hadn't done emergency-room work in years. He located a pulse and then began checking for broken bones. The possibility of internal injuries he could do nothing about now. Not here, not without X-rays and CTs and MRIs.

She was alive. No doubt the impact had given her a

concussion, but miraculously he saw no obvious injuries. He needed to get her to the hospital immediately. Standing, he glanced around for help.

No one. The accident hadn't drawn one single bystander. Without witnesses, he had no way to prove she'd stepped right in front of his car and that hitting her had been unavoidable. Figured. His normal lack of luck, rearing its ugly head.

He should have gone the direct route to Fantasies from the freeway, but he'd wanted to check out the area. His bad luck. And hers—the woman he'd hit.

But she *was* alive. Her pulse was steady, normal even. Her breathing was fine, not labored or shallow. Excellent signs.

Pulling his cell phone from his pocket, he flipped it open—and realized the battery had gone dead. "Damn it." He must have forgotten to charge the stupid thing. Unlike most other men he knew, electronics never worked for him. Everything either ran down or blew up, and he lacked the patience to make repairs.

Cursing, he shoved the phone back in his jacket pocket. Okay, fine. He didn't need paramedics anyway—he was a doctor after all. He'd take care of this quietly, without incident. No way this patient—er, woman—was dying on him. He wasn't about to add murder to his extensive litany of sins.

With the dispassionate gaze of a seasoned physician, he looked her over. Why was a beautiful woman in an evening gown strolling the sidewalks downtown at night?

Hah. Why else? Cynical, he let his gaze roam over her, taking in her tiny waist and high breasts. She was

Hispanic, lovely, and damned if something about her didn't look familiar. Since lately he'd avoided the hospital like the plague and hadn't seen any patients just before the hospital administrators suspended him, he knew he hadn't diagnosed her at the hospital. They assigned him only the weird cases, the ones no one else could figure out. He tended to remember those.

Then why…? No. He did a double take. What the hell? *Her.* The very woman he'd come looking for. He recognized her from Fantasies's Web site photos. Elena Cabrera herself. And he'd managed to run her down. Stone-cold sober, too.

Could fate slap him in the face any harder?

Again he studied her. She was more beautiful than he'd expected—the photographs didn't do her justice. On the Web, she'd looked merely attractive. But now, under the soft glow of the streetlight, her thick, dark hair complemented her creamy, olive skin. Even unconscious, in person she was compellingly beautiful.

Inside, his wolf stirred, restless. Shocked—he hadn't felt his alter ego at all in the weeks since he'd completed his court-ordered rehab—he rocked back on his heels.

Could it be he was ready to try and change? What was it about Elena Cabrera that brought his wolf self to life?

Staring at her, something clicked inside him. For the space of a heartbeat, he felt the oddest sense of connection, as though he'd been waiting for this woman his entire life.

Wha…? He snorted. Those stupid rose-colored

glasses they'd forced on him in rehab must have rubbed off after all.

She was nothing to him. He didn't know her, had never met her, and if she seemed amazingly attractive, it was only his libido talking. Too bad she *wasn't* a prostitute. He hadn't had sex since before he'd entered rehab and gone clean.

Nor would he. Yet. Until he could find one of his own kind, willing to have a bit of recreational sex, he'd stay celibate. Relationships with humans were too damn messy. His life was complicated enough without adding that to the mix, thank you.

And this woman was definitely human.

She moaned, her eyelids fluttering.

Inside, his wolf whimpered.

Weird. Rubbing the back of his neck, he suppressed the ever-constant urge to pop a pill. He often wondered why no one else seemed to realize that life was a lot stranger without the numbing haze of pain meds.

Again she stirred. He slid his hand under her head, willing her to wake. "It's all right," he soothed. "I'm a doctor. You're safe."

"Who are you?" Long-lashed eyes the color of caramel stared at him, blinking in confusion. She lifted her small hand, placing her fingers along his jaw, making him shudder. "What happened?"

"Don't move." Gently he removed her hand and restrained her. "You were hurt. I don't know how badly."

"I'm fine." Pushing him away, she tried to sit up. When her third try failed, he grabbed her elbow to help her, his heart hammering in his throat as her velvet gaze met his.

"Do I know you?" she asked. "You look…familiar."

There it was again. That strange sensation, akin to falling. Either he'd completely lost his mind, or he needed to go away on a long vacation.

"No." He shook his head. "Are you all right?" Best doctor voice. Detached, professional, infused with the perfect amount of concern. He hadn't used that voice in months.

"I think so." She swallowed. "Are you sure we don't know each other?"

Even her words made his chest tighten. "We've never met. And I really don't think you're all right."

"I don't know. My head hurts. I was walking and then…" Her lovely eyes widened. "A car hit me," she whispered. "A black Mercedes…yours?"

He nodded, suppressing the urge to use his thumb to caress her fingers. "Didn't your mother teach you to look both ways before you cross the street?"

"What?" She stared, not comprehending.

Internally he winced, wondering why sarcasm was always his first defense. Still, the words had been said and all he could do was back them up with bravado. "I wondered why you didn't look before you crossed the street."

"Hello?" She blinked. Twin spots of color flushed her cheeks a dusky rose. "Pedestrians always have the right-of-way and you were speeding. And you hit me!"

Before he could stop her, she pushed herself to her feet, weaving and wobbling. She had to clutch at his arm to keep from falling.

She tried to walk away, making it five steps before

she crumpled to her knees. "That hurt." Yet she again struggled to rise.

"What is wrong with you?" He helped steady her. "Let me take you to the hospital. You might have a concussion."

"No." She shook her head, the effort making her wince. "I can't. I'm fine. Just a little bruised, that's all. I've got to find Damien."

"You're not finding anyone right now. You're in no condition—"

"I'm *fine*." She cut him off. "Don't worry about me."

Right. He'd just slammed into her with his car, and she was fine. He didn't even have to be a doctor to know she lied.

In days past he would have taken a step back and spouted off another of his infamous sarcastic remarks, knowing there were nurses and machines to back him up. Now, he had no such things, and he wanted more than anything for this woman to be all right. Still, humility never came easy, especially to him, and he had to swallow back a retort.

Instead he hushed her. "We don't know how badly you're hurt. Why don't you let me take you to Parkland?"

"Absolutely not. I don't need a hospital." Her eyes looked huge, unfocused. "Don't you understand? Damien's missing. I've got to find my dancer." Pushing him away, to his stunned disbelief, she tried again. Weaving, she took a wobbly step. Then another. Though she moved like a drunk, she kept at it. Picking up momentum, she hobbled away.

"Wait."

She ignored him. Swearing, he stared after her in disbelief as she weaved down the sidewalk, moving away from him.

"Elena—Ms. Cabrera." He lurched after her, and even with his limp, he caught up with her easily, grabbing her arm. "Your leg, is it—?"

She froze. "How do you know me?"

"Charles Watkins is my friend." He swallowed. "Uh… Look, you're not all right. Let me—"

"I *said*, I'm *fine*." She shook off his hand. "Do you know where Watkins is?"

"No." He spoke carefully, keeping his inflection neutral and his face expressionless. "We were good friends, once. Then he took a job at another hospital and— Well, it's not your problem." He took a deep breath, limping alongside her.

"Why are you looking for him now?"

"He called me yesterday out of the blue, sounding really strange. Said he was in trouble and needed my help. He mentioned you and your club. We got disconnected before he could tell me anything else. I called the number back and there was no answer, so I went by his apartment. His neighbor said he hasn't been home in weeks."

"Sorry. I have no idea where he is." Jaw set, she tried to increase her stride, barely succeeding. Her hobble became more pronounced the faster she attempted to walk. Pain showed in the tense set of her mouth and in the hollows of her face.

Even with his bad leg, he easily kept pace with her.

Finally she gave up and simply stopped, though her

gaze continually scanned their surroundings. "What do you want?"

Here, on this darkened sidewalk in the inner city, he both marveled and disparaged her lack of fear. Despite his story, for all she knew, he could be a serial killer or rapist, intent on inflecting harm.

"I told you, I'm looking for Watkins. I was hoping you'd know how to reach him."

"No." She looked away. "We had an argument about two weeks ago and I haven't seen him since. He was using an office in my club to run a free clinic."

At least she was honest, even if she didn't say everything. He studied her closely. The most shocking thing Watkins had said before they were cut off was that he'd let her see him change. That meant he'd viewed her as a potential mate. Obviously she didn't know enough to recognize another shifter when she saw one.

Good thing for him. Watkins had said she'd been horrified. Jared intuited this had something to do with his friend's troubles.

Which led to another question. Did the woman who apparently despised shifters have something to do with Watkins's disappearance?

On the move again, she barely looked at him. "Now, if you're done questioning me, let me go. I've got to find my dancer. He was due to go on first and didn't show. I'm worried about him."

Leg aching, he used his cane to propel himself forward. "Look, you're hurt and I'm crippled." Deliberately he used the cruel word, watching her wince. "Walking unprotected in these surroundings isn't a good idea."

"Damien's apartment building is only two more blocks. It'd take longer to go back and get your car than it will to walk." She lurched forward. "Plus, they know me around here. No one will mess with us. So, you can either come with me or stay here. It doesn't matter to me."

Another curse, and he caught up to her. "Do you want to use my cane?" If she took him up on his offer, he'd be in big trouble, but he wasn't worried. People like her never did the self-serving thing.

He wasn't wrong. "No, thank you." Then she smiled, lighting up her entire face and transforming her from merely a good-looking woman to an absolutely stunning one.

Mine.

No. Such a thing wasn't possible for him. In the days after the car wreck, his mother had sat by his hospital bed while he drifted in and out of consciousness. Vividly he remembered her tears when the doctors had said he'd never walk again.

Worse, he remembered his older brother, John—an ordained priest—had been furious in his disappointment. Even his most powerful prayers hadn't been able to help Jared. Father John had washed his hands of Jared then, retreating behind his sanctimonious robes to avoid him. At least, that was how it had seemed to Jared.

Damaged shifters, especially recovering drug addicts like him, were expressly discouraged from mating. And he was damaged in more ways than one. So when he looked at this woman and thought, *mate,* he knew he was wrong. Jared Gies would never have a mate, whether human or shifter.

He looked up, realizing that while he'd been thinking, she'd continued to move and, despite her hobble, was getting farther and farther away.

Launching into a string of curses under his breath, he took a deep breath and hurried after her. "Wait—I'll go with you."

She didn't even look at him. "That's not necessary. You've made it perfectly clear you don't care about my dancer."

Panting, hating that he was out of breath and she appeared barely winded, he glared at her. "Lady, I don't even know your dancer. All I've been doing is trying to help you, but you won't let me."

They'd reached a derelict apartment building. One section of the wrought iron fence—obviously once meant to keep out criminals—had fallen down in a huge, rusted pile. The peeling paint and cracked brick made him wonder what the inside of the building would look like.

He shuddered. "Your dancer lives here?"

"Yes." In the yellow glow of the dim streetlights, her worried expression seemed softer. "He lives with his grandmother and brother, Freddie. I'm hoping they might have seen or heard from him."

He nodded. As she picked her way over the fence, he gripped his cane and debated the easiest route.

"Are you coming?" She shot a pointed look at his cane. "Or do you want to wait here?"

Mentally flipping her the bird, he struggled over the fence, using his cane to boost his still-weak leg over.

When they were side by side again, she touched his arm. "What happened to you?"

"Car accident."

At that, she stopped. "The same one Watkins was in?"

"That would be the one."

"You must be the friend he talked about. He said you were nearly killed."

Instead of a response, he gave a noncommittal grunt.

"And…" Again her gaze drifted to his leg. "He said you were in a wheelchair."

"I was." Now he did take her arm, propelling her forward. "Let's go. It's not safe here."

The fact that she didn't try to shake him off told him she, too, had noticed the group of men taking great pains to remain in the shadows.

For the first time in his life, Jared found himself wishing he owned a gun.

As they approached the first set of buildings, two of the men detached themselves from the group and moved into the light.

Jared tensed. The only weapon he had was his cane. That, and his wolf self's sharp teeth and claws.

In other words, he and Elena were in trouble.

Slowing her pace—why the hell wasn't she running? At least she had two good legs—Elena faced the men.

"Hey, Freddie," she said softly. "Lou. I'm looking for Damien."

The taller of the men snorted. Taking a closer look, Jared realized he was a shifter. All shifters could recognize each other by the energy they emitted—what some called the aura.

"You know my brother's been keepin' to himself lately. We don't hardly see much of him 'round here no more. Just comin' and goin', thas all."

Elena gave a loud sigh. "Is Mama DeLeon still up?"

"She don't go to bed till midnight most nights. Habit, she says." Freddie chuckled. "Who's the dude?"

Dude. He meant him. Jared opened his mouth to tell the younger man it was none of his business, but the hard squeeze Elena gave his arm made him bite his tongue.

"He's a friend," she said. "He's also looking for someone."

"Yes." Jared cleared his throat. "Charles Watkins. Dr. Watkins. Do you know him?"

No one responded.

As the silence began to grow uncomfortable, Elena cleared her throat. "Can I talk to Mama DeLeon?"

"Sure, come on." Pivoting on his heel, Freddie glided toward the second building. As they followed, Jared's lurching gait felt even more ungainly.

The inside of the cramped apartment was as bad as he had imagined. Though it looked clean, the dingy walls and prevailing odor of some awful, unidentifiable smell brought to mind death and decay. He shook off the awful images and focused on the tiny, wrinkled black woman huddled under a faded velvet afghan.

"Miss Elena!" Struggling to rise, Mama DeLeon finally gave up and snuggled deeper into her coverlet. She glanced at Jared. "Who's this?" she cackled. "A beau?"

"He's a friend." Elena dismissed him with a wave of the hand. "I'm trying to find Damien. He didn't show up for work tonight."

Mama DeLeon shook her head. "I knowed somethin' was wrong with him."

"Wrong? Is he sick?"

"He was. I'm worried about him. He sure 'nuff was actin' different. All twitchy and jumpy and looking over his shoulder. When I asked him what was wrong, he said nerves."

Jared shook his head. Sounded like drugs to him.

"Did you ask him what he was nervous about?" Elena's calm, reasonable tone belied her earlier panic.

"He wouldn't say. I'm worried." The old woman wheezed. "If Damien's sick, he should be here at home."

"I know." Elena patted the woman's age-spotted hand. "I'm worried, as well. But I'm looking for him. I promise to let you know when I've found him."

"You tell that boy to call me."

"I will." Kissing the wrinkled cheek, Elena let Freddie shepherd them out the door.

Once they were back outside in the chilly night air, Freddie turned to Elena. "Damien and Dr. Watkins are involved in some bad shit."

"Be specific." Jared grabbed his arm. "What do you mean?"

Immediately Freddie knocked his hand away. "Be cool, bro."

Jared froze. But his stillness wasn't due to the tall man's threat. For the second time in months, his wolf had awakened inside him and struggled to get out.

His wolf wanted to fight.

Heart pounding, Jared pushed the wolf down, closing reinforced iron bars on a mental cage. It was a trick he'd taught himself after the accident six years ago, when he'd been bedridden in the hospital. Over time, he'd found the wolf stirred less and less. Why it was stirring now, worried him. Still, he forced himself to appear calm, to focus on the other man.

But Freddie seemed to feel he'd said enough. The shifter in him appeared to sense something of the struggle inside Jared. He backed away, his expression wary.

"Come on," Elena said in what he was beginning to think of as her no-nonsense voice. "We need to go."

Since he agreed, Jared followed without a word.

Only when they'd hobbled over the fallen fence did she slow her pace. "That was crap."

He waited for her to elaborate. A second later, she did. "Freddie was trying to insinuate that Watkins and Damien had gotten involved with drugs."

He gave a shrug, remembering all the times in Afghanistan when he and Watkins had tried to drive away the horror, to override the stark death and destruction by overindulging on weed or whatever other illegal drugs they could scrounge up. "It's entirely possible."

"No." She rounded on him. "It's not. You don't know Damien. He doesn't do drugs. And do you really think Charles Watkins, with his thriving practice and good reputation, would be stupid enough to risk everything for drugs?"

"Good question." And though she couldn't know, one that hit home. Jared had risked everything and lost. Was Watkins repeating his mistake? Drugs were as good a reason as any. Or was his disappearance because of Elena? Watkins had believed he loved her, and she'd rejected him because of what he was. Now, he'd gone missing.

"Here we are." Her husky voice drew him out of his thoughts. They'd reached the street where he'd hit her, just outside the back of her club. His black Mercedes still waited, looking ominous in the dim light.

He glanced at Elena, suddenly aware that he'd nearly run her over, and she still needed to be examined by a competent medical professional. "About that emergency-room visit—"

"For the last time." She waved his concern away. "I'm fine. Don't worry. I'm not going to sue you."

His mouth twisted. "That was my primary concern," he quipped. "But really, I need to make sure you aren't seriously injured."

"Examine me yourself." Her eyes widened as she realized what she'd said, but gamely, she kept on. "I mean, you are a doctor, right?"

Slowly he nodded. Inside, his wolf stretched lazily, watching, waiting.

"Good." She flashed him a nervous half smile. "That's settled. Come inside. We'll use my office." Turning down a narrow alley between two brick buildings, she pointed to a metal-barred door with a tiny, barred window.

"Here we are." Three sharp raps, and the door creaked open. A bald man, folds of neck fat bulging, peered out at them.

"Miss Elena!" Pushing open the door and holding it, he sounded genuinely glad to see her. Jared, however, was another story. The man glared, his mouth turning down.

"Bob, he's okay. He's with me."

With a curt nod, the bouncer moved out of the way.

Feeling smaller by the moment—and more irritable—Jared followed Elena down a long hallway. The polished marble and stucco walls didn't fit with his image of a strip club—any strip club, male or female. With the ornate wall lighting and dark cherry baseboards, the place looked more like a chic hotel. A hint of his thoughts must have shown on his face.

"Fantasies is an upscale club," she told him with a small smile. "We work hard to keep it that way."

He nodded, wondering what Watkins had been doing in a place like this. Of course…he studied Elena again. Though she wasn't his friend's usual type—Watkins preferred tall, leggy blondes—she was a rare beauty. He could see why Watkins had been hanging around.

But Elena was his. *Mate. His one and only.*

Again the weird thoughts. He shook his head to clear it, his throat dry. Though rehab had mentioned possible delusions, he'd been clean long enough and shouldn't be having flashbacks.

Her limp barely noticeable now, she led the way into a large office that wouldn't have looked out of place as a CEO's den and dropped into a chair behind a massive antique desk. "Have a seat."

Continuing to stand, he eyed her. "Explain the neighborhood. Why locate such a fancy club here?"

This time, her smile looked genuine, lighting up her entire face. "When my aunt started Fantasies back in the sixties, this was a nice part of town. Sure, it's gone downhill over the years, but I won't move the club, so instead I make sure I keep the parking lot safe."

Though he raised a brow, he didn't comment.

"Are you ready to examine me?" Her husky drawl made the question sound like a come-on.

His heartbeat—and that of his wolf—accelerated. Blinking, he cleared his throat. "I'd like to wash my hands." And stall for time, when all he really wanted to do was haul her up against him and kiss her senseless.

All this politeness was beginning to grate on his nerves, but he supposed he needed to view courtesy as a necessary evil these days. He was no longer the hospital's star doctor, known for diagnosing the impossible.

"Sure." She pointed to another highly polished door. "It's through there."

He shouldn't have been surprised that she would have her own private bathroom. She owned the club, after all.

Using his cane to stand, he moved as effortlessly as he could across the room. Once there, he pulled the door open and then flicked on the light.

And nearly tripped over the body that lay facedown on the polished marble floor.

Chapter 2

A strangled sound made Elena look up. "Are you all right?" she called, standing.

"No. Uh, Elena?"

Framed in the doorway, leaning more on the polished cherrywood frame than his cane, Dr. Jared Gies looked furious. And, if she were perfectly honest, with his tall, lean body, longish wavy brown hair and ancient-looking dark brown eyes, sexy as hell. An odd sort of thought for a woman who dealt with beautiful men on a daily basis. Maybe she'd hit her head harder than she'd realized. She blinked, realizing he'd spoken. "What's wrong?"

Crossing the space between them, he took hold of her arm. "You need to call 9-1-1. "There's a…dead body in your bathroom."

It took a moment for his words to sink in. "Are you sure?" she heard herself ask stupidly. As if he, a doctor, could fail to mistake such a thing as a body, or death.

Taking a deep breath, she went to the rest room and stepped inside, absurdly grateful for Jared's solid presence beside her.

One look, and she felt bile rise in her throat.

"Damien," she said softly, dropping to her knees and feeling for a pulse, despite the fact that Jared had no doubt already done so. Nothing. Yet, he appeared to be only sleeping. "Are you sure he's…?"

"Yes. I'm sorry."

There were no marks on him, no blood, no bruising. Nothing to tell her how this had happened, how Damien had died. This was her worst nightmare, everything she'd tried to protect Damien from. Now she had to tell his grandmother and brother that she'd failed.

"Did you know?" Peering at her intently, Jared appeared to struggle to find the right words. "Did you know what he was?"

Not sure what he meant, she glared at him. "He was my friend." Her sharp tone belied her grief. Her eyes burned, but she kept her expression blank. No tears. If she cried at all, she'd do so in private, not in front of this stranger. "I have to call the police."

After the police had questioned her and cordoned off her office as a potential crime scene, Elena let herself be led to the smaller office that Watkins had been using. The officers, Yost and Trenton, were two she'd come to know and like. They wanted to question everyone who had access to her office now that they were done with her.

The words *murder investigation* made her shudder.

At least there hadn't been claw marks or teeth marks. She could safely say that the creature she'd seen Watkins become hadn't killed Damien.

But then, what had?

A few minutes later, Jared joined her.

"Now that they've questioned each of us separately, they wanted me to stay with you."

Wrapping her arms around herself, she nodded awkwardly. "Did you tell them you have nothing to do with this place?"

"Should I? Does it matter?"

"Of course." Uncomfortable with the forced intimacy, she looked away. "Sometimes you remind me of Watkins. Are you related?"

His sudden stillness seemed surreal. "No. We've just known each other a long time."

"This was his office."

Acting as if he were coming out of a daze, he glanced around, then began to prowl the perimeter of the small room, his nostrils flaring. He reminded her of a caged wolf. Werewolf? When he finally came to a stop in front of her, his intent expression unnerved her.

"What was he doing here, Elena? He claimed he did charity work, but I find that hard to believe."

"He did," she said. "He was here for a couple of hours a few times a week. He ran a free clinic for street people. That door—" she nodded at the interior door "—leads to the room he set up as an exam room."

"You know, you mentioned that before, I still can't picture it." Watkins must have changed a lot in the years since they'd been tight.

She shrugged.

"And you let him run the clinic here. Why?"

"I didn't mind." She swallowed, feeling absurdly guilty at the partial truth. She hadn't minded, not at all. Until she'd learned he was a monster rather than a man.

"He mentioned you the last time we spoke." He sounded casual—too casual. As though he lied, though how she could know this when she barely knew the man, she couldn't say.

Did he know what his friend could become? Worse— she took another look—was he like him? Was there more than one?

Ah, crap. She couldn't deal with this right now. Damien was dead. Until she knew why and how, they were all in danger.

"For whatever reason, someone removed some of his teeth. Though he could have done it himself. He was using," Jared said, as though he'd read her mind.

"Using? What? Who?"

"Damien. I think he might have overdosed on heroin, judging by what I saw. Either that, or crack cocaine."

"How do you—" She cut herself off, remembering what he did for a living. "You know this because you're a doctor, right?"

"Partially," he told her, his voice and face equally expressionless. "I also know because I'm an addict."

Stunned, she stared, not sure how to respond. Finally she took a good look at him, at the fine lines around his beautiful hazel eyes, his high cheekbones, his sensual and cruel mouth.

An addict? She couldn't have been more shocked if he'd admitted to being a werewolf like Watkins.

Giving herself a mental shake—she needed to quit seeing monsters around every corner—she swallowed. "You…you're a…drug addict?"

"I was. I'm clean now. I've just completed six weeks of rehab."

"What were you…?"

"On? OxyContin."

Pain medication. The limp. Of course. Straightening her shoulders, she rubbed the back of her suddenly aching neck. "You didn't have to tell me that. I barely know you."

"You're wrong. I did have to tell you. Because I can promise you, you're going to know me quite well."

Alarm stabbed her. Alarm, and a slow, insidious heat she wasn't sure she liked. "Is that a threat?"

"Of course not. You're missing a doctor. I need a job. Let me take Watkins's place."

"First, he didn't work for me. He did charity work here. That's it." Stupid, but all she could think to say.

"So?" He lifted one shoulder. "I've got plenty of money to tide me over."

The street people had missed Watkins. Since the free clinic had remained closed, they'd taken to hanging out in the alley outside her back door. Even Bob didn't have the heart to chase them away.

"Fantasies has always attracted an eclectic crowd," she said. "You'd be treating my dancers and the occasional customer, too. For free."

As he stared at her, she sensed something restless underneath his skin. He was worried about Watkins. Again, she wondered if this man had truly known his friend, if he'd ever seen what Watkins could become.

She studied him through her lashes. What if the beautiful Dr. Jared Gies *was* like Watkins and could change into an animal, too? No way was she letting another monster get that close.

On the other hand, she had to stop being paranoid. "Are you still a doctor?" She kept her tone gentle. "Or did you lose your license because of your habit?"

"I am still licensed. Right now, I'm on hiatus from the hospital. Once the medical board makes a ruling, they'll decide whether or not I can come back. Until then, I'm in limbo."

She could feel herself weakening. "We don't allow drugs here."

"Yeah." He jerked a thumb toward her rest room. "I can tell."

A flare of fury hit her, so strongly she nearly staggered. "Get out."

He didn't move.

Her eyes filled with angry tears. "Someone killed Damien. If he overdosed, someone else did this to him. He was murdered."

Of course he didn't respond. What could he say?

As quickly as it had appeared, her anger dissipated, a bone-deep weariness taking its place. "What do you want, Dr. Gies? Why are you here?"

"I told you. I want to find Watkins."

She waited.

"And I need a job." The sentence sounded forced, as though he'd clenched his teeth. "Something to do, something that will keep me busy. Something that will look good to the medical board while they review my case in a few weeks. Watkins's charity work fits the bill perfectly."

At least he was honest. While she tried to decide what to say, he spoke the one word that always got her. "Please."

She hated being such a sucker. But this man standing in her office, with his handsome face and ancient, beautiful eyes, was a wounded thing. While she wasn't a doctor and couldn't heal, she could no more send a broken human away than she could breathe. Which was why most of her dancers had come to her during a rough patch in their lives. Like Damien. Her eyes watered, and she pushed away her grief.

"You want to take Watkins's place and run his clinic?" She took the plunge. "Then go ahead."

"You don't expect him back?"

Her heart skipped a beat. "We had an argument, and he left. So no, I don't expect him back."

"Then I guess I'll have to find him."

"I guess you will," she echoed. "You know, I didn't consider him missing until my dancers started saying he was."

He nodded, watching her with an intent look that made her want to squirm. Eyeing him back, she felt an unfamiliar stirring low in her belly. If she'd been one of her customers—pampered, well-heeled ladies searching for a forbidden taste of the exotic—this man would have been her personal fantasy on the stage. Even now, with him simply standing near her, she had to bite her lip to keep from touching him.

Damn. Damien's death, bottling up her grief, had to be the reason her thinking was so messed up.

"Elena? Are you all right?"

"Yes." She blinked and then sighed. "Everyone's always telling me I'm a sucker for the underdog." She always had been, ever since her cousin had died.

"Underdog?"

A quick glance at him revealed he was annoyed, if his black frown was any indication. "*That* bothers you?"

"I'm not an underdog."

"Semantics." She wasn't about to argue over word choice. She had too many other things to deal with. Like running her business. Maybe work could help her deal with her grief. She glanced at her watch. "The police are finished with us, so let me show you around. You need to see what all you're going to be dealing with before you commit to taking over the clinic."

Around Elena Cabrera, Jared's usual cutting sarcasm failed him. Not once, not twice, but ever since he'd met her—or rather nearly killed her with his vehicle—he hadn't been himself.

Of course, he hadn't been himself since the original car accident.

Worse, inside, his wolf continued to stir, to want out, for the first time in years. He wasn't sure how he should react to that. Since the accident, he'd either been in the hospital, or too doped up to even attempt to change. After rehab, he simply hadn't wanted to. Now it had been six years—way too long. No wonder he was beginning to question his own sanity.

Maybe that was the reason he felt so unsettled. He'd heard that going too long without letting the inner wolf free resulted in madness. So? He'd always taken a perverse delight in being a little crazy, whether sober or flying on his pain meds.

Face it, either human or as wolf, his body would never be normal or sound again. In nature, a crippled wolf was ignored by his own Pack, or set upon by others and killed.

He supposed he should consider himself lucky that shifters were a bit more civilized than their wild counterparts, but that didn't affect his determination to avoid changing for as long as possible.

One more glance at Elena, with her thick, dark hair and huge brown eyes, and his gut clenched. As if he didn't have enough problems, the intuition he'd always trusted kept insisting she was special, his mate.

Utterly ridiculous.

"Are you all right?" Her voice was husky with concern.

He forced a smile. "Fine."

"Good. Come with me. Let me show you the rest of my club."

Feeling reckless, he followed her down the polished marble hallway to a set of gilded elevators. She pushed a button, the doors slid soundlessly open and they stepped inside.

"There are only two floors," she told him.

The elevator moved down. An instant later, they came to a stop.

"Your club is underground?"

"Yes." With that simple answer, she led him down a long, carpeted hall. She was moving naturally now, as if he'd never hit her with his car.

As they rounded the corner, he could hear a steady thump. Bass or drum, loud. And music. As they approached the massive, carved-oak double doors, the noise level reached deafening proportions.

His wolf began to pace, made uneasy by the steady thump of the bass. Ruthless, Jared fought internally, struggling and finally regaining control. Each time, doing so became more and more difficult.

Elena glanced at him. He took care to keep his face expressionless. "With a murder investigation going on, I would have thought the police would have made you close the place for tonight."

"I offered. They said there was no need, since the body was found in the private office area and not the main club. And they don't think he died here."

Odd. But no doubt the police knew what they were doing.

"Personally," Elena continued, "I'd rather send everyone home. But Val—my cousin, she's a hostess—says the employees want to work. They don't want to alarm the customers, and keeping busy is the best way to deal with grief." She bit her lip and Jared realized she was close to tears. "We're all like family here."

Once the heavy doors swung closed behind them, a tuxedoed waiter inclined his head and used a huge, gilded key to open an ornate, black wrought iron gate that separated the entry from the main part of the club.

"Come with me." Elena appeared to have regained her composure. Jared hoped she wouldn't head to the sole empty table close to the front. A discreet sign proclaimed that spot reserved. Crowds of well-dressed women occupied all the other tables.

As Jared eyed the crowd, amazed at how many of Elena's customers appeared to be well-heeled, upper-crust, Junior League types, he gradually became aware of the man on the stage. Illuminated with soft lighting, the dancer moved sensuously to the one-two beat of a country-music ballad. No strutting, leering grins or pole dancing in this routine. Instead the dancer swayed gently to the music, his dreamy, half-lidded expression seeming to suggest an imaginary lover moved in tango with his animal-like grace.

Jared frowned. The dancer was a shifter.

Stunned, he tried to collect his thoughts. Again he scanned the audience, this time more closely. The customers weren't all human, as he'd thought with his first casual glance. More than half of the women watching the show were Pack. He even spotted a few vampires in the crowd. Again he glanced at Elena. Did she truly not realize that her club appeared to be a magnet for nonhumans?

"Not the blatant, sex-in-your-face approach you expected, is it?" Leaning close to his ear to be heard over the music, Elena's husky voice sent a shuddering chill down his backbone. "The dancer that's on stage now was crying earlier, but you wouldn't know it to look at him."

His wolf snarled, then quieted.

"No." He didn't dare turn his head, knowing how close her mouth must be, knowing he wouldn't be able to resist the temptation to taste her.

Inside, his wolf began pacing, growing increasingly more agitated. Again Jared had to fight an internal battle, subjugating his wolf self to human control.

One or two of the nearest customers turned—other shifters who sensed Jared's beast so close to the surface.

Even Elena sensed something was wrong. "Jared?"

As he fought, he realized he wasn't sure how much longer he could control his need to change. Gulping air, he turned, looking for the exit sign.

"I've got to go." Heart pounding, he bolted for the door, hating his lurching, limping gait. Though Elena could have easily caught him, luckily, she didn't come after him as he found the elevator and went aboveground. The police had told him to stay with Elena, but they had his conact info if they needed him.

Outside, a light mist fell.

Uncaring, he bypassed his car, roaming the deserted, dark streets on foot, breathing hard and fast. Miraculously no one bothered him. It might have been his stride, lurching and furious, like an enraged Quasimodo, or it might have been the half-mad look he knew he had in his eyes.

Waging war from the outside in, he snarled and growled, aware that if anyone heard him, he'd sound demented. But there were no witnesses. Only the shadows and the streetlights heard his one-sided battle.

The wolf wanted out. Eventually his wolf would win.

He knew he had to change, knew he couldn't put off the inevitable much longer. But not now. He needed to be someplace where he could control the shifting, away from human eyes. Not here, not in the inner city.

He had to gain control. The shifting had to be initiated by his human half, not his wild. Otherwise, he might lose control forever. Somehow—he wasn't sure how—he knew that.

The wolf inside him snarled. Despite the ludicrous image of a wild creature limping through the city streets, his beast wanted out. Now.

His animal craved to run free and wild, to feel the damp earth under the pounding of his paws. Jared fought the desire the same way he fought his need for drugs, with all that he was.

But now, even that didn't seem enough.

Was he finally about to break?

Somehow, he found himself back at his car. Climbing inside, he drove. When he reached I-45, he pressed the accelerator to the floor. Though he knew the Trinity River bottom was not a clean area, it was close and as secluded as anywhere could be in downtown Dallas. Regardless, he had no choice. He had to find a place—any place—where he and his wolf would be able to hide once he changed.

Finally he reached the Trinity River bottom and parked in a deserted liquor-store parking lot. Then he disappeared into the underbrush. Even after dark, the humid air struck him in waves.

Wide-awake, eager and ready, his wolf snarled again.

Jared allowed himself a fierce smile. Apprehension warred with anticipation—he hadn't changed in so long and his leg was still a mess. But he was clean, drug-free and the wolf was impatient.

Underfoot, the grass felt thick and lush. He could

smell the water, the distinctive scent of fish and man, of wild raccoon and of human waste. Jared gave another savage smile. For the first time in a long while, he felt truly alive.

Dangerous.

Reaching the first group of twisted mesquite trees, he dropped to all fours, tangling his fingers in the dry grass and curled, brittle leaves. He lifted his head, sniffing the air, and eyed the night sky. Here, in the heart of the city, no stars were visible. Even the moon was hidden. The dark, smog-filled night sky suited his mood.

In the past, like most shifters, he'd approached changing with great joy and a sense of freedom. Not so now. Instead his grim resolve was full of angry trepidation.

Even as wolf, he would still have a bum leg. Unlike Watkins, who'd healed completely from the accident. Such was the detrimental part of the Halfling's existence. If Jared had been a full-blooded shifter like his friend, his body would have healed itself in record time. No limp, no pain.

How could he clear his mind if such thoughts kept crowding him? Shaking his head, he scrambled back to his feet, feeling the need to go deeper into the woods. His shirt clung to his sweaty back. Once he found a spot, he'd remove his clothing.

Skirting the bridge—his extra-keen nose detected a homeless encampment underneath—he pushed through the scraggly undergrowth and entered a thicker, wooded greenbelt. Again he tested the air. He smelled earth and leaves, freshly cut grass, the recent passage of a dog and the polluted river. No humans, not here. Good.

Satisfied that he was well hidden, he yanked off his T-shirt and shorts, placed them carefully on a flat rock, and again dropped to all fours.

Closed his eyes and willed his body to do it.

Change.

Nothing. His heartbeat thundered in his ears and he had to wipe sweaty palms on the old leaves. It had been too long and, even though he thought he knew better, he couldn't help but feel something would go wrong. The way his life had gone since the accident, something would.

The wolf inside paced, ready.

Elena's image danced behind his eyelids, proof positive that he had to try again. Once more, he dug his hands into the leaves, scraping until he found soil. He burrowed his fingers as deep as he could, felt dirt beneath his nails, then he finally lifted his hands to inhale the scent of the earth. The lazy breeze ruffled leaves and tickled his bare skin and, as his heartbeat slowed, he felt the change begin.

As his bones lengthened and changed, the first stab of pain took him by surprise. His wounded leg and knee burned, making him cry out and drop his chin to his chest.

Finally, panting and sore, he became wolf. Four paws planted firmly in the earth, his pelt the color of the moon at her zenith. As a child, he'd been told his color was a rarity, even though his mother was the same silver-white. Then and now, he was proud to take after her.

Wolf. A sense of loss struck his animal self. Solitary. Without his Pack. Worse, without his mate.

Fury made him bare his teeth. Now a wolf, he should not think of Elena. She was human. He shook himself, hoping to shed all thoughts of her.

Growling low in his throat, he moved forward. The night air held many promises—other scents, of wildlife and food. Despite this, Elena's image remained with him, unwavering.

He lifted his muzzle and howled, uncaring who heard. He was wolf again, not man. Then, as though he could excise her by doing so, he took off running, his gait stiff and awkward, unsteadily lurching into the night.

Several hours later, he returned to the same spot and changed back to man. Retrieving his clothing, he headed for the parking lot. He was exhausted, and his limp was more pronounced. Still, as he climbed into his car, he felt grimly optimistic. He'd set his wolf free. He'd tasted blood, roamed until his aching leg could take no more, and banish all human passions. He hoped.

Now maybe he could face Elena with his animal self under control. He could stop wanting to rip her clothes from her perfect body and bury himself deep inside her.

At the thought, he instantly grew hard.

Damn it. Letting loose a string of curses, he started the car, praying his erection would subside by the time he reached his apartment uptown.

Chapter 3

"Do you think he'll show?"

Elena glanced up from the time cards she was checking. Valerie, her younger cousin who worked as a hostess, lounged in the doorway, wearing a clingy, low-cut dress made of some kind of glittery mesh.

"Who?"

Valerie smirked. "The new doctor. A few grubby patients are waiting in the alley for the back door to open."

"Lining up? How is that possible? Today is Tuesday, not a normal clinic day, and Dr. Gies and I only just talked about the possibility of him taking over Watkins's clinic. He hasn't agreed yet to do it. Val, we didn't even discuss specifics."

Biting her lip, Valerie looked away. "I told Old

Tommy. He must have passed the word on to his friends. You know how that goes."

"You'd better handle it. Until Dr. Gies and I talk more, I don't even know for sure whether he's going to do the clinic."

"You're kidding, right?"

"No, I'm not." Suddenly exhausted, Elena rubbed the back of her neck. Dealing with Valerie was like dealing with a mercurial, petulant teenager, despite the fact that her cousin was twenty-five. And the police were back, talking to a few of the employees they'd missed last night. This was the last thing she needed to worry about.

"Do you expect him in tonight?"

Resisting the urge to check her watch, Elena stacked the time cards neatly and secured them with a rubber band. "I don't know. But if—when he does, send him to me."

Pouting, Valerie crossed her arms. "I was hoping you'd let me help him while he's here."

This was so not like Valerie. Her cousin usually sought ways to avoid work, not take on more of it.

"Why?" Elena kept her expression impassive.

"He's hot."

"Off-limits," Elena said, surprising even herself. She clamped her lips together to keep from saying anything else strange.

Valerie came closer, leaning over the desk. "Dr. Watkins wasn't off-limits. Why Dr. Gies?"

"Because…" What could she say? Not that he was hers, because he wasn't. "Val, I don't need a reason. And I happen to know you're seeing Luke. Leave Dr. Gies alone."

"But—"

Holding up her hand, Elena shook her head. "Go and deal with the people in the alley. After that, I think you need to get the front desk ready to open tonight."

Glaring at her, Valerie nodded. Without another word, she stalked off in her high heels.

Would Jared be back? After the way he'd bolted last night, she doubted it. Odd that a doctor could act so strangely.

But he'd hit her with his car, then discovered a body in her bathroom. All in the same night.

She couldn't blame him if he never returned. Any sane person would run as far and as fast as he could.

For herself, she kept pushing away her grief.

Poor Damien. Late last night, after the club closed, she'd gone to comfort his grandmother. Though it had been nearly 4:00 a.m., lights had still burned in the DeLeon apartment. Heart heavy, Elena had knocked on the door.

Freddie had let her in and had actually hugged her. "Grandmama was right," he'd said, his voice heavy. "She's been burning candles and prayin'. Even before the police came, she said she felt in her bones something bad happened to Damien."

They'd all had a good cry together, the older woman telling in her broken-down voice how hard Damien had tried to find a better life and how grateful he'd been to Elena for helping him.

Elena hadn't left the apartment until sunrise. As a result, she hadn't gotten to bed until nearly seven.

Sleeping until noon—five hours—hadn't been nearly

enough for her bruised body. But she'd had errands to run and things to do before going to work that night. Like buying groceries. All she'd had in her fridge had been an expired yogurt and a tub of butter.

She'd come to work early, arriving at six, moving slowly due to the aches she hadn't felt last night. Catching up on payroll and other busywork had helped keep her from thinking about Damien. And Jared. While she couldn't put her finger on exactly what, something about the enigmatic doctor intrigued her far more than it should.

You'd think she'd learn. After her experience with Watkins, she needed to be extremely careful. Maybe Jared's not showing up again was a good thing.

When nine o'clock had come and gone, she sighed and organized her desk in preparation to head down to the club area. Though Fantasies was already open, the real crowds didn't start arriving until eleven or later.

She looked up…and gasped.

"Ready to finish showing me around?" Jared lounged in her doorway, looking completely at home. With his rumpled, button-down shirt and worn, faded jeans, he looked far too appealing for her peace of mind.

With an effort, she gathered her thoughts. "You ran away last night."

"I was feeling sick," he drawled, lying and completely unrepentant. "I needed fresh air."

"You never came back."

"I'm here now." His slow smile warmed her bones. "And ready to see about running this clinic."

Part of her wanted to tell him to leave. When his

gaze locked with hers, she felt a tiny thrill of excitement. Dangerous.

Though her heart felt as if it was about to pound from her chest, she kept her head up as she moved past him.

"Let's look around the clinic. There are still some supplies—Watkins bought them with his own money, but you might need to bring in a few things. There's a medical-supply store two streets over. You also need to meet my staff." She kept her tone as businesslike as she could make it.

"No, I don't."

She started to argue but the sound of running footsteps had them both turning.

"Elena!" Rushing around the corner, long evening dress billowing behind her, Joy bleated her name. Panic showed in her wide eyes and trembling hands. "We need—" Stopping as she realized her sister wasn't alone, Joy looked from Elena to Jared, and back again.

"What's wrong?" Grabbing her shoulders, Elena wrapped her in a tight hug. "Joy, are you all right?"

Twice Joy tried to speak and failed.

"Take a deep breath." Suddenly Jared stood close. His soothing tone apparently struck the right note. Joy nodded, inhaling loudly before trying again.

"Now, what's wrong?"

"Melissa… The hospital called. She's in the emergency room. I've got to go."

"Slow down." Elena clutched her sister's arm. Joy's daughter, Melissa, had been giving her trouble since she'd reached her midteens. She'd run away from home once, and Joy worried about her constantly.

"Was she in a car accident? Is she hurt? What happened?"

Mouth quivering, Joy swallowed. Her freckles stood out on her too-pale face. "They said it's a drug overdose."

Elena swore. Though both she and Joy had tried their best to get Melissa help, the teenager had been flirting with trouble for the last year.

"Parkland Hospital just called my cell. She's in the E.R."

"What kind of drugs?" As he pushed himself away from the wall, Jared's intent gaze comforted Elena, though she didn't know why. Must be because he was a doctor.

Joy frowned. "Who are you?" She looked from him to her sister. "Have you already hired another dancer to replace Damien?"

Jared's sharp bark of laughter made Joy color.

Before Jared could speak, Elena introduced them. "Dr. Jared Gies, meet my sister, Joy. Joy, vice versa."

"Yeah." Too distracted to question his presence further, Joy swallowed whatever she'd been about to say. "I've got to get to the hospital."

"What kind of drugs did she take?" Jared repeated his question.

"They said they think—" Her voice broke. "Methamphetamines." Covering her face with her hands, her shoulders shook as she started sobbing.

"I'm driving." Elena again drew her sister close. "Valerie can keep an eye on things here. Let's go."

Joy allowed herself to be led down the hallway.

Limping, Jared fell into step behind them, uninvited. As they neared the exit, Joy realized he was still with them.

"Do you work at Parkland?" she asked.

"Yes." Jared's glare dared Elena to contradict him.

Like magic, Joy's round face cleared. "Thank God. Do you have experience with drug overdoses?"

Expression unchanged, Jared didn't even crack a smile. "Yes. I've spent a fair amount of time in detox."

Elena didn't tell her sister he meant as a patient, not a physician. If Jared wanted to accompany them, she'd let him. Even if he was suspended from the hospital, he still knew people. Her gut told her he could help her niece and, judging from the situation, Melissa could use all the help she could get.

They all piled into Elena's sensible sedan, Joy twisting her hands and rambling as Elena drove.

In the backseat, Jared stared out the window, silent.

Finally they pulled into Parkland Hospital's massive parking lot. They lucked into a spot in the front row. Hurrying across the pavement, Elena again put her arm around Joy's shoulders, leaving Jared to take up the rear.

"Hospitals are such cold, antiseptic places." Elena said inanely. She felt her sister's shoulders tense up as they neared the entrance. She massaged Joy's neck as they stepped out of the revolving doors into the vast lobby.

People stared—two women in evening gowns was not a normal sight in the E.R. Elena ignored them, hyperaware of Jared trying to keep up behind them.

Her high heels clicked unevenly as she led the way to the waiting area. Joy pulled back, her expression stark.

"What's wrong?" Elena asked softly. When her sister

didn't respond, she used Joy's full name. "Josephina? What is it?"

"I'm afraid."

"Of what?" Jared pushed past them to the counter. The bustling E.R. staff barely noticed them. "Your daughter is going to be all right. She's conscious, isn't she?"

Joy gave him a startled look. "Yes, she's conscious. But an overdose? My baby overdosed?"

"You knew she was using drugs, right? You had to. For her to get to the stage where she ODs, there had to be too many signs for you not to know."

Straightening, Joy looked at Elena, then back at Jared. "I know you're a doctor, but what business is this of yours?"

Instantly Jared's expression closed. "You're right, I'm sorry." He stepped back, away from them, his expression like stone.

But Joy didn't want to let it go. She followed him, her voice sharp. "How dare you talk to me that way! Do you have children?"

He shook his head.

"Then you've obviously never been where I am. Yes, I knew she was using. And yes, I tried like hell to stop her. Threats, punishment, I tried it all. But I can't be with her 24/7. She does what she wants and damns the consequences."

Tears rolled down her plump cheeks. Yet when Elena reached to hug her, Joy pushed her away.

Still staring hard at Jared, she swiped at her eyes. "You have no idea how I feel."

"No." His voice was soft. "I don't. But I have been

there. I know what it's like to crave something. I know what it's like to care about getting high more than anything else, not giving a damn what the cost might be."

Mouth set in hard lines, Joy sniffled. "What are you saying? How can you know that?"

Elena grabbed his arm to keep him from saying more. "He knows, Joy. Believe me, he knows."

Gaze unwavering, Joy stared hard at him. "Are you telling me you can help my daughter?"

The hope in her voice broke Elena's heart.

Jared looked down. "I don't know," he said. "But I can try." The hard look was back, the I-dare-you-to-disagree with me frown that Elena was coming to know. "Apart from running a free clinic at night, I've got nothing better to do."

With narrowed eyes, Joy studied him. She'd taken a job at Fantasies when the insurance company where she'd worked for twenty years had gone out of business. Elena considered her a loyal helper and friend and the sole person she entirely trusted.

Joy looked at Elena, wanting her opinion. Meanwhile, Jared leaned on the counter, talking in a low voice to the nurse.

"I'm not sure why," Elena said. "But I trust him. Let him try to help Melissa. Maybe he can do some good."

Digging in her purse for a tissue, Joy nodded.

"You can go in," the nurse said, smiling at Jared. "Dr. Gies can show you the way."

"Come on." Without waiting to see if they followed, Jared hobbled off.

Arm in arm, Joy and Elena followed.

At a room with its door half closed, he stopped, pinning Elena with his glare. "While we're here, you can let the E.R. doc take a look at you."

"I'm fine." Crossing her arms, Elena barely looked at him. "My hip hardly even hurts anymore. No headache, nothing." Just bruises in places she didn't care to show anyone.

"What's going on?" Joy looked from one to the other. "What happened to your hip?"

"Nothing." Darting a quick look at Jared to warn him to shut up, Elena took Joy's arm. "Let's go see Missy."

As she spoke, a woman dressed in scrubs and sneakers came out of the room. She didn't look much older than Melissa, though her name tag said she was a registered nurse. Her voice and expression kind, she held the door open for them to enter.

Jared stepped in front of the nurse. "You've already admitted her?"

Undeterred by his authoritative tone, the young woman cocked her head and met him stare for stare. "You are?"

Joy shook her head. Since she seemed incapable of answering, Elena did. "He's a friend of the family."

"Then maybe one of you should tell him you asked for the patient to be admitted to the rehab program here."

She left them after pushing the slightly ajar door all the way open as an invitation to enter.

Inside, the room was dark. No lights, no television, nothing but a lump in a hospital bed.

Elena had time to notice that the staff had raised the rails on the bed, as if Melissa were a toddler, before Jared flicked the light switch on.

Blanket pulled up to her chin, Melissa didn't even look up.

Joy hung back, shifting from foot to foot near the doorway, one fist to her mouth, struggling not to cry.

Keeping a determined grip on Joy's arm, Elena propelled her forward. "It'll be all right," she murmured.

Joy nodded, reaching out blindly to clutch at the metal bed rails, and stared down at her daughter.

Melissa's eyes were open. She stared at nothing, as though she wished she could will the world away.

"Missy?" Elena called softly. "*Mija,* we're here."

No response.

Joy began crying in earnest, this time in great, heaving sobs. Melissa didn't react.

Jared made a rude sound and yanked back the blanket. "Wake up. Time to greet your visitors."

The teenager grabbed at the blanket, clutching it like a life preserver. Otherwise, she ignored him.

"Is she…?" Joy whispered.

"She's fine." Jared went to the foot of the bed, snatching up the chart and flipping through it. "They've pumped her stomach and given her meds to bring her down. She conscious, though obviously she doesn't want to be."

"What do you know?" Melissa snarled. "Leave me alone." She closed her eyes.

Ignoring her, he continued to peruse her chart.

"Meth, huh?" He sounded disgusted—and furious. "What an idiotic way to try to kill yourself. Next time why don't you try something cleaner and quicker?"

Joy gasped, clearly outraged. She started to speak,

but Melissa opened her bleary eyes and glared at Jared, curling her lip. "Go away. I'm tired of doctors."

"He's not a—" Elena's voice trailed off, aware Jared *was* a doctor, no matter the current status of his license.

Mouth twisting, Jared flipped again through the chart, this time making notations.

"She said to leave her alone." Recovering her voice, Joy crossed to stand at the far side of the bed.

"No." Jared placed the chart on the bedside table. "I'm going to tell her how many easier, cleaner ways there are to kill herself, for next time."

Joy gasped. "How dare you talk to her that way? My daughter wasn't trying to kill herself."

He didn't look impressed. "Oh, yeah? Then what was she doing?"

"Trying to get high," Melissa snarled.

"Then why the hell did you use a needle?"

She stuck her chin out. "I didn't."

"Really." Moving with efficient speed despite his limp, he grabbed the teenager's arm, inspecting the area where the crease showed. "There. From the looks of your arm, this was your first time shooting up, wasn't it?"

Instead of answering, Melissa turned her face away. "What's it to you?" She snarled again, sounding like an animal in pain.

To everyone's shock, Jared snarled back, raising his lips and baring his teeth. Before anyone could react, he pointed to the door. "Leave. Both of you. I need a minute with your daughter."

Joy glanced from him to the bed. "I…"

Elena grabbed her arm. "Come on."

"No, Mom," Melissa pleaded, the smug expression hovering in her eyes showing she believed her mother would do as she asked. "Who *is* this man? I don't like him. Don't leave me here alone with him."

Shifting from foot to foot, Joy wavered.

"Go," Elena told her. "I'll stay and make sure she's all right." With a look, she dared Jared to argue.

Joy went, pulling the door shut behind her.

Melissa wailed, sounding like an outraged four-year-old denied a toy.

Jared simply stared, waiting. Finally Melissa fell silent.

"Good." Jared rubbed his hands together. "Let's get real."

"Who do you think you are, Dr. Phil?" she taunted.

"Look at me." His commanding tone surprised Elena. She remained silent and still, not wanting to distract her niece.

Melissa glared at him. "Why? What are you going to do? Hit me?"

He ignored the insulting comment. "I understand your kind of pain," he said, his voice remarkably soft. "I've been there."

Even Melissa looked startled for half a second, before rearranging her expression back to permanently sullen. "You don't know shit."

Jared shrugged. "Whatever. But if you want to know how to make your stay in rehab more pleasant, you might try listening to someone who's been there."

"I'm not going to rehab."

"Yes, you are. Your mother committed you."

"She has no right!"

"You're under eighteen. She has every right."

Again the teenager turned her face away. "I don't care. I'm still going to party."

"Do you really want to die?"

"No." She didn't sound certain. "But I want to have fun."

"You don't get messed up to have a good time. You're trying to escape."

Despite herself, she appeared interested. "From what?"

"The pain."

"Yeah, right," she scoffed. "You talk big, like every other adult. Liars, all of you. You don't know what the hell you're talking about."

He shot Elena a quick look. "Actually I do. I just got out of rehab a week ago. I stayed there three months."

At that, Melissa did a double take. "You? No way."

Jared slowly nodded.

"But you're a doctor."

"So?"

"Right," she snorted. "What'd you do, get caught smoking weed or something?"

"Painkillers. Vicodin, OxyContin, whatever I could get my hands on."

"But not meth." Her tone indicated her drug of choice was nothing like his. "So you really don't know."

"Meth's dangerous." He kept his voice even, as though he didn't care one way or the other. "Messes up your heart, your teeth, your brain. After you've been using awhile, you have to keep upping the dose to get your high."

"So I've heard." Looking away, she didn't seem concerned. "But I only tried it once."

"No," he corrected. "You only tried shooting it up once. I'm willing to bet you've smoked it and snorted it."

Her startled gaze and guilty expression told Elena he'd hit the jackpot.

"I started out like you." Jared's expression settled into his normal, uncaring lines. "Except my pain was physical. I was in a car accident."

"Ah, and also your drugs were prescription."

"Yes. But I abused them." Again he glanced at Elena, then swallowed hard. She watched him with interest, even knowing he felt uncomfortable revealing so much personal information in front of her.

Such an intriguing man. He drew her, like a moth to a flame. Dangerous.

"Would you like me to leave?" she asked quietly, half hoping he'd say yes.

"No. Stay." Briefly his gaze locked on hers, sending a jolt to the pit of her belly.

Melissa echoed his words. "Please, Tia Elena. Stay."

Tia Elena. Missy hadn't called her that since she was ten. Touched, Elena nodded.

When Melissa returned her attention to Jared, she pursed her lips. "That still doesn't explain how you got hooked on pain pills. So you didn't want to be in pain. I can relate to that. What's different between that and being addicted?"

"Addicted as in can't live without it. Would do anything for it. Lie, cheat, steal." He sounded weary. "Believe me, kid. I know."

"You still haven't explained *how.*" Melissa sounded petulant.

Jared gave her a wry smile. "It took a while. I had seven surgeries trying to repair my leg. When I finally got out of the hospital, I was in a wheelchair."

"That sucks." Melissa looked skeptical and intrigued at the same time. "Being in a wheelchair made you get hooked on drugs?"

He shrugged. "No. They said I'd never walk again, so I focused on doing exactly that. Now I can walk as long as I have my cane."

"Then why the drugs?" Elena asked, unable to stop herself.

Jared and Melissa looked at her, their identical expressions telling her they'd forgotten she was there.

"You succeeded. I don't understand," she said softly.

"The pain." He touched his leg. "I started out wanting to get rid of the pain."

"Then what happened?" Melissa leaned forward.

"I got hooked." The sharpness of his voice had her widening her eyes. "Taking the pain pills stopped my leg from hurting, true, but they made me feel good, too. I never thought I was lonely until after the accident. I never really cared." He seemed bemused at his own foibles.

Elena studied him, seeing not self-pity, but an honest sort of self-deprecation. Though he was not conventionally handsome, something about him was so beautiful that looking at him made her chest ache.

Melissa appeared to have decided to trust him. "You really went to rehab?"

"Yeah." Again that flash of a wry smile, once more affecting Elena like a punch to the belly. "I did," he continued. "They had to drag me there kicking and screaming. But not before I lost most of my friends and had my medical license suspended."

The starkness of his voice suddenly seemed too much for Elena. Unless she acted immediately to prevent it, in another second she'd cross the room and wrap her arms around him.

Instead she slipped out the door. She didn't understand his effect on her. After all, Jared Gies was a virtual stranger, not anyone she really cared about.

Wasn't he?

"I thought you said you would stay and protect her?" Joy's accusing tone made Elena realize she'd rejoined her sister.

"He's not going to hurt her. They're only talking."

"About what?"

"Personal stuff." Elena managed a shrug, as if Jared's revelations meant nothing to her. "Missy will be fine." Saying this, she couldn't help but wonder if Jared would be.

Ten minutes later, Jared emerged from the room and hobbled past them as though they weren't there.

Elena started after him, Joy hurrying behind her. "Jared, wait."

He glanced over his shoulder, expression annoyed.

"Tell us what happened," Joy panted, clearly winded.

Thankfully he stopped. "You want a recap? Let's see. Hmm. Your daughter takes drugs to escape, but she's convinced herself they're cool. She has no idea how harmful they are to her body, and frankly if she did, I don't think she'd care. I can't help her." Then, without so much as a goodbye, he limped out the door.

Chapter 4

"Where's he going?" Joy stared after him. "I mean, he rode with us. What's he going to do? Call a cab?"

Elena followed him, waving at Joy to wait. "Give me a minute."

Hurrying outside, she found Jared standing near the smoker's bench, staring moodily at nothing in particular.

"Why'd you do that?"

"Do what? Say I can't help her?" He lifted one shoulder. "I can't help a patient who doesn't want to help herself. If she really wants to quit, she will."

"Give me a break. She's seventeen."

"I'm not sure I'd be the best person to help her."

Elena huffed. "Then you shouldn't have come here with us. But you did, and you're already involved."

The front doors opened and Joy emerged. Marching directly over to Jared, she glared at him. "Okay, hotshot. My daughter won't speak to me. She wouldn't even say good-night. What am I going to do now?"

"She's a minor. You still have control over what she does."

"No, I don't." Expression sad, Joy wrapped her arms around her waist. "She's nearly grown. If she doesn't want to quit, no amount of rehab will make her."

"Exactly." Jared flashed Elena a triumphant look. "I was just telling your sister that."

"Ass." Elena started for the car. A second later, Joy followed. Elena refused to look over her shoulder at Jared. This complex man was precisely the kind of complication she could do without.

However, when she unlocked her car, she couldn't resist a quick peek. Moving slowly, Jared started toward them.

"He's coming." Joy had seen her look. She climbed in the front passenger seat. "What is it with that guy? He's a doctor and he said he could help."

"Give it time." Closing the door behind her, Elena considered backing out of her space and taking the car to Jared so he wouldn't have as far to walk. But Jared had nearly reached them, so she stayed put.

Yanking open the back door, Jared tossed his cane on the seat before heaving his body in.

Joy sighed, pursed her lips and looked away.

Feeling Jared's gaze burning the back of her head, Elena flicked on the radio and cranked up the volume. They drove back to Fantasies to a program featuring musical highlights of the eighties.

When they arrived at the club, Valerie greeted them, fluttering her eyelashes at Jared.

"Are the police still here?" Elena asked.

"No. They questioned everyone and left." Sliding a card across the front desk toward Elena, Val continued to stare at Jared. "Officer Yost left a card. He said he'll call you if he finds out anything. But they're thinking it's a drug overdose."

"Then how did Damien's body get into my private bathroom?"

Slowly Valerie turned her head. "I think he might have gone in there to shoot up. That's what I think."

"But there wasn't any drug paraphernalia. Unless— did the police find any?"

"No." Valerie bit her lip. "At least, I don't think they did. They didn't say."

"I'll call Officer Yost later." Pocketing the card, Elena suppressed a surge of irritation when Valerie returned her attention to Jared.

"Do you need anything, Dr. Gies?" Valerie breathed, looking at him as if she'd like to devour him.

"No, thanks." Answering for him, Elena gave her cousin a hard look to dismiss her. "You can go now."

As Val sauntered off, Elena was unable to resist glancing at Jared to see his reaction. He appeared unmoved by Valerie's blatant interest, watching Elena instead.

Again that unwelcome flame spread warmth through her chest.

"You saw the office last night. Now let me show you the exam room." Deliberately keeping her tone all business, Elena headed down the hall. "The clinic is near the back door, which makes it easy for the street people to get in. All of them are drop-ins. Watkins didn't take appointments."

"Past that bouncer?"

"Bob escorts patients to and from the clinic."

He raised his brows. "Pretty organized."

Ignoring his sarcasm, she opened the clinic door. "Here you go. As you know, this room connects to the office through that interior door." She nodded toward it, remembering being with him on the other side of it last night.

"No nameplate?"

She didn't even need to look at him to know he was kidding. "Nope. Go ahead and check out the supplies. I'm afraid Valerie jumped the gun a bit. She already had people lining up earlier for the clinic."

"Valerie?"

"The woman you just saw, my hostess. She's also my cousin."

"Ah." He nodded. "This is a family business."

"Yep." She knew she sounded flip, but over the years, she'd learned that sometimes she had to. "My aunt started Fantasies back in the sixties. When she died, she passed it on to me. I try to employ as many family members as I can."

"Hmm." He began inspecting the room.

She watched as he peered under cupboards, opened cabinets, the small closet. "I think Watkins kept the place pretty well stocked."

"Yeah." He held up a piece of gauze. "Looks like he made regular raids at the hospital."

Okay, maybe she shouldn't have been shocked, but still…

"I didn't know." Cautious, she moved closer. "How much of this stuff is stolen?"

Jared's dry laugh made her want to touch him. Instead she took a step back.

"How well did you know Watkins?" he asked.

"Well enough. I trusted him around here."

The wry twist of his mouth told her what he thought of that. "How did you meet?"

"We dated for a while." Though she knew her face had turned bright red, she forced herself to continue. "We met online."

"Dating service?"

Lifting her chin, she shook her head. "Chat room, actually. I once wanted to be a doctor."

"What stopped you?"

"Family responsibilities, mostly. And then I inherited the club."

To her relief, he didn't comment, just continued opening the last few built-in drawers. "I'll hold the first free clinic tomorrow, starting at 9:00 p.m."

"So soon?" Startled, she bit her lip. "Watkins had them on Monday, Wednesday and Friday. Can you keep the same days? Will you do Friday this week, too?"

"Let me see how everything goes." The mild tone warred with his sardonic grin. "What days are you open?"

"Every day except Sunday. Of course, Friday and Saturday are our busiest nights."

He nodded. "Do you still want me to meet your staff?"

Glancing at her watch, she realized that the performances were nearly over. Still dealing with their grief, the dancers would also be tired. They'd never forgive her if she brought Jared into the middle of their anguish. "Not now. Maybe tomorrow."

"Elena…" He caught her gaze. "This connection…"

She shook her head, about to lie for her own protection. And his. "There is no—"

"Don't." The look he gave her was so bleak it made her chest hurt. "You're right. There can be nothing between us. There are things about me…" He paused, took a deep breath and started for the door.

She thought of Watkins and how wrong she'd been about him and knew Jared was right. Maybe there were things she was better off not knowing. Still… She eyed his retreating back with longing. There couldn't be two werewolves in Dallas, could there?

The rhetorical question almost made her laugh. How had she managed to accept a reality in which werewolves actually existed? For all she knew, Watkins could be a master illusionist, along the lines of David Copperfield. With all his talk of experiments, his supposed shape-shifting could have been part of a test, with her an unwilling participant.

She was guessing she'd failed. Especially since the day after he'd morphed into a wolf, he'd disappeared. Pushing the disturbing thoughts from her mind, she headed down the hall to get back to work.

At dusk the next day, Jared again visited the river bottom and changed. As wolf, he was still frustrated at his inability to run flat out. Hoping to burn off his restless energy, as well as the constant desire for Elena, he did as best he could. The exercise as wolf would no doubt cause his leg to hurt ten times worse, but that was the lesser of two evils.

He killed a small rabbit, devouring the meat quickly, then ranged the area near the river for nearly an hour before changing back to human.

After returning home, he showered and paced his small, cluttered apartment, grimacing at the pain. Each time his thoughts turned to Elena, he imagined her reaction once she learned his true nature and forced his mind to think of something else.

He found himself staring at his home with fresh eyes, trying to imagine how Elena would see it. Bookshelves lined his walls, flanking his huge flat-screen TV, which he'd hung on the wall like a painting. Professional journals and magazines littered the top of his coffee table. Other than his reading material, the room contained no hint of his personality. Though he'd intended to, he'd never gotten around to buying artwork, and the walls were still painted the same boring white they'd been when he moved in two years ago. Though he easily could afford to invest in a house, he preferred the freedom of an apartment with a one-year lease. If he ever truly tired of Dallas, he wanted nothing tying him there.

When the darkness had grown deep and heavy, Jared drove downtown, for the first time regretting that he'd taken the apartment uptown rather than the one he'd looked at in Garland, one of the many Dallas suburbs. Even this long after rush hour, he sat in traffic on I-45 for nearly an hour before the snarl caused by an over-turned eighteen-wheeler broke up.

Turning down Mockingbird Avenue, he saw that Fantasies's parking lot was full to capacity. Though Elena had said the club didn't get crowded until eleven or later, not a single spot remained. He was forced to park in the bank next door's parking garage.

Since he'd spent a damn near sleepless night in pain and craving Elena, exhaustion swamped him in waves. Maybe this blunting of his senses would help muffle his reaction to her.

Leaning heavily on his cane, he crossed the street, keeping a wary eye out for any hint of trouble. None found him—at least not until he reached the back door of the club.

"Go around to the front," the bouncer growled. "You ain't with Miz Elena now."

Jared started to argue, decided it was pointless and began the slow, laborious journey around to the front of the building.

Rounding the corner, he saw that the line snaked out to the valet stand and down the sidewalk. Women of all ages and sizes, from well-dressed career women to edgy young fashionistas, waited in the humid night to enter Fantasies. Chattering, they laughed and gossiped. As he passed, each and every one eyed him. Scowling, he shouldered his way through the crowd, using his cane to "accidentally" bang a few ankles to move the extra-resistant ones out of his way.

The overpowering scent of multiple perfumes made his head ache, and the bits and pieces of chatter he caught indicated they thought he was a) gay or b) a pervert. No way could they mistake him for a dancer, not with his limp. Clenching his teeth, he told himself he didn't care.

Finally he made it inside the heavy leaded oak doors and approached a hostess dressed in a flowing brocade gown. It wasn't Valerie, but someone he didn't recognize.

Someone who wasn't quite human.

"Can I help you?" Her impeccable diction and flawless makeup brought to mind an upscale resort rather than a male strip club.

"I'm Dr. Jared Gies."

One perfectly shaped brow raised, she inspected him. "Shifter?"

He gave a brief nod. "I saw several here the other night."

"Yes. Fantasies tends to draw a lot of our kind." She smiled, displaying perfect fangs. A vampire. He shouldn't have been surprised. Those bloodsuckers were everywhere these days.

While he wasn't entirely comfortable with her lumping shifters and vampires into the same category, he let it go.

"Where's Valerie?"

"She's running late. My name's Olivia."

He shook her hand, finding her touch as cool as he'd anticipated. "Elena is expecting me."

"Just one moment." Talking into a microphone at the front desk, the woman relayed his information. When she'd finished, a tall, leggy brunette in a skimpy red silk dress and glittering stilettos sauntered over to him.

"Follow me please, sir."

She led the way down the hall, her heels clicking on the polished marble. At the double doors to Elena's office, she paused, rapping softly. "Dr. Gies is here."

"Show him in." Despite the fact he'd just changed—or maybe because of it—the sound of Elena's husky voice sent a caress down his spine. *Damn.*

Gripping his cane, he took a deep breath. Dipping her chin, his escort left him.

Heart pounding, he entered the room.

"Welcome back," Elena said, smiling. She'd put her long, dark hair up and wore dangling silver earrings, showcasing her impossibly long neck.

Beautiful. Absolutely beautiful.

For a moment he could only stare at her across the desk, completely unprepared for the impact of seeing her again.

Mate.

That instant, he realized he'd been totally wrong. Rather than vanquishing his desire, changing had sharpened and honed his need so much that one look from her long lashed caramel eyes had him instantly hard and ready.

Disgusted with himself, Jared shook his head and grimaced.

"What's wrong?" She recoiled a bit at his sour expression. "Are you all right?"

"Fine." He sounded as though he'd swallowed rusty nails. Clearing his throat, he tried again. "I'm fine. I wanted to check in with you before I started seeing patients. I'll need to keep some sort of records and I was wondering if you had a spare computer I could use."

At least his wolf still slept. He supposed he ought to count that as something.

Staring at him, her friendly smile gone, she tapped her pen on her blotter. "I'm sure I can rustle one up."

"How quickly?"

She glanced at her watch. "Let me call Valerie. She can help you with that."

"Valerie's not here yet. Olivia is working the front."

Nodding, she made a note on a pad. "Is there anything else?"

The professional Elena both annoyed and aroused him. He wanted to strip that facade from her, twine his fingers through her thick, dark hair and tip up her face for his kiss. Once their lips touched…

Damn. What the hell was the matter with him? Belatedly he remembered she'd asked him a question.

"I need to set a few ground rules."

When she started to speak, he held up his hand. "Hear me out. No advertising. If the hospital finds out…that might have a bearing on whether or not they reinstate my privileges. You can tell people, but you'll have to be low-key, all right?"

She nodded.

Then, because he didn't want to leave, he stared at the oil painting on the wall to the left of her desk. Vibrant swirls of angry reds, oranges and yellows warred with the calming blue background and smattering of stars.

Intrigued, he went closer. Conventional art rarely gave him pleasure and, when he found a piece that did, he bought it.

"Interesting." He meant it. The painting made him think of summer, of passion, of heat. Of…her.

He sensed her go still, watching him. When he didn't speak again, she moved up behind him.

"Do you like it?"

"I do. I've never seen anything like it." He spotted the signature in the right bottom corner and lifted a brow. "*You* painted this?"

He saw right through her careless shrug.

"Before I wanted to be a doctor, I used to want to be an artist." The last word she said in a self-depre-cating tone. "Now, I don't have time to paint as much as I'd like."

"This is wonderful," he said slowly, wondering if she had intentionally painted the raw sensuality in the swirls of color. "Would you be willing to sell it?"

Tilting her head, she stared at him. "Why on earth would you want to buy that?"

"Because it reminds me of you."

Her brows rose as she stared him down. Only the color flooding her face told him she wasn't as impervious to him as she tried to pretend.

Of course she wasn't. Anyone who could paint with such passion…

"Well?" he asked again. "How much do you want?"

She shook her head. "It's not for sale."

He couldn't help himself, he circled both her and the painting, his wolf stirring, readying himself for the hunt. "Does it embarrass you?"

"My painting? Of course not."

"Your sensuality." Again he studied her work, glancing at her periodically. "So much of it comes through in your work."

Now she couldn't hold his gaze. "You get it then. Not many people do. After all, it's an abstract."

He knew her nervous chatter was meant to distract him. But he wouldn't be sidetracked. Heat sizzled between them; surely she could feel it, too. Inside, his wolf sniffed the air, scenting her.

As though he'd totally abandoned self-control, he lifted her chin, making her look at him. When she met his gaze, he swore under his breath. The aching vulnerability in her beautiful eyes made his mouth go dry.

He could no more keep from touching her than he could stop his heart from beating.

Miraculously she didn't resist.

Drowning in sensation, he held her, her head tucked under his chin. Intoxicated at the feel and scent of her, all soft and curvy and warm, he marveled at her delicacy. Though her lush form was that of a goddess, her fine bone structure and lack of height combined not only to make him feel horny as hell, but huge and protective and tender.

Hell hounds. Emotions were the last thing he wanted. He should only be craving sex with her—hot, passionate, mindless sex. Fast and furious and sweaty.

And empty as hell.

She made a sound, moving slightly. When she tilted her face to look up at him, he covered her mouth with his.

She tasted exactly as he'd imagined—of woman and exotic spices, of sunshine and passion. Bemused, confused, and aroused more than he'd ever been, he fought himself. He wouldn't, couldn't allow this flood of sensation, of longing. Like coming home, if he'd ever known such a place.

Shivering, she moaned low in her throat, and he deepened the kiss, his body reacting to the quick catch of her breath. Her full breasts crushed against him, begging for his stroke and caress.

The wolf inside him snarled, agitated. He wanted to mate, not later, but now. Fighting him, Jared fought himself. And Elena…she had no idea what kind of battle raged inside him. Because of her. For her.

Too much. Jared felt as if he'd been thrown into the ocean, concrete blocks attached to his feet. What he'd expected to be a simple slaking of a mutual attraction had instantly become a thousand times more complicated.

He certainly hadn't expected this.

In his considerable experience, anticipation usually equaled disaster. One thing he'd learned—the more he built up something in his mind, the more anticlimactic it was when he actually got it.

He'd been dreaming about Elena for days, ever since he'd met her. Thus, their first kiss should have sucked. He'd *wanted* it to suck. Maybe then he could purge her from his mind.

But this…he groaned.

She used her tongue to mate with his. Urgent. Hot. Rubbing her body against him, she made little animal sounds low in her throat, enflaming him to the point of no control.

He'd thought he simply wanted her out of his head, but now worse, far worse, he craved *more.* He ached to bury himself deep inside her welcoming softness. To claim her, to make her his.

Mate.

No. Not possible.

Inside, his wolf howled.

From somewhere, he dredged up the presence of mind to push away.

"I'm sorry," he gritted out. "I wish I could say that won't ever happen again, but I can't." Then, having delivered a fair warning, he limped off in the direction of the clinic, trying to get himself together.

Stunned, Elena let him go without a word of protest.

When he'd kissed her, she'd gone up in flames. The paperwork that had seemed so urgent no longer appealed.

She put her hands to her still-hot cheeks, feeling like the heroine of some B-grade movie. What on earth was she going to do? Bad enough that she'd let herself get involved with Watkins—look how that had turned out—but Jared? Since when had she developed a thing for doctors?

And Jared was Charles Watkins's friend. What if he also could become a wolf? What then? She knew better than to take a risk like that.

Convinced she was being paranoid, she forced herself to calm down, to attempt to focus on the paperwork in front of her. There was an odd discrepancy with a few of the dancers' time cards, and she needed to sort that out.

An hour later, a knock on her door startled her. The door opened and Valerie peered in, eyes swollen and red, as if she'd been crying. Joy was right behind her.

"Luke didn't show up."

Elena looked up from the ledger, abandoning her attempt to balance the columns, checked the schedule and frowned as she glanced at the clock. "It's eleven-thirty. He's on in half an hour. I heard you were late. Weren't you with him?"

"Me?" Valerie sniffed. "No. I had car trouble."

"Fine. But he's your boyfriend. Call him."

"Not anymore." Glaring at her, Valerie crossed her arms. "We had a fight earlier. Over Dr. Watkins."

Elena froze. "Why?"

Valerie wouldn't look at her. "Dr. Watkins and I are only friends. But Luke thought we were sleeping together."

More drama she didn't need. She'd known Watkins was a player, but hadn't known he'd gone after her cousin. "Were you?"

"Sleeping with Dr. Watkins? Puh-leese."

Valerie was lying, Elena could tell. But right now, she didn't care. She just needed to make sure Luke was all right. "Whatever, Val. If you don't want to call Luke, I'll have Joy do it. Joy, would you give him a call?"

"I already did," Joy said. "Both his house and cell. I got voice mail both times. I left him a message to call in."

Staring at her sister, Elena knew her own fear was reflected back in Joy's eyes. They both were thinking of Damien's disappearance. Since he and Luke hadn't been friends, she probably had no reason to worry.

Still…two dancers in three days? She felt as she had years ago when her cousin had died, as if she'd failed to protect them.

Joy touched Valerie's arm. "You know Luke better than anyone. Did he use drugs?"

Shaking her head, Valerie looked grim. "No. He's clean."

"Are you sure?"

Though Valerie nodded, her expression was uncertain.

"Maybe we should step up the random drug tests," Elena said. "I'll look into it."

"Hey, maybe you can run those on Melissa for me, too." Joy sighed. "Once she gets out of rehab, that is. I hate leaving that child alone at night while I work, especially now that I know what she's been up to."

"So bring her here."

"I'd thought about it, but I don't know if it would be good for her to be exposed to so much sex on the hoof."

"Sex on the…?" Startled, Elena laughed. "You know I expect the dancers to be on model behavior when they're not performing."

"Yeah, and that part is good. But they *do* perform, and Melissa is nearly eighteen…what if she sneaks in and watches the show?"

"I'd lose my license, for one." Elena laid a hand over her sister's. "Considering what's happened, once Missy gets out, maybe you should take some time off, hang around the house—and her."

"I've been thinking about that, but—"

"What about Luke?" Valerie interrupted. "I'm really worried. He was pretty upset earlier."

The phone rang, making them collectively jump. Elena wished she could dissipate the sudden knot in her stomach.

"Maybe this is Luke, calling in sick," she said, before picking up the receiver. "Hello?"

The caller was her back-door bouncer, Bob. "You'd better get down here. I've already called the police."

Her heartbeat stuttered. "Luke?"

He sounded as if he might be sick. "Come down."

"On my way." Hanging up, she took off at a run, Joy and Valerie hot on her heels.

A small crowd had assembled around the back entrance. Mostly employees, though a few curious customers had seen the commotion from the parking lot and walked over.

Bob motioned her over. "That car came squealing up to the alley." He pointed to the black Honda. Luke's car. "When it stopped, he got out."

There, on the pavement. Black jeans, curly blond hair. Luke.

"He took two steps and fell."

Running for the body, Valerie screamed and began sobbing. "I think he's dead."

Bob grabbed Elena's arm. "Wait until the police get here."

But Elena shook him off. Pushing Valerie away, she gently rolled the man over. At the sight, she reeled back. Valerie wailed.

"It's Luke," Elena said. "He's dead."

Chapter 5

Setting up shop in the exam room, Jared couldn't shake a feeling of unease, of foreboding. He didn't have premonitions, didn't even really believe in them, yet he'd never felt such strong certainty that something was wrong. Very wrong.

At first, he thought his disquiet stemmed from kissing Elena. The kiss had been a lot of things, none of them what he'd expected. Instead of proving all they shared was physical attraction, what should have been a simple physical act made him realize he was a fool. A fool setting himself up for a hard fall.

Yet knowing this, knowing her feelings about shifters and the fact that his friend had disappeared after revealing himself to her, Jared still couldn't shake the absurd notion that she was his mate, any more than he could rid himself of his desire for her.

He wanted Elena Cabrera with a fierceness that terrified him. He craved her in much the same way he'd once craved his pain medication, like an addict.

Addictions of any kind weren't good.

Again he shook his head, trying to banish the unwanted thoughts and focus on the task at hand. Patients would be arriving soon; the first real patients he'd seen since the hospital had sent him home. That decision still rankled—he'd completed rehab of his own accord, and yet the hospital administrator had still suspended his privileges.

Inside, his wolf self snarled. That part of him also felt unsettled, and try as he might, he couldn't shake the increasing apprehension.

Something was very, very wrong.

Even as he admitted this, his stomach churned and the tension between his shoulder blades became a physical ache.

All of this was not simply because he wanted a woman.

No. His trepidation became alarm, his alarm, a blind, unreasonable terror.

Elena.

Swearing under his breath, he took off for Elena's office.

She wasn't there. Leaving her office, he startled a tall, ebony skinned man.

"Can I help you?" the man asked, his voice guarded.

Hooking his thumbs in his jean pockets, Jared nodded. "I'm looking for Elena."

The giant crossed his arms. "And you are?"

"Jared Gies. Dr. Jared Gies."

"Ah." The autocratic features relaxed. "I'm Dixon, one of the dancers." He stuck out his hand.

Shaking it, Jared asked again. "Do you know where Elena might be?"

"She's outside. Some kind of commotion at the back entrance. I'm on my way there, come with me."

His patients? Or…?

"Thanks." Jared went with him in silence.

They arrived just after the paramedics. What could only be described as a body bag lay in the alley outside the door.

Spotting Elena in the midst of the small crowd, he shouldered his way through them to reach her.

"What's going on?"

"Luke—another one of my dancers—is dead." Though she squared her shoulders, he noticed her voice shook as much as her hands.

Pushing away from him, she motioned him to follow. Once she reached the body bag, she pulled back the black plastic. "It's Luke."

Despite the catch in her voice, Jared focused his attention on the body. Luke had been a startlingly beautiful young man, with shoulder-length, white-blond hair and chiseled features.

Despite the lack of an aura, Jared suspected Luke had also been a shifter. As they all did, he'd remained in human form when he died.

Elena touched his arm. "He is—was—one of my youngest dancers. Like Damien."

"How did he die?" He directed his question to a uniformed officer.

"We don't know yet." The portly policeman who'd questioned him the night they'd found Damien answered with compassion. Officer Yost. "We suspect he might have used drugs."

"Not Luke!" Valerie sobbed. Her sharp tone made Jared take a second look. Tears streamed down her face, but she didn't appear shocked. Had she known Luke was using?

Worse, both Damien and Luke had been shifters. He took a closer look. Though he couldn't tell, this one had probably been a Halfling, too. They didn't heal the way full-blooded shifters did.

Had Elena known? Watkins had said she'd freaked out once he'd revealed his true nature. Why then, were so many of her employees and customers nonhuman?

He had to talk to Elena about it. But could he do that without revealing his own nature?

Chest aching, he helped her stand. The crowd had gone silent, watching them.

"Are you certain it was drugs?"

"Reasonably." One of the younger cops answered. "But we won't know for sure until the autopsy is completed."

"Luke didn't use drugs," Valerie repeated. "Seriously."

This time, Officer Yost's expression was stern. "No? We found this in his pocket." He held up a rolled plastic bag containing white powder. "I'm betting this is cocaine."

Elena cursed.

Jared could practically read her mind. Damien and Luke—two young men, cut down in the prime of their lives because of drugs. She probably didn't know that their Packs would have to be notified, as well as their human families.

She appeared to have no idea of their true nature.

Did she really think Watkins was the only one?

Casually he glanced around. Elena's employees, Dixon included, were congregated in a small circle, engrossed in conversation. None of them paid him any attention.

The police were all busy taking notes or talking to each other. From what he could hear, they didn't appear to think this was a crime, just a drug overdose.

Elena glanced around wildly, hyperventilating.

"Are you all right?" Jared asked her.

With a nod, she began moving away, stumbling toward the door. Immediately the circle of dancers broke up and went to her, surrounding her like bodyguards, shielding her from the curious stares of onlookers.

They pretended Jared was not there.

Inside, they herded her down the hall to her office, crowding inside. Jared pushed his way in, too, trying to stay as close to Elena as possible. With so many people, the small room felt claustrophobic, making him feel queasy. Apparently Elena felt the same way. Gripping the edge of her cherrywood desk, she inhaled loudly.

"I'm okay," she said, then repeated the words like a mantra.

The assembled dancers all watched her in silence. Most seemed intent on continuing to ignore him, but Jared noticed the shifters shooting him occasional glares.

Territorial. He understood, and let it go.

A movement distracted him and he realized Valerie and Joy had joined them also, standing near the door. When she caught his gaze, Valerie winked at him. Scowling, Jared looked away.

Finally Elena lifted her head and glanced around the room. She let her gaze linger on each man individually. When she reached Jared, he felt the touch of her eyes like scorching metal.

"Is there anything any of you want to tell me?"

Several of the men exchanged looks, but no one spoke. Finally a muscular man with spiky yellow hair stepped forward. Jared noted he was a shifter.

"I can't speak for the others, but I didn't know Damien and Luke were using, if that's what you mean."

She rubbed her temples. "Ryan, I run a clean business here. Or so I thought."

"And safe," a slender Latino chimed in, his dark eyes serious. "We always felt safe here."

Past tense. Jared noticed he'd used past tense.

"But no longer." Ryan crossed his overdeveloped arms. "Elena, none of us feel safe anymore. Two guys are dead—our friends. The police have written them off as strippers who OD'd, but we all know they weren't junkies."

He shot Jared a glare. "And Dr. Watkins has disappeared. No one's busting balls to find him, either." His direct glare changed to a challenge. "We don't like this new guy you brought in at all."

Jared shook his head. The dancer talked as though he wasn't even there.

"Dr. Gies?" Expression revealing her astonishment,

she stared at the younger man, before darting a glance at Jared through her long lashes. "Why not? You don't even know him."

"Nothing happened here until he came," another man, one of the shifters, spoke up. "We can't help but feel as if he's responsible."

"Yeah," Ryan seconded. "And if he's not responsible, then he's bad luck."

The others all murmured their agreement.

"Think about it." Ryan's earnest expression made him look about nineteen, though he had to be older. "Dr. Watkins disappears, this guy shows up and two of our friends are murdered."

Put that way, Jared had to acknowledge his appearance did sound suspicious.

"You're forgetting his leg," Elena pointed out. "How could he attack two young, muscular guys like Damien and Luke?" Bam. Though she'd meant well, with a few words Elena had stabbed him in the heart. Worse, she didn't even appear to realize.

Not looking at him, she took a deep breath before continuing. "Once he'd subdued them, he'd have to inject them with the drugs. And for what reason?"

"True." The man behind Ryan jostled the two men next to him. "Any of us could take him with one hand tied behind our backs."

That did it. Jared could contain himself no longer. Straightening, he gripped his cane. "Want to try?" he drawled. "One at a time, starting now?"

Several of the others appeared surprised, as though they truly hadn't realized Jared was there.

The shifters gave each other wolfish grins before turning to face him. "Bring it on," the first one said.

Inside, his wolf snarled. He grinned back. "Are you sure you can handle me?"

Ryan bared his teeth.

"Enough," Elena ordered. "Cut the crap. We're all upset, we've lost two of our friends in nearly as many days. We need to grieve and be kind to each other. Now, I'd like to talk to Dr. Gies. Alone. Last one out, close the door behind you."

Though they didn't want to go, she was their boss and, in the case of the shifters, their human Pack leader. Glaring hard at Jared, they left.

Jared waited until the last one had filed out and the door clicked shut. "Hell hounds. That was weird."

"Hell hounds?" She raised a brow. "What kind of expression is that?"

"A personal one." And one he hadn't meant to give away.

"I've never heard that before."

That surprised him since she was surrounded by shifters. "Never?"

She shook her head. "Not that I remember."

"Are you all right?" he asked.

"Yes. No." She rubbed her temples. "I can't think. I don't understand what's going on around here. My dancers are like family to me, and now two of them are dead."

"Evidently you didn't know them as well as you thought." He didn't know how she'd take his remark, but he had to find out if she'd known both Damien and Luke had been Halflings.

"I knew them well enough." Her beautiful caramel eyes filled with tears. "I *cared* about Damien and Luke. I tried to protect them, keep them safe. I failed."

He went very still, clenching his hands to keep from touching her. "You're their employer, not their mother. Don't beat yourself up over this."

"You don't understand." Her breath caught.

"Tell me. Make me understand."

But she only shook her head and turned away, shoulders shaking.

Because he had no choice, he gave her a moment of privacy to grieve in silence, aching to comfort her, marveling at her Herculean effort to get herself under control.

When she finally faced him again, professional, dispassionate Elena was back. Again she rubbed her temples. "This headache that's been lurking around all day is trying to become a full-blown migraine. I need to take something."

He waited while she opened her desk drawer, extracted a plastic container and shook a pill into her hand.

Though the soda on her desk had probably been sitting there all day, she used that to chase down the pill. When she'd finished, she set the can down and looked at him again. "Jared, why are you here? Shouldn't you be in the clinic now?"

How to explain the odd feeling he'd had that something was wrong. "I heard the commotion and came to check on you. I was worried about you." He gave a self-deprecating wince of a smile. "I forgot you had so many willing protectors."

She let that one go. "I've got to get to the bottom of

this. As you heard, the others think you had something to do with it."

He narrowed his eyes. "And you? What do you think?"

"I don't think so. You're a doctor. Doctors are supposed to heal."

"Not always." Her answer meant more to him than it should. Still, it wasn't enough.

"What do you mean?"

"Just like everyone else, there are good doctors and bad doctors."

Her smile trembled around the edges. "And which one are you?"

Hounds help him, he wanted her. He advanced another step, until he was close enough that his breath tickled her face. "What do your insides tell you, Elena?"

Her breath caught. He liked that she didn't back down from the intensity of his gaze.

"I don't know," she whispered. "Something about you…"

If he stayed another second, he'd yank her up against him and kiss her again.

He needed to put distance between them.

"Don't ever trust physical attraction," he snarled. "It's not safe for either of us." That said, he left her.

Fantasies closed early that night. Elena sent everyone home, keeping her composure until the last employee left the building. Valerie had left, as well, too distraught to talk coherently. Only Joy stayed.

"Go." Elena waved her sister away. "My head is pounding and all I want to do is lie down."

"No. You need company." Joy grabbed a bottle of Riesling from the fridge and two wineglasses. "Let me open this and we'll talk."

"I don't need to talk." Sinking into her chair, Elena accepted a glass of wine from her sister. Her hands shook so much the wine splashed onto her desk.

Worse, once the shaking started, Elena couldn't get it to stop.

Expression alarmed, Joy watched her over the rim of her wineglass. "Are you all right?"

The same question Jared had asked.

She gave the same answer. "Yes. No. Luke and Damien are *dead.*" Setting down her glass before more spilled, Elena covered her face with her hands. "They all know I don't allow drugs. I'd have bet my entire savings they weren't using. If Luke was doing drugs, Valerie would have known. They were dating."

"Have you asked her?"

"No, not yet." One deep breath, then another, and Elena finally was able to pick up her glass again. She took a small sip, relishing the sweet taste of the wine. "She was too upset."

"Are you going to do more drug testing?"

"I'm going to have to. I'll ask Jared to set it up for me."

Joy leaned back in her chair. "What is going on with you and Jared?"

"Nothing." She knew she'd answered too quickly. Her sister knew her too well. "There's a certain… physical attraction. That's all. The dancers think he's involved in all this drug stuff."

"And you? What do you think?"

"Oh, God. He asked me the same thing. I don't know, Joy. Seriously I don't know what to think."

Finishing her wine, Joy got up and refilled her glass, topping off Elena's. "You asked him?"

"Of course. I wanted to see how he'd react."

"And?"

Elena sighed. "He didn't really answer. Instead he asked me what I thought. He told me there were good doctors and bad ones. Worse, he said acting on physical attraction was dangerous for both of us."

"He threatened you?"

"No, not exactly. It was more of a warning, and I kind of got the impression it was directed toward himself more than me."

"Weird." Joy crossed her arms. "That the dancers are blaming him."

"His arrival did coincide with Damien's death."

"True, but do you really think he could be providing them with drugs?"

Oddly enough, the wine had made her headache subside. Elena took another sip, trying to relax. "Honestly, no. How could he? He just got here. Look at the series of events." She held up her hand. "One, Watkins disappears. Two, Jared shows up looking for him. Three, Damien dies, seemingly from a drug overdose."

"And now four, Luke also OD's," Joy finished for her. "And you forgot to mention Melissa's overdose."

"Why didn't I think of that?" Elena pushed herself out of her chair. "We need to talk to Melissa."

Expression wary, Joy stayed seated. "About what?"

"The drugs, of course. We need to ask her where she

got the drugs. Once we find that out, maybe we can find whoever is harming my dancers."

"But she didn't even know Damien or Luke."

Elena waved her sister's comment away. "Maybe not, but if she can tell us who's supplying drugs in this area, I'll bet we can find out where Damien and Luke got theirs."

"Then what?"

"Then we get them arrested."

Joy rolled her eyes. "Sounds dangerous. Maybe you should leave stuff like that up to the police."

"The police don't care. My two dead dancers are small potatoes compared to what they have to deal with. Come on, Joy. We can't just ignore this."

"I don't know…" Joy set down her wineglass. "I don't know if Missy will even talk to us. I think it depends what kind of shape she's in. When do you want to go?"

A surge of hope made Elena grin. "Tomorrow, as soon as we can get up there."

The next morning, Elena accompanied Joy to the hospital to talk to Melissa. Though the rehab program frowned on family visits in the first month, Joy had explained the unique situation and the clinic had agreed to let them visit.

A sullen Missy waited for them in a small visiting room equipped with three plastic chairs and a cheap, wobbly table. Elena hadn't seen her niece looking so good in months. She'd twisted her longish, sable hair into a ponytail and the only makeup she wore was a transparent lip gloss. Without the black eyeliner and caked-on mascara, she looked like a vibrant and healthy seventeen-year-old.

"Wow!" Elena told her.

Joy echoed the sentiment. "You look fantastic."

Missy made a face at her mom, but smiled at Elena. "Hi, Aunt El."

Twisting her hands round and round, Joy gave her daughter an awkward hug. "How are they treating you here?"

Immediately the crafty teenager returned. "Horrible." She began a litany of complaints, ranging from the food to the coarseness of the sheets. "Have you come to take me home?"

Joy swallowed. "I…No. We can't."

Immediately Melissa started wailing.

Joy looked to Elena for help.

"Missy, stop." Elena clapped her hands. When the teenager fell silent, she continued in a gentle voice. "You know we can't take you home yet, sweetheart. Not until you complete the program."

"Look at me." Missy spread her arms dramatically. "I *have* completed the program, basically. I'm clean. I'm sober. That makes me done, the way I see it."

Elena shook her head.

When she saw her words had no effect on her aunt, the teenager turned to her mother. "Mom. Take me home. Pleeease."

"I'm sorry, we can't." Sniffling, Joy dabbed at her eyes with a tissue. She didn't see the hard look her daughter gave her.

"Where's Dr. Gies?" Melissa demanded. "I want him. He knows what it's like. He'll tell you I can go home."

"He's not here." Elena cleared her throat. "Missy, we need to ask you something."

"Oh, yeah? What do I get if I answer?"

"Nothing. This is important, so please pay attention." Sharp-voiced, Elena relayed what had happened at the club, skipping any gory details. "I've got two employees dead, both from an overdose. I want to know where you got your drugs."

"Why?"

"I want to know who's supplying my dancers."

"You expect me to be a narc?" Missy's scornful tone told just how likely that would be.

Elena had to swallow her anger. Voice shaking with the effort, she clenched her fists. "Melissa Nichole. This is serious. People are *dying*. Dying! You've got to help me before anyone else gets hurt."

Missy stuck her chin out, pursed her lips and shook her head. "Would you really choose your dancers' safety over mine?"

"Of course not. I want to protect all of you. Give me the dealer's name so I can make him stop."

"Get real. What do you plan to do once you know? Go after him yourself? Then *you'll* be the one getting killed. You need to mind your own business."

"This *is* my business." Elena jammed her hands in her slacks pockets. "If you'll tell me who sells you the drugs, I'll go to the police and have him arrested."

Missy snorted. "Riiight. Then he'll get out on bail

and come looking for me. Don't you watch TV? That's how it works."

"Come on." Joy grabbed Elena's arm before she could reply, pushing her toward the door. "Visit over. Let's go."

"I'm not finished."

"Oh, yes, you are."

Once they were out in the hallway, Elena rounded on her sister. "What'd you do that for?"

Joy shrugged. "I didn't see any reason to keep agitating her. She wasn't going to tell you anything."

"She might have, if you'd given me more time."

"Dream on." Joy punched the elevator down button. "Plus, she has a point about not wanting to make herself a target. I don't want my little girl hurt."

"This isn't the movies. No one would know she told me. I'd be the one going to the police. If anything, they'd come after me."

"Maybe. Assuming the police even believed you. Either way, you'd be putting yourself and my daughter at risk."

"What's the alternative?" Elena rounded on her sister. "I can't allow any more of my dancers to be hurt."

"You are not their mother. They're adults. You can't monitor their lives 24/7."

Elena refused to believe this. "There's got to be something I can do."

"Set up the drug testing. Post your zero-tolerance policy. And find out what happened to Watkins."

This last surprised her. "Do you think he was involved in the drugs?"

Joy's creamy complexion reddened. "After you decided you didn't want to date him, I went out with him for a while, until I realized he's nothing but a player. He was dating Valerie, at the same time. I should have told you, but I was too ashamed."

Stunned, Elena could only stare. So Watkins had been seeing her sister *and* Valerie, and then had come back to her, tried to convince her they were meant to be together and shown her what he was. He was far more than a player. Should she tell her sister what she knew about him? Joy would think she was nuts if she said she'd seen the man change into a wolf with her own two eyes.

Until Watkins reappeared, she'd keep her mouth shut. There was already way too much weirdness going on around here without adding to it.

Chapter 6

Thursday afternoon, as soon as Jared stepped inside Fantasies, Elena appeared in the hallway, greeting him. She wore a dove-gray skirt and jacket, and only the vivid scarlet of her silk blouse showed the passionate nature he knew she kept hidden inside.

He wanted to rip the suit off her.

"Good afternoon." Her smile seemed lackluster.

"Yeah," he replied, hoping he succeeded in hiding the sudden instant of savage desire. "What's up?"

"I went to visit Melissa, my niece. I was trying to get her to tell me where she got her drugs."

He frowned. "Why?"

"Well, it's possible the same person sold them to my dancers."

"Possible, though not very likely. Assuming Melissa told you, then what?"

"I'd go to the police and have them arrested."

"Bad idea. All you'd do is put your niece in trouble."

"I wouldn't tell them where I got the name."

"Then they wouldn't be able to arrest anyone." He shrugged. "You can't just go to the police and tell tales on someone without evidence to back you up. And unless your niece will tell them she bought drugs from this person, their hands are tied."

"Well, she didn't tell me, so that's a moot topic."

Her disgruntled tone made him smile. "Since you closed early yesterday, how do I round up people to come to the clinic tonight?"

"They won't, not tonight. Today's Thursday. They know the clinic days."

"Tuesday night Valerie said they were lining up outside."

"She got that going." Elena shrugged. "I don't know how. But once they know for sure you're open, they'll come."

"So I'll go there and wait."

"I have a better idea." She touched his arm, sending an electric shot straight to his groin. "You need to meet my dancers."

Though he shook his head, he didn't move away. Her touch felt too damn good. "I already have."

"Not formally."

His expression must have shown what he thought of that.

"Hey, they're nice guys," she said.

"I'm sure they are." He pulled his arm free, alarmed by the way his traitorous body responded to even such a small touch. "But I don't see a need for formal introductions."

"Fine. But I thought you wanted patients. You're supposed to be running a clinic here, remember?"

"The clinic's for the homeless, you said. What's this got to do with your dancers?"

"Watkins saw them, too, when they needed medical care. That was part of the deal when I let him work out of here."

He narrowed his eyes, deciding to tease her. "Did you happen to mention that little fact to me?"

Her soft laugh made his mouth twitch with the urge to smile back. "I think so. Come on, this will take all of five minutes."

"Why not?" With a shrug, he stopped resisting.

As she led the way down the hall, she glanced at him over her shoulder. Her smile widened, containing a hint of mischief.

Again he fought the urge to yank her up against him and crush her mouth with his. Instead he concentrated on the sexy sound her stiletto heels made as she strode down the marble hall. Despite his valiant struggle, he couldn't keep up and he settled for hobbling along behind her. The view was better back there anyway, though the sight of her nicely rounded rear in the form-fitting skirt made him want to do more than merely kiss her.

Finally they reached the end of the hall. He'd thought they were going to the stage area, but once they passed through the double doors, she turned right, taking them down a short flight of stairs. At the bottom, she pulled open a metal door. He followed her inside.

Great. She'd brought him into the dancer's locker room. Tile floors, community showers, beige metal lockers and wooden benches. The air smelled of a curious mixture of humidity, perspiration and scented deodorants or cologne. Nostrils flaring, Jared left the door open behind him. His wolf didn't like this at all. Neither did Jared.

Ten or twelve men in various states of undress stared at them, unsmiling. Dixon and Ryan were there, and others he recognized from the night before. Despite Elena's presence, Jared couldn't help but notice not one man tried to cover any exposed parts. This must not be an unusual occurrence.

But seeing him, they all started talking at once, the first shock of silence erupting into unharmonious noise.

Elena climbed up on a bench and clapped twice for quiet. Instantly all the voices died down.

"*Mejos,* though some of you sort of met him the other night, I'd like to formally introduce you to Dr. Jared Gies." From her perch, she indicated Jared with a dramatic sweep of her hand, making him notice her fingernails were the same scarlet color as her blouse. "Dr. Gies will be operating the free clinic."

"Where's Dr. Watkins?" one man, a slender, wiry brunet with a ponytail, asked.

Elena cleared her throat, glancing at Jared before looking back at her employees. "I honestly don't know. He and I had a disagreement, and he left."

At that announcement, which appeared to be news to

them, the men tried to outtalk each other. Jared took this time to glance around the room, counting how many of the dancers were human and how many were…not.

The ratio seemed to tip slightly in favor of not. There were even three vampires, not trying too hard to hide their fangs.

When the noise level continued unabated, this time Jared clapped to quiet them.

"Nice to meet you," he said, aware he sounded anything but. The aggressive shifter Ryan stared him down, flanked by two other shifters.

Without formal Pack structure, they wanted to make their own. In other words, they were spoiling for a fight.

Inside, he could feel his wolf's alertness. His beast was ready for trouble. Jared snorted. From a bunch of half-naked guys? Bring it on.

Ryan looked away first. His two buddies followed suit. Victory, without a blow being exchanged.

Jared gave the rest a savage smile.

Most of them simply stared back, expressionless. The humans, sensing undercurrents but not entirely sure why, caved first.

"Nice to meet you," one human dancer finally said. A couple of the others chimed in with similar words.

Jared let his smile gradually fade away.

Undaunted, the man stepped forward, hand outstretched. Jared shook, resisting the urge to bare his teeth at the way the guy continually stared at Elena. With salt-and-pepper hair and a slightly weathered face, this dancer appeared to be the oldest of the lot. He was also the most muscular, which might explain why he still had a job.

"I'm Liam." He delivered this in a cultured, British accent.

None of the others moved.

"Oh, for Pete's sake," Elena huffed. Moving to stand at Jared's side, she beckoned them all closer.

Reluctantly they moved. Most of the human males' expressions were neutral, though a few appeared friendly. The vampires were curious and the other shifters, distrustful. Jared shook hands with aplomb, all the while trying to ignore the fact that they were grown men standing around in G-strings and brightly colored bikini underwear. He wondered if they felt as uncomfortable as he did.

The hostility from the shifters was palpable. Had they treated Watkins like this? He made a mental note to find out.

After he'd shaken all their hands, he turned to go.

"What happened to Dr. Watkins?" One of the shifters—Mark?—clutched Jared's shirt, a big no-no in Pack etiquette. "I really liked him. I don't understand why he and Elena didn't work things out."

"I—"

"How should he know?" A lanky man wearing low-slung Levi's and nothing else moved closer, his expression cold and resentful. Two miniscule fangs poked out from under his lips. "He just got here. He probably doesn't even know Watkins."

Though vampires and shifters in general had an uneasy truce, something about this one irked him. Even Jared's wolf growled.

"I'm sorry, I don't remember your name," Jared said. "How well did you know Dr. Watkins?"

"Luis. My name is Luis." Instantly the man shrugged, moving back with that effortless glide common to vampires. "I didn't know him any better than anyone else."

Several of the others snickered.

The hair on the back of Jared's neck rose as the tension in the room ratcheted up a notch.

Elena didn't appear to notice any of it.

"What's so funny?" She eyed them with mock sternness, the corners of her mouth trying not to smile. "Is there something I should know about?"

Did the immediate silence feel awkward to anyone but Jared? Intently he searched their faces, wondering if any of them knew the truth about Watkins's disappearance.

"Seriously, Luis. Spill." Elena tapped her foot in impatience.

Luis shook his head, his expression sullen. "I liked him, that's all. There's nothing to tell."

"Luis and Dr. Watkins were buddies." A lean blond man with patrician features sniffed. "Though I think Luis wanted to be more. Watkins wasn't gay, though."

Luis's dusky skin paled. "You're just jealous."

"No, I'm not."

While they bickered, Elena shook her head and glanced at Jared. "Let's leave them to get ready for tonight. Introductions are over. Come on."

He let out his breath in a whoosh once they were alone in the hall. "That was…interesting."

"Interesting?" She grinned. "What do you mean?"

"Elena, have you noticed anything…different about any of your dancers?"

"Different how?"

He seized on the first example he could find. "Luis's teeth, for one thing."

"Oh, his vampire teeth?" Her grin widened. "Part of his act. He likes to pretend to be a vampire."

Only, he wasn't pretending.

Jared tried again. "What about Ryan?"

"He's a little aggressive. But that will disappear once he gets used to you." When he started to speak, she held up a hand. "I promise you, they're not usually so bad. Give them time."

"Watkins," he said. "Have you noticed that some of the dancers are like Watkins?"

She went absolutely still, her smile disappearing. "Like him how?" Her careful tone matched the reserve in her eyes.

"Elena, I know you know." Time to cut the crap.

"Know what?" She avoided his gaze. "Listen, Watkins was one of a kind. I don't really want to talk about him—he's not here to defend himself."

"But—"

"No." The emphatic look she gave him showed him she meant what she said. "I think we're finished now. You know where the clinic is. If you want patients, I'm sure a few of them will come and see you. If not…" With a wave and an utterly false smile, she moved away.

He didn't follow. Instead he went looking for Olivia, the vampire hostess he'd met earlier.

Instead Valerie manned the front desk. She wore a skintight mesh minidress, silver stilettos and way too much makeup. Noticing him, she flashed him a smile before escorting another group of women down the stairs to the club. Olivia was nowhere in sight.

When Valerie returned, she gave him a quick, full-body hug. "You did well taking a stand against Ryan and his buddies earlier."

He nodded. "I need to find Olivia."

Her smile disappeared. "Why?"

"I need to talk to her. Where is she?"

Sullen now, she pointed toward the doorway leading to the club. "She's tending bar. She should be working the big one in the back of the room."

No point in delaying the inevitable. Nodding his thanks and ignoring Valerie's too-obvious disappointment, he descended the stairs and pushed through the double doors.

The music assaulted him first. Then the flashing strobe lights, the various scents of perfume and perspiration and alcohol. He located the bar in the far right corner and headed that way, hoping he could persuade Olivia to take a break and talk to him somewhere private.

Since she had two other bartenders to cover for her, she agreed. Instead of going into the lobby, she took him through a hallway, past the rest rooms and into a large supply room. Floor to ceiling shelves and boxes were the only other occupants.

"What's up, wolf?" She appeared curious rather than flattered.

"You probably know another dancer died. He was Pack."

"I know." Studying one long, scarlet nail, she peered

up at him through purple false eyelashes. "Watkins was Pack, too, and now he's vanished. I'm beginning to see. Damien and Luke were also shifters. You're trying to find out if someone's targeting your kind. You're a Protector."

He shouldn't have been surprised that a vampire knew about a covert Pack organization controlled by the National Pack Council. Dubbed Protectors, these Special Forces-type shifters hunted down humans who tried to expose or torture shifters. They also helped those shifters damaged by humans, but if the shifter was beyond repair, Protectors were authorized to kill. In his entire lifetime, Jared had never met one.

"No, I'm not, though I'll call them if I have to. I came here looking for Watkins," he told her. "He's my friend." His only friend, if truth be told. "And right now, I'm trying to find out how much Elena knows. Watkins told me he changed in front of her and she was horrified. Right after that, he disappeared."

"Wow." Flashing her teeth in a pointy-toothed smile, she shook her head. "I would have bet my entire blood stash that Elena didn't know. She doesn't appear to realize I'm a vamp. And she doesn't treat Ryan and his minipack any differently than anyone else."

"She's never mentioned anything to you?"

"No. But then, she and I aren't close. Valerie's her cousin. She was dating Luke. You might talk to her."

His wolf began to pace. It'd been a couple of nights since he'd last changed.

"Does Valerie know about Luke's true nature?"

"I have no idea. She knew about Watkins when she dated him." She glanced at her watch, tossing her silky black hair over her shoulder, à la Cher. "It's nearly ten, which is kind of the beginning of our rush. I've got to get back to work. Is there anything else you need?"

"No, thanks." He'd already turned to go. Looked like he'd be talking with Valerie after all.

But when he emerged from the club, he saw only guests in the reception area. He waited a few minutes in case Valerie had simply escorted more customers inside, but she didn't reappear.

With a sigh, he headed back toward the clinic. As he opened the door, his cell phone rang. When he glanced at the caller ID and saw the number, he clenched his teeth. His mother. Not for the first time he wondered if the woman had a touch of clairvoyance.

"How are you, Jared?" She sounded concerned, as she had been ever since his accident. She'd been beside herself when she'd learned he'd been suspended from working at the hospital.

Briefly he outlined Watkins's disappearance.

"Maybe this is a sign," his mother said. She'd never liked Watkins, especially after the car accident. Since he'd been driving, she'd always blamed him for what had happened to her son.

Jared refused to let her bait him. Instead he told her about the free clinic, forcing enthusiasm into his voice.

"I'm glad. Keeping busy is a good thing. Jared, I've got news." For the first time since he'd been released from the hospital, his mother sounded excited. "I've just learned they found a healer."

"They?"

"The Texas Pack Council. Eunice Tompkins's

Halfling granddaughter went to see her and she's now cancer-free!"

Hounds give him patience. "Mother, there is no such thing as a healer. That's an urban legend."

"This is real. Check your e-mail when you get home. I've sent you the article from the *Weekly Howl*."

"I'm a subscriber," he reminded her. "But I'm a bit behind in my reading."

"Read the article. Then give her a call. What have you got to lose?"

There she had him.

"Nothing," he answered, knowing his curt tone would offend her, but beyond caring. Healers were to Pack like the Loch Ness Monster and Bigfoot were to humans—legend. Stories had been told about them forever. They were always born Halflings—Halflings who could not change. Instead they channeled that energy into healing. Since wounded or ill Halflings couldn't heal themselves like full-bloods, the Pack had searched for a healer for years.

And now his mother was telling him one had been found.

A healer. The fact that none had been born in his or his father's or even his grandfather's lifetime didn't deter the Pack's belief.

If such a person existed, Jared could have hope. Absently he rubbed his leg. It had started throbbing again when he'd stood in the locker room, and now the pain was just short of unbearable. And he couldn't take pain pills….

"Read the article and give her a call," his mother repeated.

"I will," he said. "But remember, nothing is certain at this point."

"Spoken like a doctor." Though she teased, threads of sadness weaved through her voice. "Don't forget, I'm coming for Easter. I arrive on Sunday."

"As if I could, with all your nagging," he teased.

Though she usually laughed at his halfhearted attempts at humor, this time she didn't.

"I'll see you soon. In the meantime, stay safe."

After he hung up, Jared glanced at his watch. Time was crawling at a snail's pace. He hadn't had a single visitor.

Grabbing a magazine from the basket—Watkins had even stocked the familiar, outdated magazines found in every other doctor's office—he dropped into a chair and tried to read while ignoring the pain in his leg.

The squeak of the clinic door alerted him. His first patient had arrived, finally.

The girl entered the room silently, moving like a wraith, keeping close to the wall. He recognized her—Melissa, Joy's daughter. The one who was supposed to be in rehab.

"What are you doing here?" he asked. "No one under eighteen is supposed to be in this club."

"My mother works here. My aunt owns the place. And several of my mom's cousins work security. I'm safer here than I am at home."

"Point taken. Now, why aren't you in rehab?"

This time, instead of hesitant and uncertain, she gazed at him with defiance. He searched her face, looking for the telltale signs of drugs. But her eyes were clear, her breathing normal.

Clean, she must have decided she wasn't afraid of him. He wanted to applaud. How much better to face your adversaries with courage. Instead he kept his features expressionless.

"I need to talk to you," she finally said. Not asking for permission, but simply stating a fact.

If he wasn't careful, he could like this girl.

"Go ahead." He made a show of consulting his watch. "Clinic hours started a while ago and no one's shown up yet."

"They're not sure if they can trust you or not."

For some reason, that stung. "They trusted Watkins?"

She shrugged. "Must have. His clinics were always packed."

"But you're here. Does that mean you trust me?"

"No." Again she glanced at the doorway, as if expecting her mother to appear any second. "But when I inventory my choices, you're the lesser of two evils."

Reluctantly he grinned. He couldn't help it. In his former life of notoriety, it had been a long time since anyone stood up to him like this, especially a patient.

"Are you going to tell me why you're not in rehab?"

She shrugged. "I don't need it. I can stop, anytime I want. I have stopped."

"For now," he told her. "I thought the same thing once. And I did stop. Until the pain got so bad I couldn't stand it. Then—and now, sometimes—I craved my drugs. They blunted this crappy world, made my life a little bit more bearable."

"But you're clean now, right?" Squinting at him, she suddenly looked very young and uncertain.

"Yes. I'm clean now. But I don't think I could stay that way if I hadn't completed rehab. They helped me learn ways to deal with the craving."

Melissa nodded. "I knew you'd understand."

"Yeah. Though I've managed to kick my habit, and you recognized I'm one of your own kind, you're missing the point. *I had help.* Rehab. Yet you've chosen to leave rehab. Why?"

"Kindred souls aside..." she said, making him suppress a sudden grin. Her dry humor was so akin to his, she might have been his daughter, if he'd ever had one.

"Kindred souls aside," he drawled right back at her. "What do you want?" Raising both brows, he crossed his arms and waited for her to tell him.

"I just told you. I need to talk."

"Talk? Talk is cheap. Actions are what count. Go back to rehab."

Her sigh was loud and overly exaggerated. "Will you stop pushing rehab and just listen to me?"

"I'm a medical doctor, not a psychiatrist. I treat medical conditions."

"Yeah? Well, I'm a druggie," she shot back. "Like you. Only I'm scared as hell."

That silenced him. Looking her over, he noticed she wore long sleeves, even though outside it was in the midseventies. When he'd examined her in the hospital, her arms had been clean. Now, he wondered.

"Are you using again?"

"I told you I'm not." She gave him an uncertain smile. "But you don't believe me."

"Can you blame me?"

"No." She sighed again. "I suppose not. But seriously, I can quit on my own."

"Can you?"

"I want to try."

"Why?" He could only be blunt. She deserved at least that much. "When we talked in the hospital, you said you only wanted to have fun."

Immediately her expression closed down. "None of your business."

"Fair enough." He turned away. "Then why bother me with your problems? Go away. I've got better things to do."

Instead she moved closer, planting both hands on his desk and glaring at him. "You've been an addict. You're a doctor. You took an oath to help people, right? Well, I'm asking you to help me."

"Help you? If I help you, I'll put you back in rehab."

Instantly she shook her head and scowled. "Hell, no. No more rehab. I want you to help me quit on my own."

Remembering his own futile and admittedly halfhearted attempts to do the same, he shook his head. "That's not always possible. I tried, but couldn't."

"You didn't really want to."

"And you do?" He coughed. "Right."

"I have a reason."

"Really?" He raised a brow. "Care to enlighten me?"

"No." She spat the word, as though even the single syllable burned her mouth. "I'm a meth addict. And I want to quit."

"Look, Melissa. Though I know you don't want to hear this, rehab really is your best option. If you'll stick it out, it's not as bad as you think." He didn't tell her about the chill, the bone-deep coldness that he couldn't get rid of, no matter how many layers of clothing he wore. Or the shakes, the time spent crouched over the toilet, the loathing and self-hatred as he'd found himself scrambling to get drugs and getting caught.

Rehab wasn't for cowards, that's for sure. But this teenager wasn't a coward. He'd bet his life on that.

"I can't help you."

Arms crossed and face set, she continued to scowl at him. When she took a deep breath, her composure crumpled. "There's a possibility I might be pregnant."

Her words stopped him cold. As they stared across the battered desk at each other, Jared realized she was a child. An overly made-up, frightened little girl.

"Possibility?"

She chewed on her thumbnail. "Yes. I've always been irregular, so the first few months, I didn't think anything. But now…"

"You need to go to a women's clinic. They can do a quick test and tell you. I know a good one a few blocks from here."

She blew up. "That's your answer for everything, isn't it? Refer me to someone else. Are you a doctor or not?"

Cautiously he answered in the affirmative.

She leaned even closer until her face was an inch from his. He had to fight not to recoil, to push himself back in his chair and maintain a subjective distance.

"Okay. I'm a patient, asking you for help. Didn't you take some oath or something? You're not supposed to turn me away."

More rose-colored glasses. He scowled right back at

her. "I told you, I don't do counseling. If you need me to check you for STDs, we've got to have another woman present. Have you taken a pregnancy test?"

She shook her head.

"That's the first thing you need to do. Find out one way or another. If you are pregnant, that alone is a perfect reason to stop using."

She nodded. "You're going to help me, then?"

He clenched his teeth. "Looks like it."

"Thank you," she whispered, and started to weep.

Chapter 7

Elena resisted the urge to check on Jared. She kept herself busy adding receipts, working on a fourth quarter budget—anything, to keep her mind off him. When she'd done everything on her desk, she decided to go check on the club.

Shutting down her computer, she stood and headed for the door, and collided with her sister.

Joy reared back, throwing up her hands. "Melissa's gone."

"What?" Elena glanced at her watch. "It's nearly 2:00 a.m."

"I know. She took off from rehab. They just realized she was missing."

"How is that possible? The hospital has security, especially on the rehab floor."

"The security is little more than a joke. Apparently Missy decided she'd had enough and walked out."

Elena gripped her desk. "They didn't try to stop her?"

"No one noticed. They probably thought she was a visitor. You know how she is." Joy sighed. "She's a good little actress."

"Did she go home?"

"No. I've driven by the house. She's not there. And she won't answer her cell."

Elena tried to think. A scared Melissa on the run would get into nothing but trouble. Without even realizing it, the teenager could be putting her life in jeopardy.

"Did they know how long ago she escaped?"

"No. They said they can't give me an exact time. All they knew was she was there for roll call this morning."

"This *morning?* That's the best they can do?"

Joy nodded.

"Don't they have cameras?" Elena picked up the phone. "Surely someone can review the tapes and give us a better idea of how long she's been gone."

Dialing the number, she listened to the automatic message and punched in the required numbers. On the third menu listing options, she gave up and punched zero for operator.

Finally she got someone from security. Though he sounded as if he was fourteen and stoned, he promised to review the tapes and give her a call back. Eventually.

"They're not going to be any help. At least not until normal business hours."

"We've got to find her." With her pursed lips and curly hair, Joy looked like an angry cherub.

"Any chance she'd go home later?"

"No. She knows if she does, I'll call them and have her picked up."

"What about friends?"

Joy nodded. "She has a lot, but I know where most of them live."

"Make a list." Elena handed her a yellow legal pad. "Don't worry, we'll find her."

Handing Melissa a box of tissues, Jared waited until she had herself under control.

"If you do turn out to be pregnant, do you know who the father is?" he asked quietly. "The name will be enough."

"For you to do what? Have him arrested?"

"Does he go to your school?"

She looked away. "No. He's not a kid."

Hell hounds. "He's over eighteen?"

"Maybe."

Jared couldn't keep from baring his teeth. "Good thing you haven't told me. I'd hunt him down and beat the crap out of him. You are a minor, you know."

"Jailbait." Red-eyed, her belligerent stare fizzled when he glared back. With her tear-swollen eyes and red cheeks, she looked a vulnerable twelve rather than seventeen. "He told me he'd go to jail if I told."

His gut clenched. He shouldn't care, after all he barely knew this girl. But he did. "Does he know?"

"Hell, no. I don't even know for sure. Why would I tell him?"

"Are you planning on telling him?"

"No."

"Then give me his name."

Instead of answering, she slowly shook her head.

"Why not? Why are you protecting him?"

Finally she blinked, her hazel eyes focusing on him. "I'm not protecting him."

"Then what? Tell me his name."

"No. If I wanted him hurt," she snarled, "I'd hunt him down and hurt him myself."

Words of a shifter. Her response floored him and he took another long look at the girl. *Nope. Definitely human. Something was still off....*

"Where you raped?"

His question startled her enough to make her jump. "Why would you ask something like that?"

"Were you?" he pushed.

"I was unconscious," she acknowledged. "But we'd been fooling around earlier."

"Fooling around how?"

Her olive skin turned a dusky rose. "You know. Making out."

"Tell me what happened."

"I don't want to talk about it anymore." Suddenly all the air seemed to go out of her. Her fierceness vanished. Biting her lip, she seemed on the verge of tears again. "No more. Not now. Change the subject, please."

"You've got to have a pregnancy test. I'd do it, but I prefer to have a nurse present." No way was he taking the chance of a lawsuit. "The women's clinic down the street won't tell anyone."

Slowly she nodded. "I'll go tomorrow."

"Good." Busying himself with organizing tongue depressers, he hoped she would leave. His experience with teenagers was limited to those he'd seen at the hospital, and those had been few and far between.

"Dr. Gies? Can I ask you something?" She took a deep breath and, without waiting for his answer, continued. "Are you like Dr. Watkins?"

At first, he didn't understand. "Like him how?"

"A werewolf."

He froze, then slowly turned to face her. "A what?"

"A werewolf." She watched him closely. "Though he told me he preferred to be called a shifter."

His breath caught. What the *hell* had been wrong with Watkins? How many humans had he let in on his secret? And why?

He framed his next words with care. "I don't understand why he'd tell you such a thing."

"Oh, he had a really good reason." Tilting her head, she smiled. "And you haven't answered my question."

While Jared didn't like to lie, no way was he telling Melissa the truth before talking to Elena. "Werewolves don't exist," he said in a stern voice. Softening his tone, he touched her arm. "Melissa, does your mother know you're here and not in rehab?"

"No." She hung her head. "I'm sure they've reported me missing by now. She's probably driving around looking for me. I turned off my cell."

"Turn it back on and call her," he ordered. "Let her know you're safe, so she won't worry."

He waited while she did exactly that, listened as she bargained with Joy. Melissa promised she'd come home if she didn't have to go back to rehab. Apparently Joy agreed, because when the teenager hung up, her expression was smug.

"Got what you wanted?" he asked, making a mental note to talk to Joy about her weak backbone, then deciding it was actually none of his business.

"Oh, yeah. I always do."

Lack of strong parental guidance wasn't helping her stay out of trouble. Not his problem, he reminded himself.

"So," she said, leaning forward. "I called her like you wanted. She knows I'm safe. Now answer my question."

Thinking fast, he made his expression thoughtful. "No more nonsense about werewolves. If you can wait a few more minutes, I'll run you home."

She shrugged. "You don't have to. I can catch a ride."

"No. It's not safe. Another one of the dancers turned up dead here again. Another drug overdose."

"Oh, yeah?" Mildly interested, she tilted her head. "Who?"

"I think Elena said his name was Luke."

Melissa made a strangled sound. All the blood appeared to have drained from her face and she gripped the counter as if she thought she might fall. "Not Luke. Oh, God, no."

Alert now, he took her arm and steered her to the chair. "You knew him then?"

"Oh, yeah." Her bitter voice gave him the answer before she spoke the words. "His is the name you wanted earlier. If I am pregnant, Luke's the father of my baby."

"That was Missy." Joy closed her cell phone, her voice relieved. "She's all right. Thank God."

Elena eased up on the accelerator, coasting back into the right lane now that the need to drive fast had abated somewhat. "Is she sober? Or is she using again?"

"She didn't sound like she was. She's clean now." The conviction in Joy's voice made Elena worry. "She's promised to come home if I don't make her go back to rehab."

"But she hasn't completed the program."

Joy set her chin. "She told me she's clean. And I believe her."

Exactly why Elena had been worried. "I'm not sure leaving rehab is such a good idea."

"I know." Joy sighed, laying her head back against the headrest. "But if she really wants to be clean, that's all that matters. Besides, what could I do? If I'd refused, she'd stay on the run. I want my baby back home."

This, in Elena's opinion, was the root of many of Melissa's problems. Her mother wouldn't stand firm. It was an old argument between her and Joy and one she saw no point in rehashing now.

She took a deep breath. "Where was Melissa when she called you?"

Joy smiled again. "You're not going to believe this. She went to Fantasies."

Elena almost swerved into the wrong lane. "What?"

"Yeah, that's what I thought. At first, I thought she wanted to talk to you. Then I remembered Valerie works there. She and Melissa are kind of close."

"Are they?" This surprised Elena. "I had no idea."

"Yeah." Joy's laugh was completely without humor. "But she didn't go to talk to Valerie. She wanted to talk to that new doctor you have, the one who came to the hospital with us."

"Dr. Gies?" Bewildered, Elena began looking for a place to pull a U-turn so they could head back. "Why?"

"I don't know."

"Hmm." Elena thought back to the only time the two had met. "She didn't seem to like him much from what I saw."

"Nor he her. But she said she trusted him."

"Really?" Again Elena was shocked.

"Yes. But I don't." Joy pursed her mouth. "He's rude and abrasive and quite frankly, I think you should tell him to take a hike."

Again surprised, Elena ran one tire up on the curb as she completed her turnaround. "Why? He's going to continue the free clinic that Watkins started."

"Look, I know you're all about your little charity project. I also know how much money, effort and time you've put into that 'free' clinic."

"None of this is about the money."

Joy snorted. "You have a bleeding heart and Watkins probably saw *sucker* written all over it."

"You sound bitter." Defensive now, Elena concentrated on driving. "Watkins didn't get paid. He volunteered the time and I donated the space."

"I'm sure he had an ulterior motive."

"If he did, I haven't figured it out," Elena said.

Joy crossed her arms. "At least you didn't get hurt. That's something."

"Yeah." Something. Her entire family kept telling

her she tried so hard to save the world, she'd end up hurt one day.

She'd always laughed them off before. Now two men were dead. And she'd finally met the one man she didn't think even she could save.

Jared.

Despite his offer of a ride home, Melissa slipped out as quietly as she'd entered. When Jared bent under the cabinet to locate more tissue for her, she disappeared.

When he stood, the pain in his leg nearly made him pass out. A groan escaped him. Checking his watch, he clenched his teeth. Though he was supposed to stay open longer, he'd had enough. The pain had become unbearable.

In order to finish up, he forced himself to begin making notes in a file, simply labeling it *Melissa,* since he wasn't sure of her last name. A sharp tapping on the door interrupted him.

A second patient. Of course. Now that he could barely stand.

"Come in," he growled, breaking into a cold sweat as pain washed over him in waves.

His next patient—or visitor—was Valerie.

"Hey, Dr. Gies," she purred, slinking across the room. She smelled of musk and sex, as though she'd just left someone's bed.

He straightened, preferring not to let her see how badly he hurt and how uncomfortable she made him. Gritting his teeth, he crossed his arms and waited for her to get to the point.

Smiling, she circled him, reminding him of a she-wolf in heat. He kept his expression blank and bored, a major effort when all he wanted to do was snarl at her to get out.

Finally she planted herself directly in front of him, way too close. Though she'd invaded his comfort zone, he refused to give her the satisfaction of moving back, all too aware of how badly any movement would hurt.

"What do you want, Valerie?" he finally asked, though he suspected he already knew the answer.

She ratcheted her false smile up a notch. "I think you and I have a lot in common."

"No, we don't." Of that he was absolutely certain. Making a production out of glancing at his watch, he sighed. "Clinic hours are almost over."

"I know." Her smile disappeared. "Why are you here?"

"Here?"

"Yes, here." She waved a scarlet-tipped hand at the small room. "Running a clinic at Fantasies. No matter how Elena dresses it up, it's still a strip club. I checked on you. What's a doctor with your reputation doing here?"

He raised a brow. "What reputation?"

"I talked to a nurse friend who works at Parkland. Your diagnostic skills are legendary there."

"I'm looking for Watkins." In this case, letting her know the truth couldn't hurt. "He's an old friend."

"Really?" Her frown cleared. "Then you know what he is?"

Hounds help him. If one more person revealed that Watkins had told them his true nature, he was going to explode.

Still, just in case she meant something else, he had to play along.

"Of course I know what he is. Watkins is a damn fine doctor and a pretty fair human being."

"That's not what I mean."

He feigned confusion, ignoring the sweat running down the back of his neck. "No?"

"Watkins is a werewolf."

Holy effin Fido. He didn't have to pretend his shock. "A what?"

"You heard me." She crossed her arms. "And I think you might be one, too."

The only thing he could do was laugh. Long and loud, though each guffaw sent bone-jarring pain through his leg.

She patiently waited for him to finish. "Now that we've gotten that over with, are you planning to continue Watkins's work?"

"Running the clinic? Of course. That's what I'm here for."

"No." The look she gave him was full of meaning. "His *other* work."

Though he had no idea what she meant, he continued to play along. "I'm thinking about it. He called me a week ago and said he needed help. But I need more details."

Something in his tone must have alerted her. She frowned. "It's not complicated. What did Watkins tell you?"

Crap. Caught.

"He didn't." Might as well admit the truth. "I came here because he sounded desperate, and I can't find him. He never had a chance to tell me what he was working on."

Her smile made the hair on the back of his neck rise. What did Valerie know about Watkins's disappearance?

"You do know I assisted Dr. Watkins a lot, at least when I didn't have to work the front desk."

"You assisted?"

"In more ways than one." The purr was back in her voice.

Even if he wasn't in pain, he wouldn't take her up on her blatant offer. He shot her a glare, making her sultry smile falter.

"Are you gay?"

"Is that what you think if a man's not interested in you?"

Smile completely gone, she stared at him. "You're bagging Elena, aren't you?"

"Bagging?"

She shrugged. "Whatever. I don't care."

"I do." Briefly he closed his eyes, fighting the pain. He wished she would leave.

"You *are* just like Watkins, aren't you? And this time, I'm not talking about being a werewolf." Spinning on her stilettos, she sashayed over to the door. "Anyway, I'm going to see if anyone else is interested in participating. If I can find someone else, I'll let you know."

"You do that," he called after her. More and more, he felt as if he was walking on thin ice. Who knew a male strip club could have so many secrets? Worse, he had no idea how many of them might be deadly.

* * *

An overturned semi had shut down I-45. Even at 3:00 a.m, Elena was trapped in gridlocked traffic before she could exit. By the time they finally got back to Fantasies, everyone had gone home.

"Damn." Joy sagged in her seat. "I don't suppose you have that doctor's cell number, do you?"

"No." Elena pulled up next to her sister's car and parked. "I'm afraid I don't. Why don't you try Missy again?"

"She won't answer." Despite that, Joy opened her phone and hit Redial. A second later, she brightened. "Melissa! Where are you?"

Looking out her window while Joy talked, Elena wondered what Jared had said to her niece. She only hoped whatever he'd done hadn't driven the teenager back to drugs.

"She went home." Joy snapped the cell closed. "She's at the house, waiting up for me so we can talk."

"That's fantastic." Suddenly exhausted, Elena leaned her head back against the seat. "I guess you'd better hurry home."

"Are you all right?"

"Just tired." Elena forced a smile. "Go on. I'll see you tomorrow."

Joy gave her a nod and got out of the car, unlocking her own with the remote and climbing in.

Waiting until her sister drove off, Elena put her shift in Drive and headed home. Though normally she fixed something to eat before going to bed, tonight she thought she'd skip all that and let herself collapse.

When she arrived home, she didn't even bother to undress. Turning on the television, she stretched out on her couch and closed her eyes.

A pounding on her door woke her. Squinting at the clock, which showed she'd only slept twenty minutes, she pushed herself up and off the sofa and staggered to the door. A quick look through the peephole showed Jared standing outside, looking hollow-eyed and desperate in the dim porch light.

With one look, she knew the man was in some kind of crisis. But how did he know where she lived? Hesitating, she thought of Watkins and wondered if letting Jared in could be dangerous.

Then his mouth worked and he turned to go. Something inside her twisted. Screw dangerous—he needed her help.

Disengaging the dead bolt, she yanked open the door and took his arm. He didn't resist. "Come in."

Leading him into her house, she took the time to lock the door behind her. "How did you find out where I lived?"

"Internet," he gritted. "Sorry."

When she released his arm, he leaned on his cane and stared around her living room with pain-filled eyes.

He didn't even make one of his sarcastic comments, which worried her even more than the stark desperation on his face.

"Sit." Though she pushed him toward a chair, he continued standing.

Drugs? Surely not. He'd said he was clean and she believed him.

Finally looking away, he rubbed at his leg, the gesture almost automatic. A muscle clenched in his jaw and he twisted his mouth in an effort to speak. Staring at her, he looked like a wounded animal, unsure why she couldn't take away the hurt.

The next second, she realized he was trying to maintain control.

Giving him a moment, she walked around to the other side of her couch, though she didn't sit, either.

More than anything, she wanted to comfort him. And knew she could not.

"I'm sorry," he managed to say. "Maybe I'd better go."

Ah, she couldn't deny him. Not this man, not now.

"No," she told him softly. "Let me help you. Tell me what's wrong."

He only stared. But at least he didn't move toward the door.

"I might be able to help."

At first, he started to shake his head and then, apparently realizing he'd come to her, he staggered to the chair and lowered himself into the seat. Still clutching his cane, he put his head between his hands. "The pain…"

Now she understood. "You're craving a pill."

"Yes, damn it." Raising his head, he stared at her, his expression contorted. "And before you ask, no, I haven't taken one. But I want to. Damn it, you don't know how badly I want to."

Before she could speak, he continued. "Sometimes I don't see what's wrong with me taking one stupid pill to ease the pain. I'm tired of hurting. Is it so horrible just to want to be normal, like everyone else? Pain-free, just like you?"

"But would you stop at one?" She had to ask, even though she suspected they both knew the answer.

For a moment he simply looked at her, his anguish nearly palpable. When he did answer, he had to swallow twice before speaking. "Probably not. But this pain... I can't think." He cursed again. "Can't listen to music, can't watch TV. I can't concentrate on anything but this friggin' leg." Again he swallowed. "I want your help, not your pity."

"Good, because I'm not giving it. Jared, look." Consequences be damned, she moved to stand behind him, kneading his knotted shoulders. "I won't pretend to know what you're going through, because I've never been in that kind of pain. But surely, there must be something medicine can do to help you."

Head bowed, he grunted. "Not conventional medicine. Though... Never mind."

"What?" She continued to massage him, hoping her touch would somehow help. "Tell me."

With a sigh, he rolled his neck. "My mother told me about a healer out in East Texas. She thinks this woman can help me."

"Like a faith healer?"

"Sort of."

Though she waited, he didn't say more. Instead she kept kneading, massaging. He dropped his head again, letting out a soft groan. "That feels good."

"Mmm." Hearing the purr in her own voice, Elena realized she had become aroused merely by touching him. Alarmed, she stopped and stepped back.

If not for his pain, she knew how rapidly the situation could become dangerous.

"Elena?" He glanced at her. The pain made lines around his mouth. God, how she wanted to soothe him. Hell, if she was honest, she wanted to do a lot more than that.

Heart beating a rapid tattoo in her chest, she shook off her fear and resumed touching him. "Sorry. You were telling me about this healer?"

"I'm a medical doctor. I don't believe in miracles."

Ah, this she could understand. She, too, liked the world to be normal, without anything lurking in the shadows.

Like men who could change into wolves.

"But I've tried everything else," he continued. "I really have nothing to lose."

Staring at the wounded man who should still be a stranger, but wasn't, Elena wanted to cry. "I'll go with you," she said on impulse, then qualified her offer a second later. "As a friend, that is."

Pushing himself to his feet, he dragged his hand through his hair. "Maybe," he told her, leaning heavily on his cane as he started toward the door. "There's a lot we need to discuss first and I can't do it tonight."

Just like that, he left her. Staring at the door, Elena wondered why she wanted to cry.

Chapter 8

After leaving Elena's house, Jared didn't go home. Instead he drove aimlessly until he found a wooded recreation area, deserted at this hour. He parked as far from the streetlight as possible, went into the trees, stripped and changed.

Normally the sharp scents of earth and other animals he experienced as wolf were enough. Not this time. His wolf self, still hurting, was restless and uneasy. Even an hour spent hunting couldn't purge the ache in his soul. Even as wolf, Jared knew what it meant that he'd gone to Elena when he'd been at his most vulnerable.

She truly was his mate.

And he was a complete and utter idiot.

Changing back to human, he located his clothing

and dressed, unable to stop thinking of the healer. He'd read all the information his mother had e-mailed, then done his own research.

In the world of the Pack, it truly appeared this healer who could heal Halflings was real.

Then why the hell was he so afraid to call her?

The humidity continued to make his leg hurt worse than usual. Though the pain level definitely felt easier to bear than it had when he'd stupidly gone to Elena's home, he still couldn't stop wanting a pain pill. Lucky for him, he'd flushed them all down the toilet after rehab.

Once home, he slept until early Friday afternoon, then bought groceries and did a load of laundry. As had become his habit, he took a drive over to Watkins's apartment and knocked on the door. As usual, there was no answer. For dinner, he treated himself to a Chinese all-you-can-eat buffet. Then he went home and showered before heading out to Fantasies. Just the thought of seeing Elena made his heart beat faster. Dammit.

When Elena entered his office, she caught him rubbing his thigh, trying to banish the pain.

"Still hurting?" she asked.

"A little. But it's not nearly as bad as it was yesterday." He instantly remembered the feel of her fingers caressing his shoulders. Judging from her blush, she remembered, too.

"Good. Then you're all right?"

He nodded. "As good as I get these days. When it's humid like this, it's worse." He didn't tell her his leg always hurt, or that he was seriously considering calling the healer.

"Did you call that healer?"

Had she read his mind? Vaguely he remembered hearing stories of some sort of mind-communication between mates. Another thing he wasn't entirely sure he believed in.

"No," he said.

"Then, don't you know someone else? Surely there's some other treatment or therapy?"

"I've tried them all." Wincing, he used his cane to climb to his feet. "There's really nothing left."

"Except this faith healer." Elena frowned. "Are you going to call?"

"Probably. Yeah. I think I am. Eventually."

Her heart-shaped face lit up with a beauty that made his chest ache with the need to touch her. "What's it involve? Drugs? Physical therapy?"

He rubbed his chin. How to explain Samantha Herrick, Pack healer, to a human woman who didn't even know about the Pack? "I can't explain what she does. I really don't understand it."

"Oh." Her frown cleared slightly. "Well, if you've tried everything else, I suppose there's no harm."

But there was. She just didn't realize how much hinged on this healer. If she couldn't heal him, his last hope was gone forever. Not only would he never be able to claim Elena as his mate, but he'd have to face the reality of a lifetime of agonizing, untreatable pain.

Elena crossed to the phone, picking up the receiver and holding it out to him. "Why put it off? Give her a call now."

His heart thumped, missing a beat. He didn't move. For someone who didn't even know she was his mate, she sure acted a hell of a lot like one. "I will. When I'm ready."

Nodding, she replaced the receiver. "I understand. It's perfectly normal to be afraid."

"I'm not…" He stopped, unable to lie to her. "Even though she has a good reputation, I can't help but think whatever she does to heal won't work on me."

"You won't know until you try. Let me know when you're ready to give it a shot. I meant what I said. I'd really like to go with you for support." She flashed him one more quick, achingly beautiful smile.

Desire surged through him, nearly bringing him to his knees. He didn't—couldn't—respond.

Shaking her head, she walked out of the room.

Without giving himself time to think, he crossed to the phone and dialed the number he'd committed to memory. Samantha's husband, Luc, answered on the second ring. Heart pounding, Jared made an appointment for tomorrow afternoon.

A sound made him turn.

"Dr. Gies?" Hair mussed, green eyes red-rimmed, Ryan, the shifter who'd been so antagonistic the other day, stood in the doorway.

Jared froze, scenting the air. He detected none of that animosity now. "How can I help you?"

The man stayed near the door. "I'm not sick. I have a question for you. Are you like Dr. Watkins?"

"That's the second time I've been asked that, and I know you don't mean shifter."

Ryan looked over his shoulder. "Of course not. But

you said you're a friend of his. Are you planning to continue his work?"

"His work?" Time to get some answers. "I've been asked that before, too. Was Watkins dealing?"

"Dealing?" Ryan shook his head. "You think that's why he was here, to sell drugs?"

"Not really." He held Ryan's gaze. "So what do you mean?"

This time, Ryan came inside, closing the door behind him. Jared gripped his cane, just in case, but he sensed only fear on the other man's part.

He wanted to know why.

"Ryan, what the hell is going on?"

The dancer's gaze searched his face. "Damien and Luke were shifters, you know?"

"I did notice, yes."

"They were Halflings, like me. Like you. Valerie is looking for a volunteer to take their place. Why would she be doing that if you weren't going to continue?"

"Valerie asked me if I would, but refused to tell me what Watkins was doing. I've had enough." Glaring at Ryan, Jared let his lip curl. "Tell me what you're talking about."

"You really don't know." Ryan moved closer, circling warily.

Again, Jared smelled fear. "Tell me."

"Watkins was doing some kind of experiments on Halflings. Valerie was helping him."

"What kind of experiments?"

"I don't know." An almost palpable terror made Ryan's patrician features look ghastly. "But since both

Damien and Luke are dead…you and I are the only Halflings around. She told me Dr. Watkins can't use full-blooded shifters."

Jared leaned close. "Do you know where Watkins is?"

Ryan swallowed. "Not really, though he was seeing Valerie. Ask her. She likes shifters."

Dragging his hand through his hair, Jared sighed. "I don't understand."

"The experiments. I heard Dr. Watkins was going to stop them, but now Luke's dead, too."

"What are you saying? That Watkins had something to do with their deaths?"

They both heard a muted clang from the hallway, as though someone had dropped something. Ryan froze, a look of sheer horror crossing his face.

"I don't want to be next." He edged toward the exit. "Coming here was a mistake." Yanking open the door, he left.

Following him to the doorway, Jared glanced to the left and to the right. The hall was empty.

What the hell had Watkins been up to? Experiments on Halflings, on his own kind? Experiments that involved drugs and death?

He needed to talk to all the other nonhumans working at Fantasies. Surely someone could tell him what was going on. Once he'd done that, he needed to find out where Valerie lived. If Watkins was hiding out at her place, Jared would find him.

One thing was certain—he hadn't expected all of this when he'd gone looking for his friend.

Checking his watch again, he realized most of the

employees would have gone home. As should he. On his way out, Elena caught him. "Do you have a minute?"

Suddenly wary, he nodded. The dark shadows under her caramel-colored eyes brought out all of his protective instincts. He felt a sudden, violent urge to gather her close and keep her safe.

Safe? Where had that fear come from? Elena wasn't in danger, was she?

Following her down the hall into her office, he kept his mouth shut. Once inside, she perched on the corner of her desk, the move showing off impossibly long legs.

"Ryan just quit." Crossing her arms, she glared at him. "When I asked him why, he said to talk to you."

Jared shrugged. He'd tell her the truth, or as much of the truth as she could handle. "He was afraid. Apparently Watkins was experimenting on some of your dancers. Ryan was worried I planned to do the same."

"Experimenting how?"

"I don't know. I'm guessing this had something to do with the drugs." Deliberately he didn't tell her about Valerie. He wanted to talk to that one himself, without Elena letting her love of family interfere. "I'm planning to do some more snooping around to see what I can find out."

Still frowning, she finally nodded. "Please." She took a deep breath. "Changing the subject, what are you doing for Easter? It's next weekend."

Her question caught him by surprise. "Eating out." He shrugged. "Sunday I'm picking my mother up at the airport. She's coming in to spend the week with me. And Easter." Since his brother the priest was too busy with church-duties to spend time with family, he and his mom always spent the holiday together.

Her lovely eyes widened. "Your *mother?*"

"You say that as if it shocks you to learn someone like me actually has a mother."

Dusky rose flooded her face. "Sorry. You're absolutely right. I don't know why, but you seem…alone."

Alone. Once he'd prided himself on being a loner. Now, the word only sounded empty.

"Nope," he said, as casual as he could manage. "I still have some family, small as it may be. My mother and one brother."

"Is he coming, too?"

"No. I haven't seen him in years." Jared had been nothing but a disappointment for his older brother.

She cocked her head, studying him. "Why not?"

"He's a priest. He doesn't leave his diocese much. Plus, with Easter…"

Elena nodded. "He has too many duties. That's understandable."

Actually it wasn't, but Jared let the topic go. He could have used his brother's support in his struggle to kick his addiction, but support was the one thing John hadn't been willing to give, at least to his younger brother. Since their father had died when Jared was an infant, his big brother had become the father figure.

John claimed he practiced tough love.

"Do you cook?"

Jared blinked, then realized she was asking about Easter dinner. "I can, but Mom and I usually go out to eat on the holidays."

Expression thoughtful, she nodded. "You know, I just realized I don't know much about your family." With a self-conscious laugh, she studied her hands. "But then again, why should I?"

He didn't reply. The words he wanted to say would have scared the hell out of her. How could he tell her his mother was a full-blooded shifter while his father had been human? Or that his brother was one of only three Pack priests in the country?

As the silence stretched on, Jared realized she expected him to say something, he went with the partial truth. "My father's dead and I have one brother. That's all you need to know." *For now.*

His rudeness didn't seem to faze her. "Joy's my only sister, but I have tons of cousins. On Easter there'll be twenty-two people at my mother's house for dinner. Actually twenty-four if you and your mom would like to come. Here—" She wrote down the address on a slip of paper and handed it to him.

He stared, not sure how to respond. He'd made reservations for two at an upscale restaurant as he did every year.

"Uh—"

"Think about it." She waved her hand, her usually bright smile slightly dimmed with exhaustion. "The more the merrier, that's how we look at it. I don't need an answer today. We've got a week. Oh, and you should know that we don't have the usual Easter ham. We have a traditional Mexican meal—tamales, enchiladas, beans and whatever else anyone feels like making." With that, she walked out of the room.

More than anything in the world, he wanted to run after her and, right before he kissed her senseless, tell her he'd love to come to her family dinner.

Instead he pictured his mother's reaction and grimaced. Unless the healer was truly able to help him, he had no right to even think about taking a mate. Especially one who might be horrified by his true nature.

He needed to talk to her, tell her the truth. Resolute, he went to back to Watkins's office—his now, he supposed—to lock up before looking for Elena.

A light tap made him look up from where he'd been crouched by a cabinet lock. Melissa, eyes red and swollen, stood hesitantly in the doorway, swaying on her feet.

She looked as though she'd been awake for three days.

Jared gave her a hard look. "Have you been using?"

She shook her head. "No." Her voice broke. "Seriously, I haven't. I'm just worn-out."

He believed her.

"Sit." With a wave of his hand, he indicated a chair, peering into her face. "Your eyes are red, pupils dilated. If you aren't using, why do you look like that?"

Glaring at him, she spoiled the effect when her lower lip trembled. "Give me a break," she whispered. "I've been crying. That's why my eyes are puffy." She began weeping again.

Damn. One of the things he sucked at was dealing with crying females. He busied himself tidying up his medical supplies while the teenager got a hold of her emotions. He kept his back to her in case she thought he should hug her or something—he'd never been good at comforting patients. Because of his habit of delivering his diagnosis and then standing back, he'd been told his bedside manner stunk.

Melissa's shoulders shook with the force of her gasping sobs. He wanted to flee. He'd seen patients cry before, usually when they'd been told they had an incurable disease. Given the fact that Jared was only called in to diagnose when all other attempts failed, ninety percent of the patients he saw—both male and female—ended up crying. He should be used to it by now.

Only Melissa was more than just a patient. She was Elena's niece. And even if Elena could never be his mate, Melissa's connection made her family. Or Pack, in a loose, global sort of way.

Ignoring the fact that he never thought like that, Jared took a deep breath and crossed the room. Trying not to mutter and moving awkwardly, nonetheless he hugged her. She made a mewling sound, like that of a drowning kitten, and clung to him.

Hell hounds. Her tears were ruining his Egyptian cotton shirt.

"It'll be all right," he promised, though he really didn't know. "Take it easy."

Still sobbing, she nodded, keeping her face turned in to him so her tears continued to soak the front of his shirt. Uncomfortable, he awkwardly patted her back. Damn, he wished Elena would show up now to help with this. He'd even take Joy's antagonism.

Finally Melissa pulled away. Wiping her eyes, she grimaced when Jared handed her a box of tissues. "Thanks." She dabbed at her face, then blew her nose long and hard.

He waited until she'd finished before asking. "What's wrong?"

"I did like you said. I went to the women's clinic. The free one, over on Sylvania."

"Good."

She winced. "Not so much."

Though he dreaded the next question, he knew he had to ask. "Everything isn't all right?"

"My baby…" Again her voice cracked. "They say something's wrong with my fluid or my blood or something. They want to run more tests."

"What's wrong?" He grabbed her shoulder. "Try to remember. This is important."

"They found some kind of weird cells in my blood. At first, they thought the lab had mixed my sample with a dog's or something—they said my blood had canine structure. So they ran the test again. Same thing."

He stiffened, instantly alert, then cursed. "I can't believe I didn't think of that. You said Luke was the father?"

"Yes."

And Luke had been a shifter. Human tests would always reveal abnormalities, therefore Melissa could no longer see human doctors.

She had to be told the truth.

Grimacing, he closed his eyes. "You're positive?"

A single tear streaked down her cheek. "Yes. Luke was my first."

Damn. Though Melissa had asked him before about werewolves, he couldn't be sure how much she actually knew.

While he tried to frame the right words, Melissa herself saved him from having to explain.

"Dr. Gies, I know you really don't believe in werewolves, but…" She took a deep, shuddering breath. "I've got to tell you something. Something really weird. I tried to tell you before, but you wouldn't listen."

He gave her a grim smile. "I'm listening now."

"Promise me you won't think I'm crazy."

"Easy enough." He jammed his hands into his pockets to keep himself from fidgeting. Part of him had a pretty good idea what she was about to say. "I've heard plenty of strange things in my career, believe me."

"Not this weird." She sounded so emphatic, he had to smile. "You haven't promised. The last thing I need is you thinking what I'm about to tell you is some sort of drugged-out delusion."

"I promise." He didn't bother to hide his impatience. "Get on with it, will you?"

"Fine. The father of my baby is…was…" Swallowing hard, she spoke in a rush. "A werewolf. There. I've said it. I know you didn't believe me when I told you about Dr. Watkins, but it's true. There are several werewolves around here. I know it sounds impossible, but I've seen him change."

Hell hounds. How could he not have realized this? The baby Melissa carried would be half-shifter. By the laws of the Pack, he now was obligated to help her and protect her. Her child would one day belong to his people.

"I believe you." He tried to smile, the knot in his stomach tightening. "That means your unborn child is a Halfling."

"There's that word again." Elena appeared in the doorway. "I saw the lights were still on." She glanced from Melissa to Jared and back again. Moving closer, she touched her niece's slender shoulder. "I heard you say unborn child."

Melissa nodded, then started to cry. Her aunt didn't even hesitate, she gathered the teenager close, wrapping her arms around her tightly. "Shh, honey. It's going to be all right."

"She's pregnant," Jared told her. "Luke is—was—the father."

"Let me talk to her." The look on Elena's face dared him to argue, though her voice as she soothed her niece sounded calm. "We'll take care of you, Missy. And your baby." She smoothed back her niece's hair. "Sweety, does your mother know you're pregnant?"

"No. Not yet." Still shaking, Melissa bit her lip. "I've been scared to tell her."

"You shouldn't be. She'll understand."

"No, she won't. She still thinks I'm an addict. She'll say I brought this on myself."

"I promise she won't say that. But we need to be sure you don't use drugs again. You don't want to endanger the baby."

"I've quit. For the baby." The teenager started trembling. "But before, I swear, I didn't know I was pregnant. Oh God. Maybe that's why my tests came back weird." Wide-eyed, she looked past Elena to Jared, the plea in her gaze plain. "Dr. Gies, how can I find out if that's why my tests came back weird?"

"The blood tests are normal." Jared leaned back

against the counter. "Halflings have a very hardy immune system, though it's different from humans'. That's why the test results are skewed." He gave a quick glance sideways, watching for Elena's reaction. "I can order some tests of my own, and I will, but I think your baby will be fine."

"This is too weird." Melissa sounded suspicious. "You didn't even question the werewolf thing. Either you're totally blowing me off, or you believe me. Which is it?"

Jared took a deep breath, feeling as though he stood on a crumbling cliff. "*We* believe you," he said, looking from Melissa to Elena. "Don't we?"

Slowly Elena nodded, expressionless.

Melissa wasn't satisfied with his answer. Jared suspected she knew. "Why?" she asked. "Why now? You acted like I was crazy before. Why do you believe me now?"

One more quick glance at Melissa then, watching Elena all the while, he stepped off the cliff into the open. "I believe you, because I am half-shifter, too. We are part of the Pack."

Chapter 9

"Pack," Elena repeated, testing the word and tasting only ashes. She continued to stare at Jared, accepting now why he seemed so much like Watkins and wondering how she'd managed to deny it for this long. "Pack is a plural, a word for a group. There are more than one."

Slowly Jared nodded.

"There *are* more than one!" Melissa sat up straight, excitement ringing in her voice. "At least around here. There's Watkins, Ryan and Mark. Plus we can't forget Damien and Luke. Olivia doesn't count, since she's a vamp, but—"

"A *vamp?*" Heart pounding, Elena couldn't help but wonder if she was the only sane one. "You mean, like a…a vampire?"

Missy barely missed a beat. "Of course. For some reason Fantasies is a favorite with shifters and vamps. They're pretty nice people."

"Pretty nice…" Was she doomed to continue to repeat her niece? Trying to be unobtrusive, she found herself examining the teenager's slender neck for bite marks. "You say a lot of my dancers are…" She swallowed and took a deep breath. "Shifters?"

"And vampires."

"What's next? Zombies and ghouls?"

Something in her dry tone must have communicated her feelings to Melissa. Smile fading, the seventeen-year-old let her shoulders slump once more. "Wow. You really do hate shifters," she pronounced glumly. "Dr. Watkins said you did, but I didn't believe him."

"I don't hate…" Elena struggled to find the right words. "I'm just uncomfortable around them."

Through all this, Jared simply watched, his chiseled features expressionless.

"Why?" Missy cried out. "You of all people! You were always active in LULAC. You're Hispanic, Latina. You know better than anyone what it's like to face discrimination."

Discrimination? "Now hold up, little girl." Elena wished she had a glass of water. No, screw the water, she needed tequila. "First off, I've never discriminated against anyone. How could I, when I had no idea of any of this?"

"You knew about Watkins," Jared spoke up, his deep voice agitating her already oversensitive nerves. "And you fired him."

"For the last time, I did not fire him. He didn't work for me. We argued, and he…left."

"Because of what he was."

She hesitated. "I…"

"You're going to hate my baby," Melissa wailed, cradling her still flat stomach protectively. "And you're my favorite aunt."

"I don't hate anyone!" Head aching, teeth clenched, Elena looked from Melissa to Jared and back again. "Will you two stop? Maybe this seems normal to you, but this is all strange to me. You've got to give me time to adjust."

How to explain her jumbled emotions, her fears? She liked her world orderly, predictable, an oasis of calm in the middle of chaos. Watkins proving that werewolves existed had thrown such a wrench in things, she still hadn't fully recovered.

Her family always joked that she wanted to fix the world. Inside, Elena knew they were right. Ever since she'd watched a six-year-old take his last breath, she'd known an overwhelming compulsion to somehow make things better, make things right.

She couldn't deal with a werewolf, wouldn't even know where to begin. Thus, she found it simpler to pretend they didn't exist. She should have known she couldn't bury her head in the sand forever.

Shaking her head, Melissa covered her face and began to cry. Before Elena could move, to her astonishment, Jared went to the young girl and put his arm around her shaking shoulders.

"Don't worry," he told her, his voice ringing with certainty. "Your child will always belong and be loved. Pack is like that, I promise."

Pack.

The word seemed to ring in the air.

Elena felt sick. "I need some time to absorb this," she repeated. "But no matter what, I will always love your baby."

"Even if he's a freak?" Red-eyed, Missy peeked up at her.

"A shifter is not a freak," Jared put in. "I never want to hear you say that again."

Melissa nodded. Heart still pounding, Elena kissed her forehead, earning a grateful smile.

Jared's smile wasn't so pleasant. "Now that you know the truth, do you still want me to come to Easter dinner?"

Look who's coming to dinner. Madre de Dios.

"Of course," she said, wishing she sounded more convincing. Then, as another thought occurred to her, "Is your mother a werewolf, too?"

"Shifter." Both Melissa and Jared simultaneously corrected her.

Dipping her chin, Elena acknowledged her error. "Sorry."

"Yes, my mother is also a shifter. She's full-blooded, where I'm half, like Melissa's baby will be."

"But Luke was half, too. Wouldn't that make my baby only a quarter shifter?" Melissa sounded worried.

"Any shifter blood at all is considered Halfling." Jared hastened to reassure her.

Great. Two of them, in her mother's house, with her family. Though Jared hadn't yet accepted, she'd been so positive he would that she'd told her mother, who'd told everyone else. Worse, the entire family was buzzing with excitement. In all her twenty-eight years, Elena had never brought a man home for a holiday dinner. Not once. They were all speculating about what this meant.

She nearly groaned out loud. Only Melissa's expectant gaze stopped her.

Walking toward the doorway, Jared peered out into the hall. "I wasn't holding clinic tonight and the club is closed. What do you say we all take a drive?"

Melissa glanced from him to Elena. With her tear-streaked cheeks and red eyes and nose, she looked even younger than her seventeen years. "Where?"

"To a nice wooded area. White Rock Lake. I've been meaning to check that out." His bleak, tight-lipped smile tore at Elena's heart, despite everything. "I'd like to show you what happens when I change."

Elena bit her lip. About to tell him she'd already seen Watkins do that trick, her niece's enthusiastic response stopped her.

"It's really awesome, Aunt Elena. The wolves are so beautiful. You'll see."

Swallowing down the bile that rose in her throat at the thought, Elena managed to murmur words of agreement. Now she had no choice but to see and, apparently, accept.

Driving, Jared forced himself to relax. In the back-seat, Melissa had dozed off. A quick glance at Elena showed she was lost in thought. He couldn't help but wonder how she'd react when she saw him, silky pelt icy gray, white teeth sharp and long. Even lame, he took pride in his wolf shape. If his leg was whole, he'd be a prime lupine specimen.

No cars remained in the parking lot at White Rock Lake. At this hour, crime would be an ever present danger, and he knew once he'd changed he couldn't leave the two women alone for long.

Once they'd parked and he'd killed the engine, an eerie calm settled over him. He knew this was it—the deal breaker. The first—and only—time he'd ever reveal his true nature to a human. Acknowledging that Elena was his true mate had been a difficult step, but this…

If Elena rejected him—unthinkable, the idea that his mate would reject him—he'd want to die. He doubted even the healer could help him then.

"Here we are." His voice sounded artificially cheerful. Still quiet, Elena's blank stare told him she'd retreated into herself.

Stomach clenching, he went around to the passenger side, meaning to open her door for her. She beat him to the punch and was already out by the time he got there.

"Melissa's asleep," she told him. "I'm thinking we should wake her up. I don't want to leave her in the car, not here."

He glanced at the sleeping teenager. "I don't know if she'll forgive us if we let her sleep, but she's so exhausted she can barely move."

Elena chewed her bottom lip. "Will this take long?"

"The shifting? No, I can change and change back in a matter of minutes." He didn't tell her that doing so would completely drain him, or that he might have to fight his still-not-under-control wolf.

"Then lock the doors and leave her. Wherever we go, I want to make sure we have a clear view of the car."

He nodded, oddly relieved, and used his remote to engage the locks. "There. She'll be safe."

"Great." The lack of enthusiasm in her voice made him pause. Maybe pushing her for acceptance wasn't such a good thing. "Are you okay?"

"Fine." She glared up at him. "Let's get this show on the road. It's late and I'm tired."

And they'd come too far to back out now.

Staring down at her, his voice deserted him. In the moonlight her dark hair appeared as black as the sky and her eyes were shadowed. She was lovely, exquisite. His.

Again apprehension stabbed him, but there was no help for it now. Hell, he had to show her—the wolf was such an integral part of him. She had to know and understand and accept that if they were ever going to have a future.

He suddenly refused to consider any alternative.

Still, he hesitated, afraid. Unlike most of his Pack friends, Jared had always regarded the act of shape-shifting as a mystical, magical, thing. Maybe because he wasn't a full-blood and the ever-present human half still approached the wolf half of himself with awe and reverence. His savagery he accepted; after all, that was the nature of the beast.

Being a wolf, he was himself, yet different. Wolf Jared became all about scent and texture and movement.

Texture—the clinging of dew-damp leaves to his huge paws, sinking in the soft earth. Scent—animal spores, human litter, fresh-cut grass. Jared couldn't help but wonder how his wolf self would react to the scent of Elena, so close, his human mate.

"Everything will be all right." His platitude did little to ease his tension, and he doubted it helped her, either. Heart pounding, he handed her the car keys and walked a short distance, farther into the scattered groves of live oaks and silver-leaf maples surrounding the walking path.

Close to a huge, fallen oak, he shed his clothing and dropped to all fours. Leaves rustled under his hands and he took a deep breath, striving for calm. Then, glancing one last time at the silently waiting woman, he ducked his head and began the change.

Like always, colors swirled around him. The human part of him appreciated their beauty, amazed at their magic. Then, as he doubled over and bit back a moan, he forgot them.

As usual, the first sensation came instantly— stabbing pain. An awful, lancing hurt as bones expanded, lengthened. His body throbbed as he altered his shape, abandoned human man for lupine male. The wolf emerged quickly, all fur and teeth and sharpened senses.

An involuntary snarl left his throat—not directed at Elena, but simply the wolf forcing his way out.

Still the colors swirled, but wolf saw only black, white and shades of gray, and he batted a huge paw at them.

Time stood still. Then, a heartbeat later, rushed forward. The change was complete. He'd become wolf.

Lifting his head, he sniffed the wind. He scented human, yet more. Mate. Again, he tasted the breeze.

Elena. His, even now.

Turning, he padded toward her, noting with approval

that she stood her ground, even though he could see the whites of her eyes. If not for the acrid scent of her fear, he would have thought her extraordinarily brave, unmoved by his change of shape, impervious to the miracle she'd witnessed. Man to wolf.

Poised on the balls of her feet, she appeared to be trying to overcome her terror.

A few feet from her, he stopped. Tilting his head, he studied her, watching, waiting, *aching* for her to reach out her hand and tangle her fingers in the lushness of his pelt.

But instead, she crossed her arms, making no move to touch him.

Set free, impatient wolf wanted to run, to hunt. Jared knew he had only a few more seconds to retain control before wolf completely took over.

He would have to change back. Immediately.

Dropping to his belly, relishing the cool earth against his fur, Jared began the shift back to human. Wolf fought him, unwilling to relinquish control.

The struggle took a few minutes, but finally human Jared won. The reverse change ripped through him, but he bore the intense pain silently, not wanting to alarm Elena.

When he'd finished, he dressed quickly, keeping his back to the woman meant to be his mate, knowing the force of his arousal would frighten her. Turning, he ran a hand through his hair, swaying slightly on his feet as he faced her.

She still stood where he'd left her, silhouetted in shadow, the streetlight behind her. As he approached, she seemed to draw back into herself, though she didn't physically move.

"Are you done?" Her tone was cool.

With the sharp scent of her fear still strong in his nostrils, he knew her calmness was an act.

"Are you all right?" he asked, fighting back the desire rocking him. Aborted change affected most shifters that way, channeling the energy into sexual arousal. No doubt learning this would only frighten Elena more.

Silent, she regarded him, her arms wrapped around herself as though she needed comfort. Her chest heaved as she breathed, and he saw the outline of her taut nipples through her shirt.

Catching the direction of his stare, she jerked her head and turned to go.

He wanted her so badly he could scarcely breathe.

"Wait." Though his control was precarious, he grabbed her arm. She froze, still not looking at him. Though he wanted to cover her mouth with his and kiss her senseless, he made no other move toward her. This was too important. "Talk to me, Elena. Please." His voice sounded as if he'd swallowed a mouthful of rusty nails.

"There isn't anything to discuss. You wanted to show me, I saw. You're just like Watkins, though you didn't make me watch you kill some poor rabbit."

He winced. Watkins had been a fool. "You must have questions."

"No, not really." She gave his hand on her arm a pointed look. "Let me go."

Not knowing what else to do, he released her, expecting her to hurry back to the car.

Instead she walked a short distance off. "I'm not sure what you want me to say."

His gut twisted. *Tell me you found my wolf beautiful. Tell me you're no longer filled with fear or disgust. Tell me you can accept me for what I am.*

But of course, he said none of those things.

Finally her gaze met his. "Melissa's baby…"

"Will be able to do what I just did."

Her throat moved as she swallowed. "How soon? As an infant? Or does the ability come later?"

"Later. Usually by the time we reach adolescence."

"Then the child will have a normal childhood?"

He winced. "Shifting is normal, too."

Arms crossed, she gave no ground. "For you, maybe. Not for me."

His heart sank. Despite this, his body still throbbed with need. He still wanted her. Still, he kept his expression neutral. "What are you going to do now?"

A tiny frown creased her brow. "What do you mean?"

"You knew about Watkins. He told me. After he showed you, you asked him to leave Fantasies."

"Not forever." The words exploded from her. "It was late, I was shocked. I couldn't deal with it right then and there, so I asked him to leave. I didn't tell him to go away and never come back."

Startled, Jared stared. "For the Pack, showing a human our wolf means we've met our mate. Why did Watkins think that of you?"

"I don't know." Sadness rang in her tone. "We only went out a few times. We were more friends than anything. I thought. Until that night."

Exultation filled him. He'd known from the moment he'd met her that she was *his*. While he felt sad that Watkins had been misguided, at least Elena hadn't responded in kind. She was special. One of a kind. *Mate*.

Now he had to get her to accept what to her was a new reality.

"What about your other dancers? Now that you know they're not all human, are you going to fire them?"

She glanced at his car. "Maybe we should get going. It's not exactly safe here."

Though he wasn't sure he could walk, he nodded, praying his erection would subside by the time he climbed in the car.

Moving carefully, he made it to the driver's side.

Inside the car, Melissa still slept.

"No doubt she'll be furious when she wakes up and learns she missed the show," Elena said.

Now that she stood on the other side of the car, safe from his touch, Jared attempted to channel his arousal into anger. "This wasn't a show."

"I know." Her quiet tone was meant to appease him. "I'm sorry. I'll get used to all this eventually."

He unlocked the doors, watching while she slid into the passenger seat. He needed a few more minutes to feel normal. The obvious sign of his desire had faded somewhat, and in a moment or two he'd be fine.

"Are you getting in the car?" Elena asked. "I'd really like to go home."

In the backseat, Melissa stirred, yawning and sitting up. "Are we there yet?"

"Too late," Elena snapped. "He's already done his thing. It's over."

"You sound freaked out," Melissa rubbed her eyes. "It's a shock at first, I know. But pretty awesome. I'm bummed I missed seeing it."

Elena didn't reply.

Opening his door, Jared slid into the seat and started the engine. He put the car in gear and pulled out onto the street.

"Well?" Melissa persisted. "What did you think?"

"I don't want to talk about it," Elena snapped. "Not now." She said something else under her breath in Spanish.

Melissa made a rude snort from behind them. "Jared, she says she'll discuss it later."

He had a sneaking suspicion she'd said no such thing.

"Later," he agreed. "We'll talk later." She needed time to come to terms with the impossible. What she'd seen and the laws of the normal world were in direct opposition.

She was his mate. He could only hope she'd eventually accept his nature.

"Drop me off at the nightclub." Unsmiling, she wouldn't even look at him. "I'll keep Melissa with me."

"I need to go home," the teenager protested. "It's late and my mom will be worried."

"So call her." Elena's clipped speech belied her calm expression.

"I've lost my cell."

"Take mine." Rummaging in her purse, Elena handed hers over the seat. Jared noticed her hands trembled.

Melissa handed it back. "She might be asleep and I don't want to wake her up. I'm tired. And pregnant. I want my own bed."

"Fine." Elena sighed. "Let's take her to her house." Without waiting for his assent, she snapped out a series of quick directions. Joy lived in Richardson, a suburb of Dallas, and not too far out of the way.

As soon as they'd taken Melissa home and watched until she'd gotten inside the house, Jared turned to Elena. "I really think we should talk."

"A man wanting to talk," Elena snarked. "Must be a miracle. But I'm not interested. I need to get back to the club. I've got work to do before I go to sleep tonight."

Since her tone left no room for further discussion, Jared did as she asked. At this hour of the night, traffic was light. He drove fast and furious, his chest aching. A few minutes later, they exited the freeway and pulled up in front of Fantasies.

Back stiff, Elena wasted no time pushing open her door.

"Elena," he called. "I made an appointment with the healer tomorrow. If you no longer want to go, I'll understand."

Without a backward look, she marched off toward her back door.

Jared's heart sank. He knew she'd heard him, and she hadn't answered. Worse, this was the first time since he'd met her that she'd left him without saying goodbye.

Hurrying away from the car—and Jared—now that she no longer had to hide how she felt, Elena couldn't stop shaking. Great, bone-racking tremors, as if she'd fallen into an icy pond. The analogy was accurate, because she felt cold, too. So cold. Maybe she was going into shock. Who could blame her?

Shock. Worry, trepidation and…if she were honest with herself, exhilaration. Even…arousal. Because this time, Jared had been the one who'd changed.

Her man. Her wolf. Hers.

Startled—where had *that* thought come from?— Elena shook her head. Nothing would ever be the same again.

Joy would have to be told, too, since Melissa claimed to be carrying a child fathered by a…what had Jared said they were called? A shifter, she remembered.

No doubt Joy's reaction would be similar to her own.

Suddenly exhausted, she headed down the hall to her office. Once there, she closed and locked the door and dropped into her leather chair.

She groaned. Fact one: Werewolves did exist.

Fact two: Apparently there were quite a few of them.

And, fact three: Vampires were real, too.

Her head hurt. Worse, her heart felt as though someone had taken a sledgehammer and put in some serious demolition.

She hadn't realized until now how close she'd come to convincing herself that she and Jared had a connection.

Right. Why on earth was she attracted to weirdos?

Easter was right around the corner. Not only had she invited Jared and his mother, but her entire family knew. She couldn't uninvite them now.

What had she done? She'd never forgive herself if she'd exposed her family to danger. As soon as that dinner was over, she'd tell Jared she never wanted to see him again.

Maybe then she could blot out the image of him becoming a huge silver wolf from her mind. In time, she could forget the whole thing had ever happened. She'd no longer feel this ridiculous *yearning* to be with him.

Gathering up her keys, she locked up and headed to her car. The drive home passed in a daze, her exhaustion and shock making her feel like a zombie.

Pulling on to her street, her heart sank. Jared's black Mercedes was parked in front of her house.

She hit the automatic garage door opener. After she'd parked inside her garage, she debated closing the door behind her and ignoring him. But one thing she'd learned when she first inherited Fantasies was that problems didn't go away simply because you ignored them.

Waiting by the back of her car, she watched him, cane in hand, limp up the driveway. His movements were compact, full of masculine vitality. The air of isolation that normally surrounded him seemed conspicuously absent. Despite what she now knew—or maybe because of it—her pulse still quickened.

"We need to talk," he said, unsmiling.

She nodded, leading the way into the house, flicking on every single light along the way.

In her living room she faced him. "What do you want with me?"

He swore under his breath. "Elena, how can you be so blind?"

How dare he act as though something was wrong with *her?*

"I like my world exactly the way it is. Or was," she amended. "Learning reality is not what I thought is going to take some getting used to."

He watched her closely, dark eyes revealing nothing. "*Did* Watkins propose to you, Elena? Ask you to be his mate?"

"I told you, we only went out a few times."

"Then why?" he persisted. "Why would he change in front of you?"

She paused, remembering something. "Before he changed, he said something about a medical break-through he was working on. To be honest, I didn't really pay attention after I saw him become a werewolf—sorry—shifter. All I wanted was to get away from him."

Stroking his chin, he appeared lost in thought. "A medical breakthrough. Please try to remember. Any small detail might help."

"Help what? Help you find him?"

"That, too." He sounded as if the thought had just occurred to him. "Remember, Ryan told me he thought Watkins might have been performing some kind of experiments on shifters with Valerie's help."

"Are you sure about Valerie?"

With a jerk of his head, he nodded. "Please, try to remember what else Watkins might have said."

She thought back, mentally cringing as she saw again the man, a shower of glittering fireflies, then a huge, brown wolf. She remembered her shock, the absolute terror. She'd backed away, slowly at first, then once she was out of the animal's sight, at a full-out run.

Later, when Watkins had come to her in his human shape, she'd asked him to leave her alone. She'd meant for a few days.

"There was nothing else," she said reluctantly. "I asked him to leave, and he did."

He took a step toward her. Instinctively she moved back. "You're afraid of me, too." His voice held a note of mockery as he gave her a narrow, glinting glance. "Aren't you?"

"I'm not sure." It was as honest an answer as she could give. "I don't think so. But, come on, put yourself in my shoes."

He laughed, a bitter, hollow sound. "If only I could." Holding his cane, he used it to indicate her couch. "May I?"

Hesitant, she nodded, then forced herself to sit also.

"If you could become an animal, any animal, what would you choose?"

His question surprised her. "I haven't thought about that in years. When I was a little girl, I used to want to become a deer, so I could run full-out through the fields."

"A deer." His intent gaze pinned her. "Prey."

Chapter 10

Prey.

Something in the way he said that single word seemed carnal, sexual. Her blood surged, making her inhale sharply. "What do you mean?"

Instead of answering, he only smiled. The sensual beauty of that smile sent a shudder of desire through her.

That she could want him, even now, both pained and excited her.

"I think you should leave." She stood, trying to ignore her body's throbbing.

As if he knew, he made no move to go. "I want you, Elena."

Her gasp made him push awkwardly to his feet. He held out his hand. Though she made no move to take it, God help her, she didn't step away.

Instead he lightly stroked her arm. Trembling, she didn't move. Need and desire crashed through her, mingling with and enhanced by her fear.

"You want me, too." His caress was as much a command as his voice. He kissed her, his mouth surprisingly gentle when she wanted more. The brush of his lips left her aching. When he pushed his body against her, the force of his arousal made her knees go weak.

She wanted, oh, how she wanted.

Luckily she still held on to her tattered common sense. "Jared, we can't…"

He put his finger against her mouth. "Shh, no worries. I know you're confused. But I promise, we won't make love until you accept me for what I am."

Something inside her cracked, a little. "I don't know how."

He smoothed her hair away from her face, brushing his lips against her brow.

The light touch made her catch her breath.

"I don't understand. How can I still want you?" she whispered. "I was planning to send you away…."

Stark pain crossed his face. Inhaling sharply, he bowed his head. For one awful moment, she thought she saw the glint of tears in his eyes.

"I'm sorry," she said, meaning the words.

He nodded. "Me, too." Moving away from her, he gave a brusque nod. "Like I said, I'm driving out to Anniversary tomorrow to visit that healer. Call me if you still want to come."

Struggling to find the right words, Elena let him leave without saying anything at all.

* * *

The next morning Jared's phone rang at the ungodly hour of 7:00 a.m. He opened one bleary eye and grabbed for the handset, managing to croak out a garbled hello.

"Did I wake you?" Elena's throaty voice purred. Instantly his body responded, making him bite back a groan.

"Mmmph," he managed.

"I'll take that for a yes," she continued. "Does your offer to let me go with you to see the healer still stand?"

That woke him up. Maybe Elena *had* learned something yesterday to help her toward acceptance.

"Of course." Clearing his throat, he sat up. If he jumped in the shower now, he'd have time to take her out to a nice breakfast.

"Great." She sounded thrilled. "I'd like to go. The sun is shining, birds are singing. It's a beautiful day."

"I'll pick you up in forty-five minutes." He wanted her so badly he was uncomfortable. "Are you always so cheerful this early in the morning?"

She laughed, the husky sound curling around his insides like smoke. "I'm not usually a morning person, but today I appear to be." The smile in her voice would have made him grin back if he wasn't so damn aroused.

"All right." A cold shower, though unpleasant, would do wonders. "We'll get breakfast before we go."

She rang off, sounding pleased.

He hurried through his morning preparations, half worried she might change her mind. Truth be told, even allowing himself to *think* about the possibility of this healer being real terrified him. He couldn't afford to allow himself to hope for an unlikely miracle, only to be shot down again.

Because the Saturday-morning traffic was light, he arrived at Elena's house in twenty minutes. His attempt to hurry had caused his leg to hurt more. Worse, not only had his pain intensified, but his fear had him fighting the urge to call and cancel the entire thing.

He needed a distraction, and Elena provided one. When she appeared in her doorway in faded jeans and a Rolling Stones T-shirt that clung to her like a second skin, his mouth went dry. She looked…amazing. She wore her dark hair up, accenting the exotic tilt to her eyes. Her dusky skin glowed, and the light makeup she'd applied intensified her beauty.

"You look…" Desperately searching for an adjective, he hoped his tongue wasn't hanging from his mouth. "Beautiful," he finished.

"Thanks!" She breezed past him to the car, sliding into the passenger seat and buckling in before he'd even moved to follow. If she seemed a bit jumpy, he put it down to her trying to adjust. Normal. Encouraging, even.

Following her, he climbed in the driver's side. "How are you feeling this morning?" He started the car, hoping he didn't appear as jumpy as she. "I meant what I said. You look…good."

"Thanks." She glanced sideways at him. "I want you to know, I meant my apology last night. I'm going to try to have a more open mind."

"I'm glad." He gave her a quick smile. "I'm glad you wanted to come."

"I've been thinking about Damien and Luke," she

said. "Not the fact that they were shifters—I'm still trying to wrap my mind around that. But about the way they died. I don't allow drugs of any kind—I even have a random drug-testing program in place. No one—and I do mean no one—has ever failed. Now two of my dancers have died, both of suspected drug overdoses. I have to find out who brought drugs into my club."

They stopped for breakfast at a small café in Kaufman, a place run by shifters. They were lucky and snagged one of the few remaining tables.

While Jared fought the urge to take her hand across the red-and-white checkered tablecloth, the waitress poured them coffee and handed them plastic menus.

They both ordered pancakes, his with a side of sausage, bacon and ham.

This feels like…" She bit her lip, looking away.

He took a moment to admire the hint of blush in her cheeks before finishing her sentence. "A date?"

"Yes." Her gaze flew to his. "How did you know?"

"Because it feels that way to me, too."

They finished eating, and thirty minutes later they reached the bridge over the lake. A small sign proclaimed Anniversary, Population 5,546. The water sparkled in the sun, inviting and cool.

"Here we are." His stomach clenched. "Anniversary. Home of the newly discovered Pack healer." He wished he could feel more positive about this. But other doctors had tried to heal him and failed. Jared was a physician. He believed in science, not some metaphysical woo-woo stuff. If nothing in the real world of medicine worked, why did he even dare hope that a faith healer could help him?

Because he knew such things were possible. He was a Halfling and could change into a wolf. Medical science had no logical explanation for that, either.

"Nothing ventured, nothing gained," he said out loud.

"You *are* nervous." Elena squeezed his arm. "Remember this, Jared. No matter what, you won't leave here any worse off than you arrived."

He had to chuckle. "True."

"We've still got a lot of time." She glanced at her watch. "I'd like to check out the town square and maybe find a place to eat lunch later."

He agreed, choosing a parking spot in front of a crowded antiques store.

Though she didn't hold his hand, simply walking with Elena at his side made him feel, for the first time in his life, like part of a couple. Like he'd found his mate.

Mate. Again that word. If that was the truth, today they'd each taken the first step to overcoming the obstacles against them.

When they'd finished roaming the restored downtown area, Elena chose a family-owned Italian bistro for lunch. The place had delicious homemade lasagna with enough meat to satisfy even his wolf.

When they'd finished, Elena reached across the table and touched his hand. "It's twelve-thirty. Are you about ready?

Though he nodded, his heart leaped into his throat. "Might as well get this over with," he grumbled.

Jared seemed restless. Despite his attempt to continue to seem casual about the entire thing, Elena could tell. His trepidation made him vibrate with nerves. Oddly enough, she found herself wanting to soothe him, to comfort him with a reassuring touch. But, uncertain herself, she kept her hands in her lap and did nothing.

When they finally pulled up to the fifties-era ranch house nestled beneath towering trees, she wiped her fingers down the front of her jeans. Though her mother and aunts occasionally visited fortune-tellers, Elena had never been completely comfortable with New Age type things.

But whatever she'd expected—an old crone maybe, or a multibeaded love child with long hair and peasant skirts—when Samantha Herrick came to the door, she was none of those things. A slender redhead with exotically tilted brown eyes and creamy, pale skin, she was tall and willowy—everything Elena was not. Cradling her chubby-cheeked infant, she looked more like a fashion model playing at suburban mom than an esoteric faith healer.

"Hi!" Her smile was warm and welcoming, touching on both Elena and Jared. "This is my husband, Luc." She gestured to the man behind her.

Like Samantha, Luc was handsome. Tall and lean, dark-haired, he slipped his arm around his wife's shoulders, his love for her apparent in his adoring smile.

One couldn't help but like them. Elena relaxed slightly. They couldn't be that bad, could they? They both seemed so...*normal.* Exchanging a glance with Jared, she saw he'd calmed somewhat, as well.

When the introductions had been completed, Elena and Jared followed the couple into a cozy home built in the Craftsman style. Inside, a warm hardwood floor glowed and splashes of color made the simple furniture appear exotic, yet still nothing looked weird or any different than her own home. Of course, what had she expected, cauldrons and bat wings? Shaking her head at her own foolishness, Elena fingered her cross.

"Sit." Samantha indicated the overstuffed sofa, handing her baby to her husband, who gave a smiling wave and disappeared into another room. "Kyle needs to go down for his nap and Luc's going to change him. Would y'all like some iced tea?"

Elena declined.

"I'd like a glass," Jared said, and watched as the other woman moved gracefully into the kitchen. Once she was gone, he took a seat on the couch, patting the spot next to him for Elena, who shook her head.

"I want to watch from over here," she whispered. "I don't know why, but I'm a little bit uncomfortable."

"I understand." Jared looked down at his hands. "I can't believe I'm doing this."

"Nothing ventured, nothing gained." Repeating his own words back to him made him smile. He continued to smile as Samantha reappeared, handing him an ice-filled glass before taking a seat next to him.

Elena couldn't help but feel a twinge of jealousy. Samantha Herrick was beautiful and exotic and mysterious, while she herself was ordinary. How could Jared not find the woman attractive?

Yet she sensed more fear in Jared than male appreciation. His dread she could understand. He saw this woman, this healer, as his final hope at ridding himself of the pain. If her faith healing didn't work—and Elena didn't really believe it would—Elena had lost nothing. But Jared...Jared would have no hope left.

"How are you feeling today?" Samantha spoke in a soothing voice as though she understood his trepidation. This despite the fact that he wore his usual bored expression, pretending not to care.

Elena was stunned to realize how well she understood him. Somehow, after knowing him only a couple of weeks, she felt as if she'd known him forever.

Samantha patted Jared's shoulder. "You're a Halfling then? With a human mate?"

Mate? "I'm just a friend," Elena qualified.

"You know the law," Jared said, expression grim. "People like me don't take mates."

Samantha's smile widened, as though she found this amusing. "Don't be ridiculous. If it's your leg that's holding you back, I can take care of that." She continued to stare at Jared, finally taking a long drink from her glass and setting it down. "Are you ready to begin?"

"Shouldn't we go someplace more...private?" Jared held himself stiffly, as though he might pop up from the couch at the slightest provocation.

Again Samantha laughed, the sound throaty and pleasing. Elena couldn't help but smile in response— even Jared's mouth quirked at the corners.

"No need," Samantha said cheerfully. "What I do isn't the slightest bit messy."

"What is it you do exactly?" Elena asked, unable to resist.

Clear-eyed, Samantha met her gaze. Her confident

grin invited them both to share in her joy. "I touch him, and he heals."

"How's that work?" Jared leaned forward, as though the doctor part of him was interested. "Scientifically, that is."

With a slight laugh, Samantha shrugged. "I have no idea. But it does. Only on animals…and Halflings. Turns out I'm one, too. A Halfling, that is. Though instead of channeling my energy into changing, I heal."

Channeling. One of those metaphysical gobbledygook words. At least Elena recognized one, even if the rest of what Samantha said made no sense. Again Elena looked at Jared, to see how he was taking the woman's rambling. But instead of looking worried, he nodded, as if everything she'd said made perfect sense to him.

If he'd been anyone else, Elena would have feared he'd been hypnotized. As it was, she crossed her arms and leaned back against the wall, ready to watch what she felt quite certain would be an interesting show.

"Are you ready?" Samantha asked again, her intense gaze focused on Jared. This time, he nodded, his hands clenched into fists. "Heal me," he said, conviction in his voice.

Nodding, Samantha placed her hands on his arm.

"Not there," he said. "It's my leg."

"Doesn't matter." Luc's deep voice startled Elena. She hadn't seen him return. "As long as she touches you somewhere, her energy will find whatever's wrong and heal it."

Jared looked at the other man. "Your aura—are you—?"

"Pack," the other man said firmly. Elena stared.

Pack? Jared had used that word before, when talking to Melissa. Did that mean Luc was also a shifter?

"Shh." Eyes closed, Samantha continued to sit with both palms resting lightly on Jared's forearm.

The air pressure seemed to change in the room. Disbelieving, Elena glanced at Jared, then Luc. Neither man seemed to notice anything amiss. Yet the fine hairs on the back of her arm had risen, and it felt as if electricity danced across her skin.

Jared moaned.

Still touching him, Samantha whimpered. Again and then she made a growl.

"There was an accident," she said, her voice remote. "Car crash. Awful. Shattered glass. Twisted metal. Blood. Pain. Suffering. You were hurt. There's another—a full-blood. He's hurt, too, but he'll heal. You won't. You almost died." Her eyes flew open, blazing with intensity. "They didn't think you'd ever walk again."

Again Jared made a sound, a low-pitched noise that sounded like a howl. The wildness of the primitive cry sent shivers up Elena's spine. He sagged back against the couch as though boneless, his gaze unfocused.

Elena started to go to him, but Luc restrained her. "Not yet. She's barely begun."

Before he'd even finished speaking, the room filled with…fireflies? Elena gasped, remembering the sparkles when Watkins and Jared had changed. But she'd been farther away then, not surrounded. There were thousands of them, swirling and dipping and sparkling.

A closer look and she realized the sparkling lights

weren't insects at all, but something ethereal, like…
fairy dust?

She shook her head. Next she'd be looking for flying
pixies or something.

Samantha whimpered and Jared answered in kind.
Now Luc crossed to his wife, kneeling beside the couch.
She took a deep, shuddering breath, then sagged against
him. He wrapped his arms around her, supporting her,
lending her his strength as though she'd given Jared all
her energy through her touch.

Still, she did not remove her hands from Jared, who
remained unconscious.

"What have you done?" Alarmed, Elena went to him,
her heart hammering in her chest. "He's—"

"Shush!" Luc's sharp tone was urgent. "If you want
your man healed, let her finish."

About to protest that Jared wasn't her man, Elena
rocked back on her heels. Despite rational thought, de-
fying logic, on some elemental, primitive level, Jared
Gies *was* her man.

And, whether or not she believed in Samantha's
brand of healing, Elena wanted him healed.

So she closed her mouth and rocked back on her heels.

"I'm done." Samantha lifted her hands, each movement slow and deliberate, as though full of pain. Luc slid
his arms under her, lifting her as if she weighed nothing,
and carried her away from the couch.

"Please excuse us," he said to Elena, though he had
eyes only for his wife. "She needs to rest." Still carrying
Samantha, Luc disappeared down the hall.

Jared reclined against the sofa pillows, still motionless.

What to do, what to do? Climbing to her feet, Elena climbed up onto the sofa, taking Samantha's place beside him. The healer claimed to have finished—did that mean Jared was healed?

"Jared?"

No response. His chest rose and fell as he breathed, but his eyes remained closed.

She tried calling to him again. "Wake up. Please."

He grunted, taking a deep breath and slowly opening his eyes. "Elena?"

"I'm here." She leaned close. "Are you all right?"

The emotion in his gaze made her heart skip a beat. "Are you—?"

He covered her mouth with his. Hungry. So hungry.

Shuddering, she tried to break away and found she could not. Or would not. He claimed her, devoured her, and had they not been in someone else's living room, she would have surrendered herself to him willingly.

He took and she gave. His lips seared her, possessing, acquiescing, reaching her inner core, her soul.

"Elena," he murmured her name, as breathless as she. "Elena?" The dawning wonder in his voice made her smile, despite everything.

"Jared, let me go." She managed to speak against his mouth. "You've been through a lot."

As he hesitated, confused, she found the strength of will to pull away.

Staring at her, befuddled, she saw the exact instant comprehension dawned in his eyes.

"What?" He glanced around wildly, springing up and swaying on his feet. "Where's…?"

"Her husband carried her out. She said she'd finished." Elena tried not to watch him too closely, not wanting him to realize what she waited for.

"Am I…?" He took a tentative step forward, then another. Frowning, Jared glanced down at himself. Then, a stunned look replaced the confusion on his handsome face. "The pain. There is no pain."

He spoke with so much wonder, Elena's eyes filled with tears.

"I don't believe this." He ran his hand over his leg, probing. "When she touched me, I felt a burning deep inside at first, but then I must have passed out. I don't remember anything after that first touch."

Before she could stop him, he kissed her again, quick and hard. "She healed me. She really healed me."

Pushing himself up, he moved around the room, testing his leg, though he still used the cane.

Joy shone from his dark eyes. "The bones are holding. For the first time in years, I'm not in excruciating pain."

"You can get rid of the cane," Samantha said from the hall doorway, smiling an exhausted smile.

He glanced at her, then down at his cane.

"You're right." He tossed it on the floor by the couch.

Elena moved to help him, worried that at any second, his leg would fail. He waved her away. Taking another step, he let his left leg bear the full brunt of his weight, his wary expression showing he was bracing himself.

"No pain. It never came." In disbelief, he stared at Samantha. "It's gone. How the hell—?"

"Hell had nothing to do with it." Samantha stepped forward, kissing him on the cheek. Exhaustion showed in the tight line of her mouth and the circles under her eyes. "Go with love, my friend."

"Thank you," Jared told her. "I mean that with all of my heart. "You've taken away the pain."

"How long will this last?" Elena asked. "I mean, is it permanent?"

Samantha nodded. "Yes." She gave Elena a long look. "I can heal physical injuries. As to the other, that healing will be up to you." Then, still smiling, she opened the door, weaving slightly on her feet.

What had she meant by that? Before Elena could ask, Jared grabbed her hand, pulling her with him out the door.

Chapter 11

They'd barely made it out of the neighborhood before Jared turned down a wooded street. He turned right on a gravel driveway, ignoring the No Trespassing sign and once they were out of sight of the road, he coasted to a stop. He couldn't wait another moment.

"What's wrong?" Elena sat up, eyes wide with alarm.

Gently he unfastened her seat belt and pulled her to him. "I'm going to kiss you." That was all the warning he gave before claiming her lips.

He was whole again. A complete man. Now, he had the right to claim her.

If she would accept him.

Every pent-up emotion, adrenaline, relief and a dawning sense of wonder mingled with his desire for her.

Angling her chin up to his, he kissed her deep and long, mate to mate.

Her breath caught. Quivering, she wound her arms around his neck and kissed him back. Her lips were warm and sweet, vibrant and passionate.

Sliding his hands across her dusky skin, he eased the lacy cup of her bra aside. She gasped as he took her swollen nipple into his mouth, arching against him, her head back, eyes closed.

Beautiful. So beautiful.

His.

She shuddered, moaning. The noise she made—low, animalistic—sounded like Pack. Her scent—that of arousal—inflamed him.

Though his body throbbed, he forced himself to go slowly. She had to be certain that this was what she wanted, that *he* was what she wanted. All of him, right here, right now and forever and always.

Mate.

"Jared." She used his name to invite, as well as to demand.

Pulling her against him, he let her feel the strength of his desire. She gave a low cry, reaching for him and caressing the length of him through his jeans.

At the first tentative touch of her hand, he convulsed, his body nearly giving in to release like a teenage boy at his first time.

Hell hounds.

"Wait." Capturing her hand with his, he held her away.

Taking great, ragged gulps of air, he struggled to regain control. Only then did he allow himself to touch her.

Slowly, carefully, he stroked her, sliding his hands down her torso, lingering at the waist of her jeans. She moaned, low in her throat, her eyes dark with passion.

"I'm ready," she said, parting her lips for his kiss.

At her words, raw desire clawed at him. Heartbeat thundering in his ears, blood boiling, still he held himself back.

"Are you sure?" he asked, gravel in his voice, knowing fierce hope and need showed in his face.

There was no hesitation in her slow, answering smile nor in the press of her mouth to his neck. "I've never been more certain of anything in my life. Make love to me, Jared. Make love to me now."

His control slipped. Somehow, some way, he managed to hold on.

Slowly. Slowly.

Unzipping her jeans, he eased his hand past the lacy band of her panties. Ah. Sleek, wet, ready. For him.

Eager, she wiggled, helping him remove her jeans. He slid her panties down, his own body so inflamed he felt as though he might explode. When she touched him, tugging at his zipper, he couldn't help surging against her hand.

Somehow, she freed him, yanking his jeans past his hips. Mouth still mating with his, she straddled him, gasping as she took his entire length deep inside her.

"Wait," he gritted. The seductive smile she gave him in response was all it took to shatter what was left of his tenuous grip on control.

He pushed up. Again. And again. Despite their reversed positions, he pounded into her, hard and claiming, while the small part of his mind that could still think wondered if she realized what this lovemaking meant.

In case she didn't, he spoke the words out loud. "I claim you, Elena Cabrera. You're mine."

At his words, she clenched her body around him, bathing him in the honey of her agreement.

"Mine," he repeated, as the last vestige of his control shattered. Lost in her, consumed by her, he reached shuddering ecstasy with his arms wrapped around his mate.

There would be no going back now. They belonged to each other.

Sunday dawned a replica of Saturday, bright and sunny; a perfect day for a newly healed man to go for a run in the park. Grinning to himself, unable to believe his good fortune, Jared dressed in a lightweight pair of sweats and took off.

As his feet pounded the pavement, his wolf woke and stretched. He could sense his other self's interest, though the wolf would have to wait to run—Jared planned to save that pleasure for later in the day, when his mother could join him.

He had a few hours before he had to pick her up at the airport and couldn't wait to surprise her with his newly healed leg. Too much time had passed since he'd last seen her and, though the chasm between them had been entirely of his own making, he'd missed her.

They had a lot of catching up to do. The last time she'd seen him, he'd still been an addict and full of resentful, bitter rage. Since then, he'd kicked his addiction, found his mate and gotten healed.

His mother would be thrilled. Too bad his brother, John, wouldn't be with her. That would be another rift Jared himself would have to heal.

Now, clean and sober for the first time in years, he could finally admit the distance had been his own fault. After the accident, he'd gone AWOL from family and friends, unable to bear the pity in their expressions when they looked at him. Only Watkins had hunted him down, wallowing in guilt since he'd been the one driving. Watkins had been the only one Jared had let hang around, even though Watkins, being full-blooded, had healed quickly, while Jared had nearly died. Secretly Jared's bitterness had fed off his friend's remorse.

Finishing his run, he hurried home to shower and dress for his drive to the airport.

As he toweled off, his phone rang. He glanced at caller ID, then grinned. Elena. Maybe she wanted to ask if she could go to the airport with him.

"Jared, I'm glad I caught you." As usual, her husky voice sent a jolt of pure lust straight to his groin.

"Me, too," he murmured. "How are you?"

"Umm…" His heart sank. Her tone sounded cool. "I think we need to take a step back. Things are going too fast."

Stunned, he gripped the phone and tried to think.

"Since your mom's coming to town, why don't you take the week off from the clinic and hang out with her? I think that'd be a good thing for both of us."

"Maybe for you." He sounded harsher than he'd intended.

"For both of us."

"But last night—"

"I need time, Jared. Time to think." Now there were tears in her voice. "Last night was special. Very much so. I've got to make a decision and I need to be clearheaded when I do. I can't think very well with you around."

He wondered if he was supposed to be grateful that she'd thrown him that crumb. Then, because he had no choice, he agreed. Time apart. He wouldn't show up at Fantasies the entire week.

Replacing the phone in its cradle, he got dressed, strode on his newly healed leg to his car and drove to the airport, no longer reveling in his newfound freedom from pain.

Once there, he parked and hurried into the terminal. Frustrated and full of an odd combination of anticipation and dread, he waited outside the baggage area for his mother. When he saw her striding through the crowd, stylishly cut and highlighted head towering over most of the others, his heart caught.

Meeting his gaze across the crowd, her startling blue eyes were full of so much unconditional love that his throat closed.

"Jared." Her perfume washed over him as she wrapped him in a violet-scented hug. She still wore the same perfume—the delicate scent had always suited her—and he felt a wave of nostalgia for his childhood.

"It's been too long." Her entire face lit up. "You look fantastic."

He smiled. "I have a lot to make up for."

"Shh." She touched her finger to his cheek. "None of that. I'm here, you're clean and things can only get better."

Frustrated, he shook his head. "There's so much I need to say."

"No." She gave him a tender smile. "Let it go, Jared."

"But—"

"I forgive you." Just like that, she wiped the slate clean. Staring at her, he felt as though an immense weight had been lifted from his chest.

"I love you," she said, hugging him again. "And I've missed you so much."

"I've missed you, too." He cleared his throat, finally doing as she asked and letting go of his guilt and his shame. Shifting his weight from foot to foot, he waited for her to notice the absence of his cane.

Her eyes widened. "Your leg… Did you go to the healer?"

"Yes."

Before he could elaborate, she squealed. Unmindful of others' stares, she hugged him again, laughing out loud.

"Amazing."

"I think so, too." And that was putting it mildly. "There's someone I'd hoped for you to meet." Briefly he filled her in on the situation with Elena and the missing Watkins.

"She's afraid of shifters?" Her indignant tone made him smile.

"Yes. But she's my mate. She'll come around. Her niece is pregnant with a Halfling."

His mother sighed. "Do you love her?"

The bluntness of the question took him by surprise. "Of course I do. She's my mate."

"Are you certain?"

The bags began tumbling down the ramp to the carousel, saving him from answering. Isobel pointed to a large, hot-pink suitcase. "There's one of mine. The other matches it, but is smaller."

Once he'd snagged them both, he turned to go. Keeping pace even in her four-inch heels, she followed him out the double doors to his car.

After stowing the two suitcases in the trunk and waiting for her to fasten her seat belt, Jared started the car.

Watching him, his mother laughed, the husky sound making him think of lazy childhood summer afternoons, swimming pools and bright colored Popsicles. "You never answered my question. Are you absolutely sure this woman is your mate?"

"More certain than I've ever been in my life."

"Then you have to fight for her. True mates only come along once in a lifetime. I know you, Jared. You don't give your love easily. If you truly love her, then she's worth fighting for."

He took a deep breath, finally speaking his greatest fear. "I haven't been so great at fighting lately."

"I think you're wrong about that." She gave him a smile to soften the sting of her words. "You've been a fighter all your life, and never more than lately. You struggled to gain your sobriety and won. You fought for your health by going to see the healer. Surely you can wrestle this relationship into place."

Her choice of words made him smile.

"When am I going to meet her?" Leaning forward, her perfectly made up, unlined face made her look much younger than her fifty-two years.

Feeling reckless, Jared let his smile widen into a grin. "She's invited us both to Easter dinner with her family. I accepted."

"Excellent." With a sigh, Isobel leaned back in her seat and fluffed her spiky, sable and gold-tipped hair. "What time are we expected?"

Something in her voice…

"What are you planning?"

"To help you," she said simply. "Surely I can help show Elena shifters are nothing to be feared."

"Absolutely not." He shook his head. "Oh, no, you're not. The last thing I need is you scaring the hell out of Elena. She's still in shock over seeing me change."

"You must be certain, then. But you're being a bit overprotective, aren't you?"

"Maybe." He refused to be baited. "I think you would be, too, if the situation were reversed."

She conceded the point with a short bark of laughter. "So you want me to promise to keep my mouth shut, right?"

Since his mother rarely kept her promises where he was concerned, he gave up. "I'm pretty sure she regrets even inviting us. Now all I can do is hope you don't screw up my life any more than it already is."

"Regrets? Why?"

"She kind of freaked out when she saw me change."

Rather than condemning him, Isobel shrugged. "So? That's pretty usual between mixed mates."

"Evidently Watkins showed her first."

She narrowed her eyes. "Why? Because he sensed she was yours?"

"He never saw us together. And even if he had, Watkins is my friend. He wouldn't do something like that."

Isobel snorted. "I think you're wrong. Trying to steal your mate is exactly the sort of thing Watkins would do."

He let that one go, changing the subject and pointing out various local landmarks.

Once they arrived at his apartment, they stowed her bags in the guest room. Jared took her to his favorite deli for an early dinner, and then to the river bottom.

"Here's where I go to change."

Looking around dubiously, she raised a brow. "Is it safe?"

He had to be honest. "Probably not. But I haven't had any trouble yet. I've been careful not to be seen."

She nodded and got out of the car.

He took her to his favorite grove of trees, keeping an eye—and nose—out for any humans. Backs to each other, they made quick work out of shedding their human accoutrements and changed.

Then, side by side, two huge, silver wolves ran into the twilight.

One week later, mother and son drove to Elena's parents' house for Easter dinner. Jared had nearly held his breath all week, waiting for Elena to call and rescind the invitation, but she hadn't. He took it as a good sign.

If he had reservations about meeting Elena's family, his mother appeared to have none. Immediately upon arriving, she swept into the small, brick house like royalty minus the entourage.

Elena's family had gathered in the living room and

Isobel was in her element, smiling, hugging and exclaiming over everyone as though they were long lost friends.

They all appeared to love her.

But, while they fawned over his mother, they stared at Jared. He stared back, then glanced around the crowded room, looking for Elena. Here, she blended in. Like Elena, the women of her family were all petite and delicate, with the same patrician bone structure and dusky olive skin. They were all lovely, though none could compare to Elena. Even though they'd just shared mind-blowing lovemaking, he wanted her again. And again. He had to clench his teeth and force himself to think of other things.

Like the way her family eyed him. He felt like a giant moving awkwardly among them, but he wanted to find her before his mother did. Searching the kitchen with no luck, he returned to the living room to find that all the men had vanished. Now what had he missed?

Valerie sidled up to him. Even at a family gathering, she'd dressed in a slinky red dress. "Dr. Gies, welcome. I've been thinking about you."

"Thanks." He didn't want to encourage her, so he kept quiet and continued to scan the room, searching for the one woman he needed to see.

"She's in the bathroom," Valerie drawled, giving him a wry smile. "Watch down that hallway and you should see her shortly." Muttering about his taste in women, she moved off, hips twitching in an exaggerated sway.

A door opened at the end of the hall and Elena emerged. She raised her head to find him watching her and frowned. Unsmiling, she brushed past him, nodding at Valerie.

"Well." Valerie's bright red lips twitched in a smile. "I guess that's that. You might as well join the rest of the men." She pointed him toward a long hallway. "Through there," she said. "They're playing pool in the game room. There's a fridge stocked with beer and I'm sure they have plenty of snacks."

Jared nodded but couldn't help glancing once more toward Elena. Silent in the midst of a crowd of chattering women, she'd turned her back to him and appeared to be busy rearranging something on the antique sideboard near the wall.

He couldn't tear his gaze away. She'd worn a pale yellow cotton sundress, the soft material flowing around her lush shape like a sensual veil. She'd arranged her dark hair into a thick braid, making him long to undo it, combing through the silken strands with his fingers. "Elena." He called to her, knowing she heard by the way she stiffened. Then, pretending to be unaware of him, she drifted off, chatting and laughing with the other women.

"Go." Valerie touched his arm. "I'm guessing you two had a fight and she's still freaked out about it. Give her time. We Cabreras have to simmer awhile."

The scent of Valerie's musky perfume made his nose twitch and his head ache. Nodding, he couldn't resist peering around her one more time, hoping for a glimpse of Elena.

Instead he spotted his mother in the midst of the crowd, watching him. Her artfully coiffed blond head stood out from the others like a gazelle among white-tailed deer.

At the analogy, his wolf snarled.

Valerie raised her head, her nostrils flaring. "Did you—?"

"No." Taking a deep breath, he straightened his shoulders. No way Valerie, a human, could have heard his beast. Thanking her and ignoring her narrow-eyed gaze, he headed down the hall to meet the male part of Elena's family.

Jared had come. Heart pounding, she felt his gaze burning like a brand in the back of her head. Despite the way he'd rocked her world the other night, since she'd told him she needed space and he'd stayed away all week, she'd halfway believed he wouldn't show. Now she had to admit she'd hoped he would.

And he'd brought his mother. The woman looked… normal. Avoiding her, Elena studied the other woman from a distance. Despite their different coloring, the resemblance to her son was startling, from the high cheekbones and intense eyes, to the elegantly athletic way they moved. Though Elena had never thought of Jared as beautiful—he was far too masculine for that—his mother was exquisite.

She looked nothing like a werewolf. But then, neither did Jared.

Irritated at herself, Elena headed toward the game room, supposedly to check on the appetizers she'd set out for the men. In actuality, besides avoiding Isobel Gies, she wanted to make sure her father wasn't torturing Jared.

Halfway down the hall, her sister intercepted her.

"Looking for Jared?" Joy asked, grabbing her arm.

"Give him a break. Valerie told me how you gave him the cold shoulder. What are you two fighting about anyway?"

Great. Before they even ate, the entire family would be gossiping about her.

"Shh." A quick glance toward the kitchen showed no sign of Maria Cabrera. "I don't want Mama to hear."

"Why not?" Joy didn't bother to lower her voice. "You know she's in there with his mother, interrogating the poor woman. They both look expectant, like they know something's up."

"Like what? Why?"

"I don't know. Maybe because this is the first time you've ever invited a man over to meet the family?"

Elena groaned. "That kind of nonsense is just what I don't need."

"Hey, what'd you expect? You're the one who invited him."

"What on earth was I thinking?" Elena shook her head, glancing toward the kitchen. Neither Isobel Gies nor Mama had emerged, which meant they were still talking.

"I'm sure Jared's mother can handle Mama." She tried to sound convincing.

Joy snorted. "Do you? You know Mama won't rest until she's uncovered every last detail of gossip. She was thrilled to find out you have a serious boyfriend."

"He's not a boyfriend."

"Whatever." Grinning, Joy waved her away. "You know Jared can't avoid Mama forever. She's like a dog with a bone. Poor Jared will think he's meeting the Spanish Inquisition."

"Hey." Munching on stuffed celery, Melissa drifted into the hall. "Who's that tall, model-looking woman?"

"Jared's mother," Joy told her, still grinning.

Melissa's face lit up. "Really? Did you invite Dr. Gies, too?"

"Yes, she did," Joy chimed in before Elena could answer. "And your gramma is talking to his mother alone in the kitchen."

"No way." Missy winced. "Yow."

"I'll say." Glumly Elena glanced down the hall. From the sounds of things, the men were having a great time. "I haven't even met her yet."

"Why not?"

"Too scared," Joy put in. "You never knew your aunt Elena was such a chicken, did you?"

"I'm not scared." But both Melissa and Joy knew she was lying. "I just need time."

Immediately Melissa nodded. "Because of the wolf thing?"

Elena winced. "Shh."

"No one knows what I mean."

"Now I'm curious." Putting her arm around her daughter's shoulder, Joy gave Elena a hard look. "What's up, sis? Spill."

Glaring at Missy, Elena shook her head in warning. "Have you told your mother about—"

"Not yet," Melissa yelped. "Later, okay?"

"When?"

"Not here. At home."

Expression mildly curious, Joy swiveled her head like a spectator at a tennis match. "What's going on, you two?"

"Nothing." Seeing the desperate plea in her niece's eyes, Elena knew she had to change the subject quickly. "Jared and I aren't even dating. I like him, that's all. I figured he had nowhere to go for Easter dinner, so I invited him. His mother happened to be in town, so I invited her, too."

"Riiight." Melissa gave her a grateful look, conveying her thanks. "You must be more serious than you admit. Meeting the parents? Come on, Aunt Elena."

"Missy." Shooting the teenager a warning look, Elena glanced at the kitchen again. "I'm thinking I ought to rescue the poor woman, but I don't want to draw Mama's attention to myself."

"She looks pretty sophisticated," Missy said.

Joy took the bait, allowing the change of subject. "She looks just like him. She's really thin." She sounded envious. "And did you see her shoes? They must have four-inch heels."

"They're designer." Tone bored, Melissa went into the parlor and flopped down on the sofa. "Jimmy Choo, from the looks of them. Probably last year's style." Grabbing the remote, she began channel surfing.

"Try not to be intimidated." Grinning back, Joy patted Elena's arm. "Even if she is gorgeous and looks way younger than I'd imagined his mother would. Now, go and find your man. It's almost time to eat."

Shooting her sister a go-to-hell look, Elena hurried away, heading down the hall toward the men.

Valerie intercepted her. "I want to talk to you about Jared," she said. "I know you said hands off earlier, but I didn't know he was your boyfriend."

"He's not my boyfriend." Speaking through clenched teeth was more difficult than it seemed. "We're not even dating."

Valerie pounced. "So he's free to see whoever he wants?"

Trying to ignore the twinge of jealously in the pit of her stomach, Elena shook her head. "Don't try to start trouble."

Valerie smiled her brilliant, cat-that-ate-the-canary smile. "I'm not. Either you're dating or you're not. Which is it?"

"Got to go." Elena made her escape, barreling into the game room, her mouth going dry at the sight of him.

Jared stood near the side of the couch, looking acutely uncomfortable. Her chest constricted and she swallowed, hard.

"Hey, baby girl!" Her father motioned her over. "Come here and talk to me."

Internally she cringed, hoping she wasn't in for a barrage of questions in front of Jared. Externally she kept a pleasant smile on her face, as though she hadn't a care in the world, and strolled over.

"What's up, Pop?" She kissed his cheek. "Do you need another beer or something?"

"No." He shot her a glance full of annoyance. "Your young man told us about what's been going on at your club."

Damn. Thus far she'd managed to keep her parents sheltered from all that. She must have forgotten to mention her desire to continue to do so to Jared.

"Why didn't you tell us?" her cousin Jose leaned

forward, his expression intent. "We can come out and guard the place."

She sighed, knowing to argue would be to fight a losing battle. "Can we talk about it after dinner?"

Her cousins nodded—all seven of them.

As if on cue, her mother appeared in the doorway. "The food's ready," she said, then stepped out of the way as all the males rushed for the door. She followed them, leaving Elena alone with Jared.

Chapter 12

Elena felt her face heat as he studied her.

"You look beautiful. I've missed you." His gaze caressed her. She nodded, trying to get up the courage to admit she'd missed him, too. When she didn't, he gave her a sad smile. "What do you think of my mother?"

"I haven't spoken to her yet."

One dark brow rose. "I think we need to rectify that."

As if he'd called her, his mother turned the corner. "There you are." Beaming, she smiled at her son before turning the focus of her knowing blue eyes on Elena. "You must be Elena. I've heard so much about you. I'm Isobel Gies."

Smelling of expensive perfume, she grinned at Elena without reservation. "You're quite lovely," she said.

Up close, his mother looked even more chic and beautiful. The slight tilt to her eyes gave her an exotic look. This combined with her high cheekbones and long legs made her look like a former runway model.

Elena was short, dark and well-rounded. Her best feature was her hair and the dusky color of her smooth skin. Despite her new yellow Easter dress and three-inch matching heels, next to Jared's mother, she felt drab and uninteresting.

Elena reached for the older woman's hand, meaning to shake it, but Isobel surprised her by pulling her close for a quick hug.

As they broke apart, Jared's mother cocked her head, her gaze sweeping over Elena top to bottom. "My son has good taste," she said, smiling. "I'll be honored to have you as a daughter-in-law."

This said, she walked away, joining the others in the other room.

"What…what did she mean?" Elena asked, her voice sounding strained, even to her own ears. "Surely she doesn't think…"

Jared shook his head. "I wanted to do this my own way, and much more slowly. It's a long story."

"Elena?" This time, her own mother reappeared, her no-nonsense gaze brooking no argument. "Come on. It's time to eat. Everyone is waiting for you two." She stepped closer, eyeing Jared. "Since my daughter has no manners, let me introduce myself. I'm Maria Cabrera."

Jared hugged her, carefully avoiding Elena's questioning gaze. When they broke apart, Maria led him by the hand down the hall to the buffet, shooting her daughter a stern look over her shoulder.

Elena knew that look well. It meant, *No more trouble.*

Everyone filled their plates and sat at the enormous oak table Elena had inherited from her mother's sister. Her father said the blessing, and they all dug in.

Her mother had cooked both chicken enchiladas and chile rellenos stuffed with beef. Aunt Marabel had brought her famous tamales. Everyone had contributed something—black beans, taco salad and soft tacos were among the repast.

Jared heaped his plate and then proceeded to polish it off, following her cousin Raymundo back for seconds.

Somehow, Elena made it through the meal, managing to stuff small morsels of food into her mouth and go through the motions of pretending to enjoy the feast, all the while hyperaware of Jared sitting next to her as she turned his mother's words over and over in her head.

Had he told his mother they were engaged?

Finally the women got up and started clearing the plates.

"We'll have cake and coffee in a little while," Maria Cabrera announced. "And my homemade flan."

"I'll help with the dishes," Isobel Gies said. "The rest of you go and relax."

Even Jared appeared startled at this. Elena grabbed him before her father could. "Let's go outside and walk off some of this food."

The entire family watched them. Clearly having no choice, Jared nodded.

Chatter resumed as Maria and Isobel started collecting plates. Elena motioned to Jared to follow her, ignoring Valerie's long, scarlet nails tapping on the table.

Once outside, Jared waited while Elena quietly shut the door behind them. They walked to the end of her driveway and a few feet down the sidewalk before she turned to face him.

"Look, Jared, maybe we shouldn't see each other anymore."

He froze. Raw hurt glittered in his eyes. "How can you say that? Especially after what we shared?"

Though she flushed, she held his gaze. "What we shared is part of the reason I say this. Didn't you think that was a little…intense?"

"Intense?" He stared at her as if he couldn't believe his ears. "Of course our lovemaking was intense. We're mates. Why would you want it any other way?"

She shook her head. "We barely know each other."

"We're good together." His words were the truth, and she knew it. Her gaze slid away.

Fidgeting, when she once again looked at him, she tried to make her expression resolute. "This entire thing has got me worried. What did your mother mean? What have you told her? You'd better start talking."

Hostility? From Elena? He'd expected trepidation, even curiosity, but what the hell?

She still didn't want to see him again? After the way their bodies had made each other sing? He'd known she had intimacy issues, but come on. They were perfect together. Meant to be.

Trying to collect his admittedly nonplussed thoughts,

he tried to school his expression into something soothing. He knew his frown intimidated people, though he doubted it would bother her.

With her arms crossed and her caramel eyes spitting fire, she looked as though she wanted to launch herself at him in attack. He half wished she would, because he wanted nothing more than to kiss her hard and passionately.

She thought she could walk away? They were *mates*. The tie between them wouldn't be so easily broken.

"My mother is indulging in a bit of wishful thinking," he finally told her. "She knows I don't give my heart lightly."

"Give your heart?" Expression startled, she shook her head. "Please don't go there."

"I would fight to the death to protect you," he said softly.

She swallowed. "That's not the point."

"Of course it is. Why would you want someone who didn't love you?"

"Jared, I can't deal with this whole werewolf thing."

"Give it time."

Slowly she raised her head to meet his gaze. Then, to his surprise, she placed her hand on his chest, over his heart. He caught his breath.

"When you're a wolf, do you attack and hurt people?"

"Of course not. I'm a doctor. I took an oath to heal."

Head tilted, she didn't look convinced. "In the movies—"

"This is real life, not a movie. I'm not a monster."

"This is the freakin' twilight zone!"

Lowering his head, he brushed a kiss across her mouth. "You're mine, Elena. Never doubt that."

Her eyes drifted closed. "Mmm. I can't think when you do that."

The low-voiced admission pleased him more than anything she'd said so far.

"How about this?" he teased, tracing the soft outline of her mouth with his tongue. She exhaled softly, parting her lips, opening for him.

Just like that, she shattered his control.

Crushing her to him, he claimed her mouth. She returned his kiss, gripping the front of his shirt, rubbing her body against the front of him with wild abandon.

Passion, savage and intense, made him growl low in his throat.

"Oh." She pushed him away, her chest heaving. "See? That's weird. Scary. I can't deal with that!"

Dazed, he blinked. "I would never hurt you." Reining in his arousal—not an easy task—he took several deep breaths. Once he had himself under control, he tugged her softly back to him. Then he kissed the tip of her nose, trailing kisses down her cheeks to the hollow in her throat where her pulse beat so erratically.

Elena pushed out of his arms. "You know, we do have things to discuss. Not just about us, but about what's going on at Fantasies. The last thing I need is for all of my male cousins to show up wanting to play vigilante. The police let me know that autopsy results on Luke and Damien show they died of drug overdoses."

For one more heartbeat, he allowed himself to savor

the lingering scent of her, the taste of her lips, the heightened color in her cheeks. Then, taking a deep breath, he nodded. "Let's start with Valerie. How involved was she with Watkins?"

"They were sleeping together, I think. She also dated Luke, but not Damien. She's, uh, interested in you." She swallowed. "She told me so, earlier today."

"Not interested. You're my mate, no one else. Still, I think we need to do some more checking on her. She's very involved." Quickly he told her about Valerie's visit to the clinic and her claim that she had been helping Watkins with his experiments, whatever they might be.

"But you don't have any idea what he was doing?"

"No." Jared swore. "He's always been pretty easygoing. This stuff with drugs, performing experiments on his own kind…that's not the man I thought I knew."

Her somber expression matched his own. "People change when they get involved with drugs. You know that."

He sighed. "I know. Most likely, he's the one who supplied the drugs. We just don't know why." He thought for a moment. "Assuming Watkins is still alive, maybe he had to go into hiding. He could still be running things from wherever he is."

"We've got to question Valerie. Obviously she knows more about what's going on than anyone else." She sighed. "I hate this. Literally hate it."

"Elena, you've got to be careful. We don't know how deeply she's involved. Two men are dead and one is missing. I don't want anything to happen to you."

Eyes wide with shock, she stared at him. "She's my cousin. She would never…"

Jared said nothing, letting her realize on her own.

"Oh, no." The awful look in her eyes told him she'd reached the same conclusion as he had. "That would mean…"

"Exactly."

"Valerie might be a lot of things, but a killer?"

He shrugged. "Until we know for sure, we've got to be careful. But I do think we should ask her about Watkins's experiments."

"Together." Her tone left no room for disagreement. "Let's see if we can get her alone before we leave."

With her color high and her eyes glowing, she looked vibrant and alive. He couldn't help himself—he kissed her again.

With a soft sigh of acquiescence, she welcomed him, openmouthed.

When they broke apart, he actually felt weak in the knees.

"Damn," he said, trying to catch his breath.

"Damn," she echoed. Then, her eyes widened. "Crud. Here comes my sister."

Jared raised his head to see Joy bustling down the sidewalk toward them. She'd spilled something at dinner on her white, stretchy top, and her hair stuck out in all directions, as though she'd been running her hands through it.

When she reached them, she shot them both a look of disgust. "What do you think you're doing? Putting on a show?"

Without pausing a beat for them to answer, she continued. "Why on earth are you two making out on the sidewalk, in full view of the house?"

Jared winced. Simultaneously he and Elena both glanced at the front window.

Most, if not all, of her family peered out at them. Grinning widely, Melissa waved.

"Great," Elena muttered. "Just what I don't need."

Jared put his arm around her shoulders. She shrugged him off. He couldn't help laughing, earning him a dirty look.

"How am I going to explain this?" she groused.

"Maybe you'd better start with telling them you're engaged," Joy snapped. "Papa is furious."

Elena looked stricken. "What about Mama?"

"She and Isobel Gies are whispering together in the corner. I think they're planning your wedding."

"That's ridiculous! We're not—"

"Elena." Jared cut her off midsentence. "Will you marry me?"

Joy gasped. Elena merely narrowed her eyes. "Stop kidding around. This isn't funny."

"I'm serious." And he was. She was his mate. Why pretend otherwise? His entire life had changed. Healed. he could start over. And first he wanted his mate.

Dropping to one knee in front of her, he grabbed her hand. "Will you do me the honor of becoming my wife?"

Behind him, Joy made strangling sounds. Focusing only on Elena, he ignored her.

Belatedly tugging her hand free, his mate slowly shook her head. "Oh, no, you don't. You're not doing this to me."

"Everyone is still watching you," Joy warned. "Jared, get up!"

Jared continued to watch Elena, knowing his expression revealed clearly how he felt about her.

"No," she whispered, her stricken face breaking his heart. "No. I will not marry you. It's too much, too soon, too fast."

Backing away from him, she tripped over a crack in the sidewalk and fell. He leaped from his knees in a futile attempt, trying to catch her, but she landed solidly on her bottom.

After a moment of stunned silence, Joy began to giggle. Glaring at her sister, Elena pushed herself to her feet, dusting off the back of her dress.

He stood, too. He'd torn his slacks and scraped his knees.

"I'm fine." She waved away his attempt to help her. "Better than you, I think."

"I'm okay." But he wasn't. He felt like she'd ripped his heart from his chest.

"Your knees are bleeding," Joy pointed out. "And your khakis are ruined."

The front door slammed open. Melissa came running out, grinning broadly. "Wow! That was exciting! Are you two going to make an announcement now?"

Elena opened her mouth, then closed it. Face set, Joy stepped in between her daughter and her sister.

"I think—" Before she could finish the sentence, the entire Cabrera family poured out the still-open front door and, everyone talking at once, surrounded them.

"Congratulations!" Her father pounded Jared on

the back. "Welcome to the family!" Enveloping Jared in a bear hug, he was joined by his two brothers, Elena's uncles.

Once released, he was surrounded by the cousins. There were too many to count, and way too many names to remember. Jared accepted their congratulations, though with each one the knot in the pit of his stomach grew worse.

He glanced over at Elena and saw that his mother and hers had pigeonholed her between them. The two older women took turns rapid-firing questions. Elena looked both shell-shocked and horrified.

"Where's the ring?" Melissa wanted to know.

Still smarting from Elena's reaction, Jared shook his head. "I haven't bought one yet. I wanted Elena to choose her own."

At the sound of her name, Elena met his gaze. "Excuse me," she told the mothers, sliding out from between them, and with a forced smile, she waded through her cousins and aunts and uncles until she reached Jared.

Valerie sidled up next to them. Lines of anger made her appear older than her years.

"You lied to me!" She glared at Elena. "You said you two weren't involved."

"We…"

"Are now," Joy interjected, stepping in front of Valerie. "You need to settle down."

Giving Elena one final black look, Valerie stomped to her car, got in and, with a screech of tires, took off.

Something in Elena's face… "Are you all right?"

"No." She scowled. "Far from it. In fact—"

Joy grabbed Elena's elbow. "Come with me," she ordered. "Both of you."

Still involved in their planning or celebration or arguments, no one in the family seemed to notice as Joy, Elena and Jared returned to the house. Except Melissa, who started to follow them. One look from Joy made her stop.

Once inside, Joy pushed them both toward the couch. "Sit."

Elena dropped like a stone, her expression an alarming mixture of shock and horror.

"I'll stand," Jared growled. "Look, I can fix this—"

"You're engaged." Joy shook her head. "Whether you like it or not, you are."

"He asked. I answered no!"

"Well, you didn't tell them." Joy rubbed her temples. "Now Mama is already planning the wedding, and Pops thinks he's getting a new son-in-law who can play pool."

"We have to fix this." Elena glared at him. "Right now."

"Repairing the damage will be simple." Hurting and furious, Jared began to pace. "All Elena has to do is tell the truth. She refused my proposal."

"I didn't get a chance to tell them anything." Now Elena pushed herself to her feet. "This is all your fault. If you hadn't kissed me—"

"Will you two stop acting like children and let me talk?" Arms crossed, Joy waited until they both watched her. Jared had never seen Elena's sister like this, her face alight with purpose.

"For today, I think you both need to stay engaged. Wait." She held up her hand when Elena started to argue. "Hear me out. It'll be easier to go along for now. You can let them down later, when you're not so outnumbered."

"No." Jared crossed his arms.

"Absolutely not," Elena echoed.

"Think about it. Can you face our entire family and tell them there won't be a wedding? You'll make mama look like a fool."

Silence.

"I don't know." Voice weak, Elena appeared to be considering the idea of letting the engagement stand.

Temporarily. And for all the wrong reasons.

Jared knew he had to get out of there. His throat felt tight and absurdly, his eyes seemed about to water.

She didn't want him. His own mate didn't want him.

"Call me when you decide." He tossed the remark over his shoulder, putting on his best I-don't-give-a-damn face.

He strode outside and over to his mother, who was still animatedly discussing wedding plans with Elena's mom, and grabbed her arm.

"We've got to go," he said, trying like hell to sound polite.

Isobel Gies frowned. "Not yet. I'm not finished talking—"

"Now."

"Is everything all right?"

"I'll explain in the car." Turning, he took Maria Cabrera's hand. "Thank you so much for the wonderful dinner. I've truly enjoyed meeting you."

Bewildered, Maria looked from Jared to Isobel, then peered beyond Jared to search for her daughter. "Where is Elena?"

"She's in the house with Joy and Melissa." Still smiling, he gently steered his mother toward the car. "Thanks again."

Isobel waited until they'd pulled away from the curb to turn on him. "All right. Now what have you done?"

Clenching his teeth, he glanced at her. "Elena and I are not engaged."

"Of course you are. We all saw you propose."

"You didn't hear her answer."

She tilted her head. "Hell hounds. Are you saying she turned you down?"

"Are you in the mood for another run?" he asked, pretending not to hear the question. "I'd love to have the company." Plus, wolves didn't talk.

Slowly she nodded, then sighed. "Sure. But don't think you can avoid discussing this forever. I'm only here another couple of days."

"There's nothing to discuss." He didn't bother to hide his grim tone. "Oh, except Elena's sister is trying to get her to *pretend* to be engaged."

"Pretend? Why?"

"Because of what's been going on at Fantasies."

"Ah, the male strip club. You know, I think I want to see this place."

He rolled his eyes. "For hounds' sake, Mother."

"Seriously. You're going there tomorrow, right? You can take me with you when you do."

* * *

Elena had never known she could be so deliriously happy, angry, confused and depressed, all at the same time. Dropping her head in her hands, she groaned. "I don't know what to do."

"Then tell him no," Joy insisted. "Again."

"I'm not sure I can."

"Why not? Don't tell me you have feelings for him." Elena swallowed. "I…"

"He loves you," Melissa insisted, earning another disapproving stare from her mother. "I can see it in his eyes."

"You're young," Joy put in. "And full of romantic ideas. Jared has an agenda of his own."

"Which is?"

"I don't know." Forced to admit the truth, Joy looked even more unhappy. "Either way—"

The front door opened. Face flushed, Valerie stormed inside. Ignoring everyone, she went directly to the chair where she'd left her purse, retrieved it and slammed her way back outside.

"She's going again." Melissa peered out the front window. "She sure is mad about nothing."

"She'll get over it." Joy squeezed Elena's shoulder. "Are you all right?"

Elena lifted her head. "I don't know. Why on earth would Jared propose to me? We barely know each other." She clenched her hands together so the others wouldn't see their trembling.

If anything, Joy's frown deepened.

Elena sighed. "Joy, I know you're overprotective,

but you're the one who said I should continue to pretend to be engaged."

"I know, but I didn't realize you cared."

"I don't—" She started to protest, but again the front door opened. This time, the entire family poured inside, surrounding her and all talking at once.

"You'd better decide," her sister muttered in her ear. "Either tell them the truth now, or let them continue planning your wedding."

Elena lifted her chin. "You're right." She swallowed. "I'm not saying anything for right now."

Surrounding her, the women chattered excitedly. One by one, starting with her father, the men hugged her and gave her their congratulations. As soon as they were finished, they disappeared down the hall to the game room, obviously glad to escape the loud, giddy women.

When all the men had gone, Maria banged on a metal pot to gain their attention. "Time to get to work. We've got a lot to plan. Everyone grab a chair and get started."

Still talking animatedly, they began pulling up chairs. Aunt Helen brought paper and pen, her daughter, Connie, began pouring coffee.

Only Joy, Missy and Elena didn't move.

"Mama, what are you doing?" Elena shook her head. "We haven't even set a date."

"She doesn't even have a ring!" Snatching up Elena's hand, Joy held it aloft.

"Exactly." Elena jerked her hand free. "It's way too early for—"

"I've been waiting for this for twenty-eight years," Maria proclaimed. "Let me enjoy myself. *Mija,* we've got some serious planning to do."

Elena shook her head and backed away, feeling the lie must surely show on her face. "Later, okay? I've got to go."

She bolted for the door before anyone could stop her.

Feeling as though she'd dodged a bullet, she drove home, planning to take her phone off the hook and open a bottle of wine. Maybe with a long, relaxing bubble bath, she could vanquish the tension headache she felt starting.

Then maybe she could decide what to do about Jared.

Chapter 13

The next afternoon, his mother returned from shopping while Jared was getting ready to leave for the clinic.

"Are you heading to Fantasies?"

At his nod, she grinned. "Excellent. I'm going with you." Setting four large department-store bags on the table, she rubbed her hands together. "Like I said, I've always wanted to see inside one of those male strip clubs."

"No way."

She gave him a sharp look. "I thought hunting last night would make you less tense. But you seem even more jittery. What's wrong now?"

How could he explain his unfounded sense that his life was once again spiraling out of control? He didn't know why, or how, but he'd long ago learned to trust his instincts.

Beside that, the last thing he needed was Isobel poking around things at Fantasies. In addition to the danger, he and Elena needed privacy to work things out. Having his mother witness the tension between them would make it that much worse. Especially if she felt the need to try to help, which she would.

"Elena and I need some alone time."

"So?" With her arched brows and hands on her elegantly clad hips, she looked exactly as she had when he'd been small. "I won't bother the two of you. I just want to see a show."

"It's not safe."

She narrowed her eyes. "What do you mean? I know about the two dead dancers. I'll be on guard. No one will bother me. I'm just another middle-aged woman wanting to take in a show."

"An adult show. Don't you think that makes me uncomfortable?"

"Give me a break, Jared. You're a doctor, for hounds' sake. Why would you care or be bothered if I want to watch a bunch of young guys dance?"

"And strip."

"So? When the Pack changes, we all strip. This won't be the first time I've seen a naked man."

She was right. Damn it. With a groan, he gave up. "Fine. You can go. I have to leave in a few minutes. Do you think you'll be ready?"

"I'm ready now."

He sighed. "Sure you are."

His mother smiled. "Okay. Give me a few minutes."

When she emerged fifteen minutes later wearing a

black leather miniskirt and five-inch heels, he couldn't help but laugh.

"What?" She raised a brow.

"Those dancers won't even know what hit 'em." Holding out his arm, he led the way to the car.

Some mothers might have had a problem entering a male strip club. Not his. Head held high, Isobel exited the Mercedes with grace and stalked across the parking lot like royalty in her stilettos.

Once inside, he took her arm, steering her down the hall toward Elena's office.

"This is really nice," she murmured, taking in the polished marble floors, the elegant rugs and contemporary artwork. "Completely unexpected."

Elena's office door was partially closed, just enough to hide her desk from the hall. He tapped on the wood, pushing it open all the way.

His heart stuttered when Elena got up from her chair and came around the front of her desk. She wore a form-fitting, cream-colored pantsuit. "Jared. And…Isobel. What are you doing here?"

His mother's wolfish grin made Jared's heart sink.

"I want to see a show."

Clearly surprised, Elena looked at Jared.

"I don't need his permission." Isobel laughed. "He's my son, not my mate."

Jared shook his head. "Humor her," he whispered close to Elena's ear. "She goes home tomorrow."

With a soft sigh, Elena turned her face so that her nose touched his. Her pupils darkened, making his gut tighten and his mouth go dry.

"None of that!" Isobel pushed at both their shoulders. "You can play kissy-face later, while I'm watching the show."

Elena's caramel eyes widened, then she laughed. "I wasn't about to kiss him. I was going to tell him off."

"Right." Isobel's disbelieving tone matched her eyes. "And if I believe that, I'd have to be completely gullible. Which I'm not."

Jared suspected Elena had no idea what she'd been about to do. The look on her face had mirrored his own desire. She wanted him as intensely as he wanted her. And she wasn't happy about that. No doubt she still wanted to call off their pretend engagement.

Enough time alone with her, and Jared suspected he could convince her otherwise. But his mother was right. Now was not the time or the place.

Hoping his expression showed none of his hunger, Jared looped his arm around Elena's waist and pulled her close. The scent of vanilla mixed with female tantalized him. "What time does the first show start?"

She held her body stiffly in his arms. Not looking at him, she glanced at her watch. "In about an hour."

"That long?" Isobel sounded disappointed.

"We run happy hour from nine to ten. Free appetizers and bargain cocktails. If you'll follow me, I'll get you a seat." Stepping away from Jared, she took the older woman's arm.

"Jared, come keep me company," Isobel ordered. "I don't want to sit by myself."

So much for her promise to leave him alone. He cursed under his breath, knowing she was setting him up, yet not sure for what. "Sorry. I've got to get ready in the clinic. Plus, I have no interest in watching men prance around in G-strings."

If anything, his mother's grin grew wider. "I don't care. I'm only going to be here until tomorrow. I hardly ever see you."

"I'll try to join you later," he said, knowing he'd do no such thing. "Don't forget, I have a clinic to run. Maybe Elena could visit with you during the show?"

"Of course I can," Elena said smoothly, nothing but pleasure in her expression. "Have more people started showing up for the clinic?"

Since she knew they hadn't, Jared glared at her. "A few," he lied. "Once word gets out, they'll start coming in droves. I wouldn't want to miss out on that."

"We wouldn't want you to." Isobel patted his hand. "We can visit more later."

Jared breathed a sigh of relief. He couldn't imagine anything more uncomfortable than sitting with his mother while she ogled seminude strippers. "I'll be in the clinic if you need me," he said.

Still avoiding looking directly at him, Elena nodded. "Come with me, Isobel. I have a private table with a good view. We'll be sitting there."

Again, Isobel swung her gaze from one to the other. "The two of you need to get over yourselves. Life is too damn short for games."

Elena smiled and said nothing. Jared could tell she was biting her tongue out of respect for his mother. He, however, had no such compunctions. "Our business, Mother. Not yours."

Isobel only laughed. "I'm done." She took Elena's arm. "Lead the way."

Watching the two women stroll off, Jared rubbed the back of his neck. He couldn't shake the feeling of foreboding. Something big was about to happen—and whatever it was, it wouldn't be good.

Since the public part of Fantasies hadn't yet opened, Elena had to flick on the lights when they entered the club. While Isobel admired the polished parquet wood dance floor, Elena started pulling the retro-metal chairs down from where they'd been upended on the top of the tables. A second later, Isobel began to help her.

"What's the dance floor used for?" Isobel asked.

"In between performances, the men dance with the customers, earning extra tips."

"In their G-strings?" Looking properly horrified, Isobel also looking intrigued.

"No. But even though they wear slacks and white cotton button-down shirts per my dress code, they exude sex appeal." Elena grinned. "Dancing with the dancers, as I advertise it, is one of Fantasies' most popular draws."

Chuckling, Jared's mother slid the last chair in place. "I can well imagine."

To her surprise, Elena found herself laughing along with her. She waited while the other woman inspected the rest of the room.

"Amazing." Isobel hopped up and strode the length of the runway. With her long-legged stride and high heels, she looked as though she'd be at home in a fashion show with expensive designer clothes draped over her lean body.

"It's a lot like when I used to model," she said, confirming Elena's suspicion.

"The design was deliberate." Everyone liked the stage. The platform resembled something from a beauty pageant, with a long runway and circular end. That way, all sides of the room felt as though they had good seats.

Now that the room was in order, Elena led the way to her private alcove near the front by the stage.

"This is nice." Isobel ran a hand over the polished oak table. "Not at all what I expected."

"Thank you. My aunt started this club over forty years ago. I worked summers here while I was in college. She was determined to make Fantasies the most elegant strip club in Texas, maybe in the United States. I've continued to further her vision."

"Your aunt owns this?"

"Owned. She died while I was in college. Even though she has grown children—my cousins Valerie and Salvador—she left Fantasies to me."

"Really?" Isobel pursed her lips. "That must have caused hard feelings between you."

"No, not really. Salvador is in the peace corps, working in Africa. He couldn't care less. And Valerie has her own interests. She works here as a hostess, but she never wanted to have more responsibility than that, even when her mother was alive. Everything worked out for the best."

The heavy double doors opened and the bartender, a slender Puerto Rican who went by the stage name Augusto, arrived. At Elena's request, he brought over a chilled bottle of her favorite Riesling and two glasses.

Elena found herself studying him. Was he human or…?

"Human." Smiling, Isobel took a taste of her wine. Her perfectly shaped eyebrows rose. "Good white."

"My favorite." Elena took her own sip. "I'm glad you like it. How did you know what I was thinking?"

"About the waiter? You have an expressive face. Tell me—" Isobel leaned forward "—would knowing which of your employees are shifters change the way you feel about them?"

Twirling her glass in her fingers, Elena pondered the questions. "I'd wondered that myself. But now, getting to know you and your son, I'm finding I think of shifters as just more members of the human race."

"You know what, I think I like you." Isobel chuckled. "Now I see why my son wants you."

Face heating, Elena managed to thank her. "I, er, like you, too."

"Yes, but…" Isobel touched Elena's hand, her expression serious. "Do you love my son?"

Flabbergasted and nonplussed, Elena used her wineglass as a shield. "Our relationship is…complicated."

"Love is not complicated. Either you love him or you don't."

"It's not that simple."

"Yes." Isobel drank deeply, before placing her glass on the table. "It is."

"Love is…" Clearing her throat, Elena tried to find the right words. She failed, and all she could do was shake her head.

"When I met Jared's father, I felt as if a lightning bolt had hit me. My entire life, my plans and directions, my routine, all of it was thrown into the winds." Isobel sighed. "But obviously, we worked everything out. Oh, like any young couple, we had our share of problems. Who doesn't? But our bond was strong enough that we were able to conquer them." Isobel rested her chin in her hand.

"What happened to him? I'm assuming he was human, since Jared refers to himself as a Halfling."

Isobel looked away, then met Elena's gaze head-on. "He died when Jared was two." She took a deep breath. "I've never gotten over him. Like our wild relatives, shifters mate for life."

Elena winced.

"I saw that," Isobel declared. "That's why I'm worried about my son. If you can't handle this now, how will you feel once you meet his Pack? Or when you spend hours alone at night because he's out hunting?"

"To be honest with you, I don't know." Taking a long drink of her wine, Elena sighed. "I'm attracted to him, definitely. But I've never been one to leap before I look."

"Sometimes you have to take chances, go with your heart."

Elena thought of her little cousin, of the pain and grief her aunt had suffered when he died. Her aunt had proved she hadn't blamed Elena by leaving her Fantasies, but...

"I still feel as if I have a lot of work to do to repay the universe." Seeing Isobel's puzzled look, she explained what had happened so many years before.

"But of course that wasn't your fault." Isobel covered Elena's hand with her own. "And I really don't understand what any of this has to do with loving my son."

"My world was turned upside down when my cousin died. After that, I vowed to do all I could to keep things the same, to keep things normal." She bit her lip, then bravely continued. "People changing into wolves isn't normal."

"It is to us." Isobel smiled. "Maybe all you need is time to get used to the idea."

"Maybe. Jared's rather persuasive. I'm still not sure about any of this. Were you sure when you married Jared's father?"

"Oh, yes." Blinking, Isobel's mouth worked and Elena saw she was close to tears. "I've never been so happy before or so since. I'll never again experience anything like what he and I shared. I miss him. Every day I feel like half of me is missing."

She leaned forward, her intent gaze locking on Elena. "I want the same for my son. I've thought long and hard about that, ever since I learned how he feels about you. He loves you, Elena. And Jared doesn't give his love lightly."

Love. Despite herself, Elena couldn't stop herself from reacting to Isobel's statement. A shiver rippled along her spine, so strong and sudden she knew Isobel saw.

"I— Honestly I'd been thinking of trying to break away from Jared."

Isobel looked horrified. "Break away? How does one break away from one's mate?"

That word. *Mate.* She liked the sound of that.

"What does that mean, mate?"

"See. Everything in you resonates to the sound of that. Jared feels he's your mate, and you're his. You should consider yourself lucky," Isobel said dryly. "When both mates have shifter blood, they can read each others thoughts. Because you're human, you don't have to worry about that."

"How is a mate different from a spouse?"

"We are blessed if we find our mate. But if our mate rejects us…well, it's devastating."

Inexplicably Elena's eyes filled with tears.

"Shh." Isobel patted her arm. "Don't worry. I think you'll find a way."

Elena nodded, still unsure. "Maybe it would help if you could tell me more about shifters. I know next to nothing, and Jared told me that what I've seen in movies and read in novels is all wrong." She glanced at her watch. "Though maybe you can do that later. We don't have much time before the show starts."

Isobel grinned. "I'll give you the abbreviated version. We have enough time for that." Placing her hands flat on the table in front of her, she took a deep breath.

"We shape-shifters are an ancient race. Not werewolves—as you've noticed, we hate that term. We don't howl at the moon, nor are we compelled to change because the moon is full. As you said, we're a race, just like humans, though definitely a minority. We've successfully integrated ourselves in society and live normal lives. We call ourselves Pack."

"How many of you are there?"

"No one knows for sure. We don't do a formal census, and obviously 'shifter' isn't included on the U.S. census questionnaire. We're scattered all over the country."

Trying to digest it all, Elena swallowed. "Only in the U.S.A.?"

"No. Europe. Asia. Africa, too."

"Basically you're everywhere."

Isobel nodded. "And have been for centuries."

"How is it no one has discovered any of this? Surely with that many…"

"Oh, we've had some close calls, believe me. The ones who know write books, tell stories. Most rational people dismiss them as crackpots."

"Are you immortal?"

"No. Though we heal much faster, our life spans are the same as yours. We live, we die, just like you. We eat, sleep and breathe. Like you. The only difference is that we can change into a wolf at will and you can't."

Crossing her arms, Elena tilted her head, regarding Isobel thoughtfully. "If that's so, then why do you keep your existence a secret?"

Isobel took another long drink of her wine, twirling the glass in her hands. "If humans were to discover the Pack's ability to shape-shift, we know they'd panic and attempt to destroy us. It's happened before, long in the past, when we once made the mistake of letting them know the truth of what we are."

Belatedly Elena again refilled the older woman's glass. "But I'm human. What…how…?"

"Interracial marriages are more common than you would think. That's why there are so many Halflings, children born to a human and a shape-shifter."

"Like Jared."

"Yes." One corner of Isobel's mouth lifted in a soft

smile. "Halflings can change, though they aren't as strong. Still, among our people they are welcomed and loved."

"Loved." Elena nodded. "Like my niece's baby will be."

"Yes. That's all that matters. So again, I'll ask you. Do you love my son?"

Feeling her face heat, Elena shifted nervously in her chair. Jared's mother deserved an honest answer. Yet how could Elena give her that, when she herself didn't know?

The early shift DJ swung into the room, a man known as Veep. With his dreadlocks and penchant for beads and fringe, he resembled a young Bob Marley.

"Evenin'," he said, flashing both women a brilliant smile. "I'll be ready to go before the doors open, Ms. Cabrera."

Elena nodded, casting Isobel a sidelong glance. The older woman grinned.

"Yes. He is shifter."

"I—" Music blared, cutting off Elena's response, as well as whatever else Isobel might have wanted to say.

As the song died down, Elena leaned across the table. "I hope you're ready. The show's about to start. First, they'll unlock the doors and the hostesses will lead the guests in."

"You never answered my question," Isobel said.

Elena pretended not to hear.

As another techo-dance number came on, the heavy oak double doors were thrown open. Valerie and Olivia led clusters of women inside, some giggling and embarrassed, others determined to snag their favorite ringside table. They were as diverse a group as Elena's dancers, ranging from barely twenty-one to grandmotherly, jeans clad to formally dressed in business suits and cocktail dresses.

Isobel tugged on Elena's sleeve, motioning her to lean closer. "Were they waiting outside?" she yelled, trying to be heard over the music.

"Yes," Elena shouted back. Most nights a fair-size crowd had assembled by the time Fantasies' doors opened at nine. But the true rush didn't start until ten or eleven.

The lights dimmed. Cheers went up from the assembled women. Those just entering scrambled to find their seats.

The music changed from techno to blues, a John Mayer song with a heavy, throbbing beat.

The first dancer, a new hire who resembled Brad Pitt from his *Thelma and Louise* days, strutted on to the stage. He wore the required tuxedo and tails—Elena wouldn't let her dancers wear more elaborate costumes until they'd proven themselves.

As she settled back to watch him perform, Elena's pager went off, vibrating against her hip. Since her staff had been instructed only to page her if a situation was urgent, this wasn't good. She could only hope something hadn't happened to another of her dancers.

Heart pounding, she pushed to her feet, grabbing a cocktail napkin and a pen. "I've got to go," she scribbled, sliding the paper across the table.

"Will you be back?" Isobel mouthed.

Since Elena had no idea, she only shrugged. "I'll try."

Returning her gaze to the stage, Isobel waved her away.

As soon as she exited the dance floor, using the private back door, Elena used her cell to called Valerie.

"I'm heading for the front. What's up?"

"The police are here again." Valerie had apparently forgotten her hostility. She sounded mildly hysterical.

Elena's stomach dropped like a stone. "Has something happened to another dancer?"

"No, no, nothing like that. They want to look around," Valerie said. "They have a search warrant."

Since this was so minor compared to what she'd been imagining, Elena took a deep breath. "I'll deal with them. Where are they?"

"I showed them to your office about five minutes ago. Out of courtesy to you, they said they'd wait until you arrived to start."

Reversing direction, Elena headed toward her office. They could search all they wanted—she had nothing to hide—as long as it helped them find the drug-dealing murderer.

The same two officers, Yost and Trenton, had taken seats across from her desk. They both looked up when she entered, waiting until she'd crossed behind her desk.

This time, Yost's friendly smile was conspicuously absent. "We've received credible evidence that drugs are being dealt out of this establishment." He held out a piece of paper and waited silently while she read it.

After inspecting the warrant, Elena handed it back. "I'll let you get busy." She stepped around her heavy oak desk. "Do you mind if I watch?"

"Of course not," Trenton replied, since Yost seemed disinclined to talk. He pushed himself out of the chair and headed down the hall, leaving his partner to follow.

While she couldn't quite put her finger on the

reason, something was off with the two men. She shrugged the thought away. No doubt Yost's sour mood was completely unrelated to this search. If only she could feel the same way about Trenton's obvious jubilation.

They started with the dancers' locker room. Since the early shift had just started and all her employees were either out on the floor serving drinks or waiting in the wings to begin their set, the room was empty.

Good. She'd prefer none of her employees knew about this search, especially if any *were* using drugs.

Crossing her arms, Elena watched as the two officers and three assistants methodically went through each locker, every cabinet, even searching inside the washer and dryer and the stack of clean towels near the showers.

To her immense relief, no drugs were found. She crossed her fingers that her luck would hold. She preferred to deal with any drug users herself, rather than going through the police. She'd fire them, but offer them a chance to enter rehab. If they could come clean and stay that way, they'd still have a job waiting when they finished.

Since this was a much better alternative than prison, she figured most of them would take her up on her offer.

"We'd like to see your break room next," Officer Trenton said. "Please, lead the way."

Heading down her hall with the troupe of uniforms following her made Elena feel like the Pied Piper. She bit back a smile at the reference, knowing Trenton would never understand, even if she were to explain her thoughts to him.

Once they reached the kitchen, she stepped back. "Here you are."

Yost nodded, his hangdog expression beginning to wear on her nerves. Trenton, on the other hand, bounced off the walls, as though each room they searched energized him.

The police searchers made short work of going through the kitchen, the break room and the pantry. She watched from the hall as they began to search everywhere but the bar and dance floor, wondering why she felt so violated.

"Are you okay?" Jared came up beside her and slipped his arm around her waist. She leaned into him, inhaling his familiar, masculine scent. For the first time since all this had started, she felt at peace, confident, as though Jared had loaned her his strength.

Stunned, she pulled away, then caught herself. Maybe Isobel was right. Maybe she needed to let down her walls a little.

"I'm fine." She inclined her heard toward the uniformed officers. "I'm not worried—I have nothing to hide."

"What are they searching for?"

"I assume drugs." She shrugged.

Jared frowned. "Did you see a copy of the warrant?"

"Yes. I didn't really look at it."

He drew back, his dark gaze shuttered. "Ask if you can see it again."

"But why? I don't think—"

"Almost done." Officer Yost came over. With his normally friendly expression dour, he seemed like a different man, one out of place amid the intently bustling searchers.

Jared squeezed her shoulder.

With a sigh, Elena gave in. "Officer Yost, may I take another peek at the search warrant? My *fiancé* here—" she indicated Jared "—wants to know what you're searching for."

At the word *fiancé,* Yost appeared at a loss for words. His mouth worked, but no sound came out. He cleared his throat, shooting a glance at his partner for assistance.

"He wants to see the warrant? I bet he does." Officer Trenton stepped forward, his mocking tone completely inappropriate. "Especially since we're searching the clinic next." He spun on his heel and strode away, heading to assist the others trying to move a heavy filing cabinet so they could look behind it.

Shoulders sagging, Yost remained rooted in place. Staring at Elena, he searched her face before exhaling loudly. "Fiancé? When did this happen?"

Jared tightened his arms protectively. "Easter Sunday."

"Really?" Though Yost's tone sounded mild, his expression wasn't. "Congratulations." Back stiff, he walked away, barking out orders directing the rest of his searchers toward the clinic.

"What the heck was *that?*" Elena couldn't believe it. "Officer Yost has always been friendly before. He's the one who called to tell me about the autopsies. What happened?"

"I think he's jealous." Jared pulled her closer. "He wanted you for himself."

Since they were alone, Elena knew there was no longer any need to pretend anything. Yet she felt reluctant to leave his side, which confused her. Pushing him away, she took off down the hall after the police team. Jared followed close behind.

For some reason, the search seemed more thorough in the clinic. The searchers yanked open drawers, dumped the contents on the floor and rummaged through before moving on to the next. They upended canisters of gauze and cotton balls, emptied boxes of sterilized syringes, though they thankfully didn't tear open the individual bags.

"We received a tip about this place," Office Trenton said casually. "And if we find what we're looking for, your fiancé will have some explaining to do."

"You won't find anything here." Jared sounded confident. "Only medical supplies. I don't keep any personal belongings here."

"We'll search anyway."

Jared shrugged. "Suit yourself."

This time Yost stepped forward. He looked almost apologetic as he glanced from Elena to Jared. "Our search warrant doesn't include this, but would you mind if we searched your vehicles?"

Suddenly they'd made this thing personal. Furious, Elena started to protest. But Jared tossed the man a set of keys. "Go for it. Mine's the black Mercedes parked out back."

"Jared." Elena grabbed his arm. "You don't have to—"

"Yes, I do." He gazed down at her, his expression unreadable. "They won't find anything. Like you, I have nothing to hide."

Trenton grinned. "What about you, Ms. Cabrera?"

Though she knew they'd find nothing in her car, at this point it was a matter of principle. "You're not touching my vehicle until you come back with a warrant. Understood?"

Narrow-eyed, he nodded. Snatching Jared's keys from Yost, he strode toward the door. With one final apologetic look at Elena, Yost followed him.

Jared cursed under his breath. "Do you get the feeling…"

"That something's wrong? Yes. Come on." Propelling him forward, she headed toward the door. "Let's go watch and make sure they don't damage your car."

They arrived as Trenton opened the Mercedes's door and two officers searched the interior. Yost talked quietly. Yost remained behind, by Elena's side, while Trenton and crew began the search.

"Do you smell that?" Jared asked, his nostrils flaring. "I recognize that smell. It's…" He grabbed Elena's arm. "This is not good."

Yost raised his head. Looking for all the world like a bloodhound, he sniffed the air. "I'd say you're right, Dr. Gies."

Even Trenton's cocky grin wavered as he opened the trunk. As soon as he peered inside, he recoiled and gagged. Then he swore.

"Better call for backup," he said, a tinge of nausea mixed with the triumph in his voice. "There's a body in here. From the looks of things, it's been dead awhile."

Chapter 14

As they slapped the cold steel handcuffs over his wrists, Jared could think only of Elena. Even though seeing the shock and pain in her huge caramel eyes felt like agony, he couldn't bear to look away.

Elena. Mate. Beloved.

Her mouth worked, as if she meant to voice a protest. But, caught in the surreal circus of police and bodies, she froze. Watching him. Because she had no shifter blood, he couldn't read her thoughts and had no idea what she felt. Disappointment? Disbelief? Anger? All emotions coursing through him.

Surely she didn't believe he'd killed anyone. He wished she'd go back inside, get away from here. He didn't want her to see him like this.

Next, he thought of his mother. While Yost read him his rights in a monotone voice, Jared prayed she wouldn't come outside. He could guess how she'd react. No matter how he'd disappointed her in the past, he was still her cub, her youngest child. She'd be furious, and her first instinct as a mother would be to lash out at those who hurt him. The last thing he needed was for her to go all feral on him.

Could things get any worse? He imagined they were about to.

"I didn't do this," he said, to no one in particular. "Someone set me up."

Yost didn't comment. Trenton snorted.

Jared glared at the officer, daring him to say one friggin' word. The other man thought about it, then shook his head and turned away. Yost finished reading the Miranda and asked Jared if he had any questions.

Shaking his head, Jared muttered a no.

If there was a God… For the first time in a long time, Jared began to pray.

"I didn't do this," he said again.

"I know you didn't." Elena, standing beside the squad car, looking both fierce and determined. "And believe me, we're going to prove that."

Then, to his shock and disbelief, she leaned in and pressed a firm kiss on his mouth.

"Don't worry," she murmured. "We'll figure out something."

Was that love he saw in her face? Trust shining from her eyes? He didn't dare hope, especially not now, when things were going so horribly for him.

"Come on, buddy." One of the junior cops tried to close the door. "We've got to take you in and have a little chat."

"Wait." Elena stepped in front of him. "Is he being charged?"

"Not yet," Yost said glumly, steering her out of the way. "But he probably will be. Preponderance of evidence and all that."

The last thing Jared saw before the patrol car pulled away was Elena's beautiful, serious face, full of determination.

Watching as the police led Jared away, Elena actually looked down to make sure her chest hadn't been ripped wide-open. As she stood frozen, unable to move or think or cry, the remaining officers got busy securing the area with yellow police tape, waiting for the Crime Scene Unit to arrive. Most of them had grim faces, trying not to show a reaction to the stench of decaying flesh.

Despite the awful smell, Elena tried to move forward to peer into the trunk. She'd just caught a glimpse of something—a familiar pinky ring—that made her gasp when two uniformed cops stopped her.

"Crime scene. Sorry," said one.

"I still don't know the body's identity." She tried to see past them, to get one more look, but one grabbed her arm and forcibly turned her around.

"Neither do we." Moving to her side, Trenton gave her a narrow look. "The medical examiner will have to determine that. The body is really decomposed."

Decomposed.

"That proves what Jared said. He didn't do this." Dragging her hand through her hair, she struggled to keep her voice neutral. "The odor is awful, unbearable."

"So?"

"I've been in his car recently and there was nothing—no smell."

Trenton shrugged. "Maybe he just moved the body into his trunk this morning, on his way to dispose of it."

"But why park here? Why risk someone complaining about the stench and being found out?"

"Who knows? Sometimes we never can figure out what these guys are thinking."

"These guys?"

"Perps." Trenton's smile widened. "You know, criminals."

Wanting to shriek aloud at the policeman's stupidity, Elena bit her lip and said nothing.

"Enough," Yost said, touching his partner's arm. "Leave her alone."

Shaking his head, Trenton moved away. Meanwhile, Yost continued to stare at her. "Are you okay?"

She blinked. "Not really." Then she remembered, things were about to get even worse. Jared's mother was inside, watching the show. How on earth would she tell Isobel that her son had been arrested?

Raising her chin, she squared her shoulders. Most of her employees, except those actually working, clustered around the back exit, watching her.

"Do you need anything further from me?" she asked the policeman.

"We'll need you to make a statement," he said, scratching the back of his neck. "But we can do that when we're finished here."

She didn't even bother with a reply. Turning, she marched to the back door and her waiting employees.

They all began speaking at once, peppering her with questions.

"Not here." She raised her hand. "In my office. Now."

They fell into step behind her.

Once she reached her office, she stepped aside and motioned them all in. It would be crowded, but they'd fit. Once the last dancer had filed inside, she closed the door and waited until they were all watching her.

"The police came here with a search warrant, looking for drugs." Her grim voice let them all know, in case they'd forgotten, how she felt about that.

"Did they find any?"

"No. Not this time." She let her hard gaze linger on each of them, looking for signs of guilt. "But as you could see, they found a body in Dr. Gies's trunk. Do any of you know anything about that?"

Again they all started talking at once. Waiting, she scanned each of their faces, looking for any sort of a hint that they might have known.

When they finally quieted down again, she sighed. "The police can't tell yet, but I think the body might be Dr. Watkins."

"Why?" Dixon asked. "Why would you think such a thing?"

"I saw a pinky ring." Elena shuddered. "The dead man had a pinky ring just like Dr. Watkins's."

"So, Dr. Gies is a murderer," Dixon said, his voice smug. "I thought so."

One or two others agreed.

"No," Elena protested, glancing around the circle of her employees and wondering if she really knew any of them. Were even the shifters siding against Jared? "He's not."

"Dr. Watkins was his friend." Ryan stepped forward, expression fierce. "I don't think Dr. Gies did this."

With a feeling of relief, Elena studied him, remembering Jared had said he was Pack.

"Oh, yeah?" Dixon crossed his arms. "If he didn't kill Dr. Watkins, who did?"

"I don't know." Elena fought the panic clawing at her throat. She wanted to believe in Jared so badly it hurt. "Why don't you help me find out?"

Several others murmured their agreement. A few more shook their heads and voiced their dissent.

"You know what?" She paused, waiting until they all went silent before continuing. "Those of you who want to help me, let me know. It appears to be up to me to prove the cops wrong. I've got to find the real killer."

Luis spoke up. "Really? What are you going to do now?"

Taking a deep breath, she willed herself strength. "Find Jared's mother and let her know what's happened."

She headed toward the club, dreading what she had to do.

Isobel rose when Elena entered, then hurried across the floor to meet her. Elena took her arm and led her out the private entrance into the hall. "I need to speak to you."

"What's wrong?"

Leaving nothing out, Elena filled the older woman in.

Shock turned into anger as Isobel listened. "Hell hounds." Then, before Elena could respond, Jared's mother lifted her chin and set her jaw. "Well, I'm not going home now. You and Jared need my help."

Jared paced. They'd put him in jail. Hell, what had he expected? There'd been a body in his trunk, after all. Though he'd told them he hadn't killed anyone so many times he felt like a caricature of a bad cliché, they hadn't believed him.

He wished he could shake the feeling that being in jail was his karma catching up to him. That too many years of self-indulgence, not caring who he hurt or how badly, had given him exactly what he deserved.

If not for Elena, he suspected he might have been more accepting of his fate. But because of her, he would fight and win. He hadn't killed anyone, which meant the real murderer was still out there and a threat to the woman he loved.

Being kept in this ten by nine cell until a judge somewhere could decide whether to allow him bail was driving him insane. But he couldn't escape—even if he became wolf, he couldn't squeeze through the metal bars. His desperation was so great he still considered trying. If he were ever to have a prayer of proving his innocence, he had to escape. But how?

They hadn't even let him have his one phone call. In retrospect, he supposed he was glad. He didn't know what he'd do if he called Elena and she refused to speak to him.

"You have a visitor," the gruff-voiced, female jailer

announced, moving out of the way so Jared could see the dark-haired woman standing behind him.

Elena.

Blinding joy filled him, even though he didn't know whether to feel shame…or relief.

"Your mother's with me." She moved closer to the bars. "I asked her to give us a few minutes of privacy before she came in."

His mother. Crap. He closed his eyes, then opened them again. "Send her home."

"She won't go."

"She has to. I've disappointed her enough." To his shame, his voice broke. "She's going to need a ride to the airport."

Elena's serious expression made him want to kiss her until she smiled. She shook her head. "Not now. She says she's staying until she gets you cleared of this. I'm voting for simply getting you out of jail. One step at a time." When she did finally smile, it looked weak.

He couldn't blame her. The entire police force had decided he was guilty. It would take a miracle to get him out now. The guard had told him she doubted the judge would even set bail. Her smug smile made him want to howl.

One step at a time. He repeated Elena's words, finding calm determination.

"Tell my mother to go home. She doesn't need the stress. She can't help me now."

"She's your mom. Of course she's not going to leave." Elena took a deep breath, her expression serious. "They've identified the body. It's Watkins."

Swallowing, he looked away. "I'd hoped…" He didn't finish the sentence. She had to know that he'd hoped against hope the dead man hadn't been his friend.

"The police are formally charging you with his murder. They say they've got enough evidence to go to the D.A."

Her tone reminded him of the way he used to be—flat, emotionless. That way nothing could touch him, nothing could hurt him. Until he'd met Elena and realized how beautiful emotions could be.

"They're wrong." Taking a deep breath, he struggled to suppress a shudder, but failed. "I didn't kill Watkins." Desperately seeking insouciance, he tried for a grin. From the look on Elena's face, he only half succeeded.

"Jared…"

Bracing himself, he watched her. Here it came, what he'd been expecting all along. She didn't have any reason to trust in him. He'd never given her any.

Gaze locked with his, she crossed her arms. "I believe you," she said softly.

Dumfounded, he could only nod.

She moved closer, until she'd pressed herself against the bars. "We need to figure out how his body ended up in your trunk. He was a large man. It would take more than one person to lift him."

Taking a deep breath, he tried to pretend his blood wasn't roaring in his ears. She trusted him—him. Until that moment, he hadn't realized how awesome something like that would feel.

Jared cleared his throat. "Someone is trying to frame me."

"I agree." She accepted this without question, making him love her even more. "Any idea who? Or why?"

"I don't know."

"Then I guess I need to find out." She gave him a hard look that made him want to kiss her long and deep.

To keep from doing exactly that, he dragged his hand through his hair. "I have no motive for killing Watkins. He was my friend. Pretty much my *only* friend. They've got to keep looking."

"What do you think, that they'll miraculously find the real killer and let you go? I'm pretty sure that since they have you, they've stopped looking."

He had no choice but to concede the point. "Let's make a list of my enemies." His self-depreciating laugh was painful to his own ears. "Not counting all the doctors, nurses and patients I pissed off at Parkland Hospital, let's start with your dancers. You've got several that don't like me." He gave her a hard look of his own. "You know who they are."

She nodded. "Shifters and humans." The casual way she spoke made him realize she'd grown more accepting of his kind.

"And Valerie. She was involved in those experiments—whatever they were—with Watkins. She even tried to recruit me."

"Valerie's harmless." Elena shook her head. "She's family. She wouldn't do anything to hurt you or Watkins."

"Luke was dating her."

"I know. So?"

"She doesn't seem too broken up about his death."

"She was, even though they'd already split up. She cried for days. Plus, my cousin has always been fickle."

"Elena, I know she's family, but please—don't assume anything. Talk to her. She knows the truth about whatever experiments Watkins was working on."

He took a deep breath, hating himself, but knowing it had to be said. "I have a feeling she knows what happened to Damien and Luke, as well. Obviously there's a lot more going on here than just dancers using drugs."

Chewing her bottom lip, Elena finally nodded. "Fine. I'll talk to her."

"Be careful."

"You, too. As soon as the judge sets bail, I'll get you out."

"*If* he sets bail."

"Oh, I think he will." She winked. "He's dating one of my other cousins. She's promised to talk to him." Pushing away from the bars, her expression sobered. "Let me send in your mother. While you two talk, I'll make some calls and see what I can get done."

Isobel entered the room with her head up and her color high. Fury radiated from her. The instant Jared saw her expression, he knew she barely held her temper in check.

"Easy, Mom," he cautioned. "Now is not the time to make waves."

Her nostrils flared. "Someone is trying to frame you," she growled. "When I find out who, I'm going to rip them apart, limb by limb."

"Settle down."

"I don't want to settle down."

After twenty minutes of hard argument, he managed to convince her to take another flight home. He thought. One could never be certain with his mother. "This is going to be a long, drawn-out process," he told her. "While I appreciate your support, there's really nothing you can do. Go home and come back when and if I need help. I promise Elena will keep you posted."

Isobel said nothing, finally shaking her head and leaving.

After everyone had gone, Jared tried to sleep. But his wolf, edgy from all the amplified emotions, wouldn't let him. The beast inside didn't understand why they couldn't change and hunt.

In the morning, the guard told him the judge would set bail soon. Two hours after this news, Jared had another visitor.

Valerie. She came alone, a baseball hat pulled low over her face, her shoulder-length hair tucked under it. She wore a loose, man's cotton shirt and baggy jeans. With her basketball shoes, she could easily have passed for a teenage boy. He wondered if that was her intention.

"Elena sent me to post your bond." Her low voice sounded sullen. "I came to get you out."

Startled, he searched her face, finding no answers in her closed-off expression. It made no sense that Elena would send Valerie.

The guard behind her unlocked the cell door. "That's right. You're free to leave."

As the door swung open, Valerie motioned him out. "Let's go."

He followed her through the hall and through three

electronically locked doors. Several guards waved them on, so she had to be telling the truth.

"Why didn't Elena come herself?" he asked.

Valerie didn't answer. "Come on," she ordered. "We don't have much time."

Unimpeded, they reached the front desk. Signing him out, Valerie waited for the buzzer before pulling the door open. "Hurry. I brought my friend's van."

They hurried across the parking lot. When they reached the white panel van, she opened to back door. "In here."

He balked. "I'd rather ride up front. In fact, I'd rather call a taxi." He began backing off.

"Don't be stupid." Valerie crossed her arms. "Elena sent me. She said to tell you if you want to find out who really killed Dr. Watkins, then to do what I say."

Since Jared suspected Valerie might be the killer, he doubted Elena had said any such thing. Still, since she'd gone to such elaborate lengths to set him up for the murders, he doubted she would hurt him. Hell, maybe she might even confess.

Reaching a quick decision, he climbed in the back of the van.

Instead of going around to the drivers' side, Valerie got in after him.

"What are you doing?"

She grinned. "We're gonna let you have some fun."

At first, he thought she was making a pass at him. Talk about bad timing. Too late, he saw the syringe just as she plunged it into his arm.

He jumped, cursing. "What the hell is that?"

"What do you think?" She grinned a vicious grin.

"I'm putting you out of commission for a while. This is even better than your former drug of choice. The kiddies call it cheese."

Cheese was a mixture of black tar heroin and cold medicine. Highly potent and frequently unstable, too high a dosage had gotten dozens of kids killed.

"I'm screwed," Jared said, already feeling dizzy.

Her grin widened. "In more ways than one. You've got something I need for the experiment and once I've taken it, I'm going to set things up so there's no doubt you killed Watkins and the rest of them."

"But you posted my bond. They saw you…" Already his tongue had gone thick.

"No, they saw a young man. I used fake ID. They'll never connect me to you."

"Why?"

"We were close on the experiment. Actually it's a spell. We had to use drugs to get them to agree."

Climbing into the front seat, she started the engine. "Watkins wanted to stop when he saw what the drugs were doing to the Halflings, but he got hooked on his own mixture. He killed himself, Jared. Accidently, I think." She shrugged, uncaring. "With drugs."

"How'd you get him into my trunk?"

"Junkies will do anything for a fix." Her grin was pure evil. "A couple of street people helped me out. I paid them back with such pure drugs they suffered fatal overdoses."

"What's the ex…ex…?" He tried to finish his question, but couldn't wrap his tongue around the word *experiment*.

It didn't matter. Valerie told him anyway. "I'm using magic. I found an old book of spells in a used bookstore. The right mixture will help me become a shifter. Luke helped me by impregnating Missy. I need bone marrow from a Halfling fetus. That's the final ingredient that will turn me into a wolf."

Impossible. Horrified, he tried to speak, to tell her so, but couldn't. He closed his eyes, opened them and watched the rise and fall of his chest, amazed he was still breathing.

Time became meaningless. When he woke—or he thought he might be awake—he couldn't move. He spent an eternity lying flat on his back staring up at the sky in wonder.

Or was it the sky? Ceiling? Despite something niggling in the back of his brain, exultation and joy flooded him.

He was high. Finally, at long last, gloriously high. The whens, whys and hows seemed irrelevant. Deep inside, he'd been craving this. The pleasure of gratifying his needs felt immense.

Happy. So happy. Then why the tears streaming down his face?

If not for the nagging sense that there was something else, something he should remember, he thought he could laugh out loud.

What was the thing he needed to remember? He had no idea.

Elena.

Who? Sluggish, he shook his head, struggling to hold on to the name.

Elena. Mate.

A low growl escaped him. He rubbed his eyes, feeling grit, struggling to stand. Once on his feet, he swayed and the world spun.

Floating. He fought himself, fought the dizziness, the drug. Must. Concentrate. Must.

Elena.

Briefly his head cleared. With a sudden clarity he remembered his arrest, the jail, Valerie with the needle. Then nothing, until this.

Where was he? He tried to look around, the movement causing such vertigo, he staggered and fell to his knees. Damn this. He couldn't seem to clear his head. And…did he smell smoke?

Elena carried her steaming cup of Seattle's Best coffee to her back porch and tried to relax.

Ignoring the twelve messages concerned relatives had left on her answering machine, she'd gone to bed an hour after getting home, without eating. Despite her craving for sleep, she'd spent a restless night, tossing and turning, haunted by images of what could happen to Jared in jail.

She had to get him out.

Her phone rang. Again. Glancing in disinterest at the caller ID, her heart sped up when Dallas Police flashed on the display.

A few minutes later, numb and in shock, she put down the phone.

Jared's bail had been set. He'd already posted bond and left.

Wherever he'd gone, it hadn't been to her.

Quickly, she phoned his apartment and spoke to Isobel. He hadn't contacted his mother, either. Isobel hadn't heard from him.

Heart pounding, Elena paced, trying to settle her jangly nerves. Where would Jared have gone? And why would he have disappeared without a word to her?

Something was wrong. Whoever had engineered this whole thing had some sort of master plan. Whatever it was, she was certain Jared wouldn't come out on top of things. She feared that before all this was over, he'd end up dead.

Glancing at her cell phone, she checked the charge. Jared had the number. If he could, she knew he'd call.

In the meantime, nothing would be accomplished by sitting around waiting. She'd go out and look for him, praying she could find him before something worse happened.

She'd start by going to Fantasies. Maybe one of the other shifters would have an idea where Jared might have gone.

Heat. He felt fire, red-hot flame, licking the soles of his feet, wanting to consume him. The drug kept him from caring, but he forced his eyes open and saw a wall of fire maybe ten feet away.

An inferno. Still doped up, he laughed out loud. He'd finally made it to hell, where he belonged.

Still, he got to his knees. He wasn't ready to die. And the devil couldn't have him—not without a fight.

He had to get away. Or at least try.

Stupidly blinking, he remembered enough to keep his

face low to the ground—not difficult when he'd passed out on his stomach.

Something in his arm hurt. Glancing down, he saw a huge bruise and marks from a needle. This time, he'd bet Valerie hadn't given him more drugs. She'd taken his blood, how much he had no way of knowing. Probably a lot, which would account for his weakness. She'd even left the rubber tourniquet tight around his forearm.

Cursing, he yanked it off. Coughing smoke, trying to breathe, he looked around, knowing he should be wild to run, to escape. Dimly he registered the overturned can of gasoline near his feet

"What the…?"

Where was he? The thick smoke made it hard to tell. He climbed to his feet, willing his strength to return, at least enough to carry him out of the inferno.

Elena's club. He was inside Fantasies. In the room he'd used for a clinic. He recognized what was left of the built-in countertops.

Evidently Valerie had brought him here, then set the place on fire with him inside, setting it up to make it look like arson gone bad. Fire was one of the only ways to kill a shifter. Obviously Valerie had known.

Pushing himself on his hands and knees, he began to crawl in the direction of the door. He hoped.

"Jared? Are you here?"

A voice. Familiar. Beloved. As he tried to concentrate, an image flashed into his face of a beautiful woman with olive skin and dark, lustrous hair.

Elena. His mate. The fog clouded his mind began to lift. If she was here…she was in danger, too.

He *had* to clear his head. Somehow…overcome…the drug. *Somehow.*

"Jared?" she called again. This time he recognized fear rather than hope in her voice.

Hell hounds. He couldn't let her risk her life. He had to save her.

Chapter 15

Gathering every ounce of his strength, he covered his face with his shirt and pushed to his feet. At standing height, the smoke was worse, thick and choking.

"Here," he rasped, then rethought. "No! Elena… Get out! Now!" Doubling over as a spasm of coughing hit him, he tried to determine from where her voice had come. Every cell in his body urged him to get outside, away from the heat and fire and smoke, but damned if he was going without his mate.

"Jared?" she called again.

Where the hell was she? And why weren't the ceiling sprinklers doing their job?

Lurching forward, he spotted her silhouette in the doorway on the other side of the room. The flames hadn't reached her yet.

She saw him at the exact same instant.

"Jared!" Joy mingled with fear in her voice. To his disbelief, she started toward him, as though she thought she could walk through fire.

"No. Get out," he rasped. "Hurry. Go."

"Not without you." She kept coming, until only ten feet—and a wall of flame—separated them. Black smoke billowed between them, making it hard to see or breathe.

Coughing, she held out her hand, then swayed. "I don't—" Before she finished, she crumpled and fell to the floor.

His heart stopped. He had to get her out. He started toward her, fire be damned.

Flame exploded, shooting across his line of vision, searing his back. Instantly he dropped, praying Elena hadn't been incinerated.

The smoke. Damn it. Hard to see. To breathe. Moving forward, unsteady, he pushed in to the fire, ignoring the pain.

Reaching a still-unconscious Elena, he grabbed her under both arms and pulled her toward the door. The heat was intense. If they stayed too much longer, they'd both die.

The smoke-filled hallway was even worse. He couldn't see more than a foot in front of them.

Keeping low to the floor, he dragged her in the direction of the back entrance.

A loud pop signaled fire breaking through something. The wall?

Miraculously they made it to the steel exit door.

Pushing at the metal bar to open the door, Jared realized it had been locked from the outside.

"Hell hounds," he cursed, though Elena couldn't hear him. There had to be another way out, if only he could think. Still weak from loss of blood, the drug Valerie had given him…still hampered him.

Maybe if he changed… *If he changed to wolf…* Would the act of changing purge the drugs from his system? He had nothing to lose if he tried, and everything to gain.

Head down against another rush of dizziness, he took a deep breath, tore off his clothes and began.

Without waiting for the thought to leave him, he dropped back low to the ground. Willing his body to change, to become wolf *now,* he fought to not sink back into the calming oblivion caused by the drugs.

An instant later, he was wolf, staring at his human mate passed out again on the floor. He couldn't scent her, not with the acrid smell of the smoke filling his sensitive nose.

Using his teeth, he grabbed hold of Elena's leg, clamping on to the denim and praying the material would hold. Pulling, he succeeded in dragging her maybe six inches before the material tore.

Leaving her for a moment, Wolf Jared crept along the smoke-clogged hall, belly low to the floor. The marble tiles were hot; a testimony to the searing heat.

Yet once in the hall he realized, though the black smoke and lack of lighting made seeing more than a few feet in front of him impossible, the fire still seemed to be confined to the area around the clinic.

For now.

If he didn't find a way out, they'd die from smoke inhalation long before the flames ever reached them.

"Jared!" Elena. The sound of her voice had him pivoting on all four legs.

She was awake. Forgetting he was wolf, he ran.

"Jared?" Elena appeared, crawling through the smoke toward him, her face half covered with a wet cloth. When she saw the wolf, she froze, then nodded.

"Jared?" The question wasn't really a question. "Help me get out of here." She coughed. "I have a key, but not sure I'm strong enough to use it. Change back."

He thought she'd look away when he began the change, so he rushed it, praying the time he'd spent as wolf had expunged the drugs from his system.

Man again, he grabbed his boxers and stepped into them, then dragged on his jeans.

Elena stumbled, then fell. Looking up at him through the smoke, she tried to speak, but only succeeded in a fit of coughing. She handed him a key.

Moving quickly, he scooped her up and carried her to the door.

The heat was getting worse.

Fumbling, praying, he finally succeeded in fitting the key in the lock. The door swung open. Behind him, fueled by fresh air, the fire swelled.

He stumbled, but grabbed Elena and got them outside, agonizing as she went limp in his arms. Laying her carefully on the small patch of grass between the sidewalk and the street, he began immediate CPR, praying silently all the while.

If he lost Elena, he wouldn't want to go on living.

Behind them, the fire roared, consuming the old building, destroying mortar and wood and anything else in its path. In the distance he heard sirens coming closer, proving help was on the way. Still, he didn't stop, determined to ensure that his mate would live.

As the fire trucks and ambulance drew nearer, Elena opened her eyes. "You can't stay," she rasped. "If they find you here, they'll put you back in jail."

He ignored her. No way was he leaving her side until the paramedics arrived and he knew she was okay.

"What happened?" Brow furrowed in concentration, she grabbed his arm. Quickly he told her about Valerie, how she'd sprung him from jail, only to drug him and try to kill him in the fire.

"The prison will have cameras." Elena sounded satisfied. "They'll prove what you've told me."

Warmth spread through him as he realized she'd accepted his explanation without question. "She was dressed like a boy and used fake ID."

"They can enhance the video. I'll make them aware of what happened."

"She's setting me up." He remembered something else she'd said. "She said she needed something else from me, though I don't know what it was." Quickly he outlined the crazy story Valerie had told him.

"I won't let her do this to you." Elena kissed him. "To us."

He nodded, hoping they'd believe her. "Be careful." He kissed her back.

As Elena had predicted, the police followed the firefighters and paramedics. As soon as he saw Elena on oxygen and being checked over by the medical workers, he turned to face them.

Officer Yost stepped in front of him, service revolver drawn. Jared held up his hands. "I'm out on bail."

"Your bail's been revoked." Officer Trenton slapped on the cuffs, his expression inscrutable. "You're under arrest."

"For what?"

"Let's start with adding arson to your list of charges," Trenton said in a conversational tone. "The fire department is sending over their arson investigator."

As Jared got into the patrol car, he glanced over his shoulder, searching for Elena, wanting to see her one last time. But the door closed and the car drove away.

His enemy had infiltrated the jail the last time and could do so again. If she did, Jared was certain Valerie would kill him this time, eliminating the witness.

What he couldn't figure out was what Valerie planned to do next. Somehow, he was betting she'd move against Elena.

She'd said she needed one more thing…he struggled to remember. Something about… His heart stopped. No. Melissa's unborn child. Surely Valerie wouldn't hurt the teenager just to get to the baby.

He had to call Elena. Before it was too late.

Elena had done some fancy talking to avoid going to the hospital. After dealing with the arson investigator, who'd confirmed that they'd located an accelerant, and her insurance agent, who informed her they would pay nothing until a thorough investigation was completed, Elena finally let her shoulders sag. She needed Joy, needed her rock-solid, sensible nature.

But several attempts to reach her sister hadn't worked. Joy didn't answer her home phone or her cell. Melissa was also strangely unavailable.

Rubbing the back of her neck, Elena headed for her car. She'd run over to Joy's house and check on them on her way back to the jail to see Jared. Paranoid, maybe. But after all that had happened, she'd feel better once she knew for sure they were all right.

Joy's place seemed deserted. No cars in the driveway, no answer when Elena rang the doorbell. She tried phoning again while parked in the driveway, but had no success.

As she set off again, her cell phone rang. Joy—finally!

"We're at Parkland Hospital," Joy said, before Elena finished saying hello. "Someone attacked Melissa and tried to drag her into a van."

"Where?"

"In the shopping mall parking lot. A man saw and helped her escape. But she's hurt." Joy sounded as though she fought back tears. "I don't know if she's okay, or the baby."

"I'm on my way." Closing the phone, Elena made a U-turn at the first intersection and headed in the direction of the hospital.

"One phone call," Jared pleaded. "I know I'm allowed at least that."

The guard's stony face told him he didn't have a snowball's chance in hell.

"Come on, man." Jared tried again. "Someone's life depends on me making this call."

The man snorted, then wiped his nose with the back of his beefy hand. "Try again, dude." He rolled his eyes. "I wasn't born yesterday." And he walked off, leaving Jared locked in the cell.

"I have to call Elena," he yelled to the man's disappearing back. "If I don't, someone else might die."

Pacing his cell, Jared considered his options. He had one shot. True, Pack law forbade it, but he didn't give a rat's ass about Pack law right now. Not when his mate was in danger.

If he could get a guard—any guard—to open his cell door, he could make his phone call, tell Elena about the danger and then change. As wolf, Jared could outrun humans anytime, though he couldn't outrun their bullets.

At least a regular gunshot wound or two wouldn't kill him. Only silver bullets or fire could do that, which Valerie had obviously known. He supposed he should be thankful that she hadn't had a gun.

From his last stay in this jail, Jared knew the guards changed shifts every six hours. His best chance would be to hope for a different guard.

He was in luck. He watched as the stone-faced guard exchanged keys with a younger, taller man. Waiting until he was certain the first guard had left, Jared went to the bars of his cell.

He'd try another tactic.

"Excuse me, sir?"

Tapping his nightstick against his thigh, the man came over. "What?"

"I haven't made my one call yet. I'd like to do so now, if that would be all right with you."

Evidently his polite, deferential tone pleased this guard. "Let me check the log book to make sure you're telling the truth. If you're not lying, I'll see what I can do."

He strolled off. Jared could only hope he'd return.

Melissa was unconscious, the huge bruise on her cheek a testament to her ordeal. The doctors were running tests and until they got the results, all anyone could do was wait. Joy hadn't called the rest of the family— no one knew about Missy's pregnancy and she didn't want them to find out until they knew how Missy was doing.

Though Joy didn't want to leave Missy's room, Elena convinced her, saying that ten minutes wouldn't hurt anything. Joy was so tightly wound, she looked as though she could shatter. Elena wanted to distract her and help her regain some semblance of calm before Melissa woke.

Arm tucked firmly in her sister's, Elena hustled Joy down to the hospital cafeteria.

Since dinner hour was long past, they had the austere room almost to themselves. Steering Joy through the checkout line, Elena kept up a steady stream of chatter, all of it filled with positive, hopeful comments.

"Missy will be fine. They'd have her in ICU if it was something serious."

"True, but what about the baby?" Tears rolled down Joy's plump cheeks. "She just told me," she sobbed. "And I really am looking forward to being a grandmother. Even though Missy will pull through, the doctors said there's a chance she might lose the baby."

As Elena was about to answer, her cell phone rang again. She glanced at the caller ID, intending to let the call go to voice mail, but when she saw the readout said Pay Phone and Justice Center, she punched to answer.

"Jared?"

"Yes. Where's Melissa?"

Startled, she told him what had happened.

"I'm certain Missy's attacker was Valerie." He didn't waste time on pleasantries. "I'm not sure why, but she needs another Halfling for her experiment, whatever it may be. She took my blood and I know she wants something from Melissa's baby."

Shocked, Elena jumped to her feet. Across the table, Joy poked her fork aimlessly into her salad, oblivious.

"But—"

"Trust me on this." The urgency in his voice galvanized her. "Don't leave Melissa alone, not even for a second. I'm not sure what Valerie might do."

"She's alone right now," Elena whispered. "Oh my God, Joy and I are in the cafeteria."

"Go!" he urged. "Run."

Snapping her phone closed, Elena grabbed her sister. "Joy, come on. We've got to hurry."

Joy looked up, uncomprehending. "Why? What's going on?"

"I'll explain on the way." She took off running, trusting Joy to follow. Sprinting, Elena headed past the elevator, planning to take the stairs.

But Joy, right behind her, pushed the button and miraculously, the doors opened immediately.

The ride to the sixth floor seemed to take an eternity. Heart pounding, Elena explained what Jared had told her. Joy clutched her hand in a death grip. Even though she felt too agitated to stand still, Elena forced herself to offer her sister whatever comfort she needed.

As soon as the elevator doors opened, they took off running, skidding to a stop in front of Melissa's room.

Back to them, Valerie had sneaked into the room and was leaning over the bed, a pillow in her hand.

"Stop!" Elena ordered. "Get away from her."

Valerie spun, still clutching the pillow. "I…"

Elena rang for a nurse. "I want Melissa checked out immediately," she barked into the intercom. "Stat."

Joy pushed past Elena, shoving Valerie aside. "She's family, Val. What have you done to my daughter?"

"What have I—?" Valerie frowned, attempting to bluff. "Surely you don't think…?"

"Jared's still alive," Elena told her bluntly. "He told me everything."

A nurse came bustling through the door, her sneakers making no sound on the linoleum. "Can I help you?"

Joy explained her worries, asking the nurse to thoroughly check her daughter. The woman glanced at Valerie and Elena, then went to the phone and punched a series of numbers.

"What are you doing?" Valerie asked, standing and appearing poised to flee. Fury sparked in her eyes and when she looked at Elena, her gaze was full of hatred.

"I've called security. All of you please stay where you are."

"I will." Defiantly Valerie crossed her arms. "I've done nothing wrong."

An alarm on one of the machines hooked to Melissa began shrieking. The nurse pushed a button on the console and turned to them. "You all need to leave the room. An emergency team is on the way."

Before she'd even finished speaking, a group of people burst through the doorway, pushing a shiny metal cart.

In the confusion, Valerie slipped out into the hall and took off running.

"Don't let her get away," Elena shouted at two orderlies rounding the corner. "She tried to kill a patient!"

Without hesitation, the two men grabbed Valerie, holding her by the arms while she kicked and screamed. When security arrived, the officers walked her back toward Elena and Joy. The orderlies stayed with them as backup.

"What did you do to Melissa?" Elena asked. "Tell me, so we can tell the doctors."

Valerie made a rude sound and an even ruder gesture.

Another group of people—doctors and nurses—rushed past them, heading for Melissa's room.

"They're too late." Valerie smirked. "Nothing can help her now."

Elena grabbed her cousin by the front of her shirt. "What did you do to her?"

Glancing at the clock on the wall, Valerie laughed. "Your precious Missy's not in any danger. I gave her misoprostal to induce labor." She laughed again. "Hell of a nice way to have a baby, don't you think? She's unconscious. She won't feel a thing."

"Misoprostal?" Elena looked to an orderly.

"It's a drug sometimes used to induce labor."

"But," the other orderly chimed in, "high doses of it have caused uterine ruptures, severe vaginal bleeding, shock and even fetal and maternal death. There are lawsuits out there. How far along is the patient?"

"Barely five months. That's too early, isn't it? The baby will die."

"A preemie in Homestead, Florida, survived after just twenty-two weeks in the womb. It's possible." But his tone indicated it wasn't likely. He pulled a walkietalkie from his belt. Speaking softly, he relayed the information to someone. "Now at least the team working on her will know what they're up against."

Elena's throat ached. "Is there any chance—" Her voice broke. "Any chance they can stop the labor and save the baby?"

The man met her gaze. What she saw in his expression wasn't encouraging. "I'm sure they'll do all they can."

"The baby will die." Unbelievably Valerie appeared happy at the prospect. "It has to. I need the bone marrow from its body."

Horrified, Elena stared. How had she missed her cousin becoming a monster?

"Why?" she asked.

Valerie smiled. "I found an old formula in a sixteenth century book of magic. It's a powerful spell. Each ingredient has to come from a different Halfling."

Elena shook her head. "Do you hear how crazy you sound?"

"I'm not crazy," Valerie snarled. "I want to be able to change into a wolf, like them. I had everything I needed. Damien's teeth, Luke's hair and skin, Jared's blood. The only thing I need is a Halfling baby's bone marrow. Luke got Missy pregnant on purpose, just so I could use the baby's marrow. But when Watkins found out, he said enough was enough. Turns out he didn't even believe in the spell. He said he couldn't let me hurt an unborn baby."

"You're not getting my grandbaby's bone marrow." Joy stepped forward, face furious. "I can promise you that."

"I have to," Valerie pleaded, her expression crafty. Madness shone in her brown eyes.

"Luke was helping you?" Elena couldn't contain her disappointment. She'd liked and trusted Luke.

Valerie laughed. "He thought he loved me. Until Damien accidentally overdosed. Then, Luke freaked out. He still helped me get the body into your bathroom. But both he and Watkins claimed they wanted to stop me. I couldn't let them do that, now could I?"

"That's why Dr. Watkins disappeared, isn't it? You killed him."

"No, I didn't." Valerie smirked. "I made the man a slave to drugs. He never left my room."

"He was your prisoner."

"Mine and the needle's. The man couldn't even think for himself, he stayed so loaded all the time."

Elena turned away, unable to bear looking at her cousin any longer.

"You have everything that should have been mine,

Elena," Valerie continued. "Even Watkins thought he wanted you instead of me. Luckily you didn't want him. Once I become a shifter, I will finally have something you won't."

"You killed them all?"

"Not hardly. Damien did it to himself. I helped Luke along with a little injection. And Watkins, he said only a silver bullet or fire could kill him, but he was wrong. I injected him with way too much heroin, and he overdosed. Guess he wasn't so much of a super werewolf after all."

"Now you're trying to kill Melissa."

Valerie shrugged, unconcerned. "She should be all right. I just want the baby."

The security men exchanged a look. One of them glared at Valerie. "The local police have been notified."

The two orderlies also exchanged uneasy glances. One rolled his eyes. "At least she can use insanity as a defense."

Anger helped Elena hold back her tears. Gazing at Valerie, the cousin she'd known since childhood, she struggled to understand. "But why, Valerie? Why would you want to do such a thing?"

"As if you don't know," Valerie spat. "I hate you. *Hate* you. My own mother loved you more than me. Mother should have left Fantasies to me, not you."

Finally the police arrived. After the security guards informed them of Valerie's actions, the police handcuffed her and led her away.

"I'm not finished," she shouted over her shoulder at Elena, struggling with the officers. "I can't leave until I finish the spell."

Elena dug in her purse until she found Officer Yost's

card. Now that Valerie had confessed, she needed to see what she could do to get Jared set free.

He hadn't been too late. Jared breathed a sigh of relief. When Officer Trenton had come personally to release him, he'd filled Jared in on the doings at the hospital. Valerie was in custody and everyone was safe— if the baby could survive the early birth.

The police officer had even been kind enough to drive Jared to Parkland Hospital and drop him off.

Exiting the elevator, Jared spotted Elena and took off running. She met him halfway, flinging herself into his arms. His heart sank when he realized she was crying.

"What is it?" He held her tight. "Is Melissa…"

"They're working on her now." She gestured down the hall. "They've got two medical teams in there. Valerie gave her something to induce labor."

"What?" He asked the question urgently. The doctor part of him flared to life. "What did Valerie give her?"

She spelled the name of the drug. "An intern told me there could be other, even more serious consequences."

The drug was familiar to him. He didn't tell her some of the horror stories he'd read about in medical journals. "If they can save Melissa—"

"But the baby…" She wiped at her eyes. Lower lip trembling, she tried hard not to break down completely. "It's too early. The baby will die."

"There have been cases…"

"I know." But she didn't sound hopeful. "They told me."

He grabbed his cell phone, punching in a number.

Speaking in a low voice, he relayed his information tersely, extracting a promise to hurry.

"Samantha's on her way from Anniversary. She should be here in thirty to forty-five minutes."

"Samantha? The healer?" For the first time hope shone in her eyes.

"Yes. This baby will be a Halfling. Samantha can help make sure the preemie survives. There'll be a long hospital stay, of course, but if anyone can help…" He prayed he was right and also that the baby survived long enough for a healer to help. Healers could only heal, they couldn't bring back the dead.

Now the tears flowed in earnest. "Thank you." She grabbed his hand tightly. "Come on. Let's find Joy and tell her."

"I've got to speak with the doctor in charge of Melissa's case. He needs to delay delivery as long as he can."

He let her lead him down the hall to Melissa's door. Joy was outside the room. Since the medical staff still worked frantically, they wouldn't let family members in.

"Wait here." Jared pushed open the door.

"Hey, you can't—"

The attending physician recognized Jared. "I won't ask what you're doing here, Dr Gies." Professional respect rang in the other man's tone. "But since you are, we don't need a diagnostician. She's contracting and dilated enough to give birth. It's doubtful the infant will sur—"

"The baby will live." Jared let his firm tone tell all the people in the room that he would accept no alternative. "I'm bringing someone else in. We need to delay delivery as long as we can."

The other man stared. "What difference does that make? A few minutes more or less won't matter. It's too early."

"She's twenty-eight weeks along." Jared spoke with authority. "Not beyond the realm of possibilities. After all, that baby in Miami was only twenty-two weeks."

Melissa cried out, her body arcing off the bed. Her eyes opened, finding Jared. "What's wrong? What's happening?" She shrieked again. "It hurts!"

Jared grabbed her hand. "Everything's going to be all right, Melissa." He used the comforting, assured tone of a caring medical professional. "Don't worry."

"My baby?" Expression frantic, she watched his face. "What about my baby?"

Jared lifted his chin. "We're trying to help her."

"Her?"

He couldn't say how he knew. "Yes, her. You're going to have a daughter."

For a brief moment, elation shone in Melissa's flushed expression. "Her name is Nichole," she said. Then another contraction hit her, and she screamed.

Despite their best efforts to delay, little Nichole was born thirty minutes later, just ten inches long and weighing nearly eleven ounces. The nurses rushed her to the preemie room, where she'd be placed in an incubator.

"Pray for her," one of the nurses said bleakly as she bustled out of the room.

Frantic, Melissa struggled to sit up. "What will happen now? What will happen to my baby?"

Jared glanced at his watch. "I've got help on the way. A Halfling healer." Quickly he explained about Samantha. "If anyone can help Nichole, she can."

Finally Joy and Elena were allowed into the room.

"Samantha should be here soon," Jared said.

"I've filled Joy in." Elena put her arm around her sister's shoulders. Joy was looking completely stunned. "Do you really think she can save Nichole?"

Jared nodded. "She's a healer. This baby is Pack. If anyone can find a way, she can."

His pager went off. "She's here. I'll go get her."

"Wait." Elena grabbed his arm. "I'll go with you."

He shook his head. "No. I've got to get her into the preemie room, which is a flagrant breach of security. You stay with your family. Melissa needs you. Joy needs you, too."

Slowly Elena nodded.

"I'll send her husband to stay with you."

Again, Elena agreed.

Jared could feel her watching him as he hurried off.

Once Elena and Joy began to call, news spread fast in the Cabrera family. They started arriving at the hospital while Jared and Samantha were still in the preemie room. Samantha's husband, Luc, had chosen to wait in the cafeteria, telling Elena good-naturedly that Jared's emergency call had interrupted his dinner.

Elena couldn't have eaten to save her life. She'd left Joy watching over a sleeping Melissa and tried to see into the preemie room, but a nurse turned her away. Though this nurse grumbled to Elena about Dr. Gies ordering the neonatal nurses out of room, she said she'd seen him save so many lives that she trusted him despite his suspension. She told Elena she believed he'd do his best to save the tiny newborn, though quite frankly her compassionate expression spoke more loudly than words. The nurse didn't believe such a premature infant could survive.

Just in case, as Missy's mother, Joy gave her permission for Dr. Gies and Samantha Herrick to take care of baby Nichole.

Elena returned to the waiting room, trying to make small talk with her parents, who'd paid Missy a quick visit before settling in to wait. Every few minutes, the elevator doors opened and more Cabreras emerged.

Soon, every seat in the small waiting room had been taken. A kind nurse rustled up more plastic chairs, which helped, but the crowd overflowed into the hallway and close to the nurses' station.

Isobel Gies arrived shortly after, looking once again as though she'd stepped from the pages of a glossy fashion magazine.

Elena mustered up a weak smile for Jared's mother but said nothing, unable to tear her gaze away for long from the preemie room down the hall. A small cluster of nurses still peered through the windows, effectively blocking the view. They reminded Elena of vigilant angels, watching over their tiny charges.

"He brought the healer in there to heal the baby," Elena whispered.

Isobel nodded, patting Elena's shoulder. "Don't worry. Everything will be all right."

But time seemed to move at a crawl.

Finally the door opened and Jared, his arm around a clearly weak Samantha, emerged. He half-carried her over to the crowded room, settling her on a chair.

As if he'd been paged, Luc appeared and gathered his exhausted wife in his arms. "Did it go well?"

The room fell silent as everyone waited for Samantha's answer. She licked her lips, tried twice to speak and, failing that, finally nodded.

"Let me get you home." Luc's tender expression reflected the adoration he clearly felt for his wife. As though she weighed nothing, he scooped her up in his arms and carried her off, dipping his chin in a goodbye to Jared.

Immediately the entire family began talking at once.

Jared crossed to Elena and took her hand. "Nichole's going to be fine. She'll have to stay in the preemie unit awhile, but eventually she'll be strong enough to go home."

Relieved, Elena leaned forward and brushed her lips over his mouth. Her kiss was slow and soft and as full of love as she could make it.

Behind her, someone cleared her throat.

"Mother!" Jared rose, bringing Elena up with him. "I thought you agreed to go home."

"Like I would ever leave while my son was in jail!" Sniffing, she leaned forward and kissed his cheek, then she also kissed Elena's. "I'm so glad you found each other," she declared. "Elena, tell him about your little cousin who died."

"Please, Mom," Jared cautioned. "Not now."

Elena grinned at Isobel, feeling like a coconspirator, though they hadn't even talked. Her entire family watched avidly, all except Joy and Melissa. What better time than now to start the rest of her new life?

"Jared," she said, tugging on his arm. "I need to ask you something."

He swung around to face her. "Go ahead."

Enjoying the shock on his handsome face, she dropped to one knee in front of him. "Jared Gies, I love you. Every single bit of you. You're the other half of my soul. You asked me once before, and I didn't give you a real answer, so I'll ask you here, now. Will you do me the honor of becoming my husband?"

Apparently speechless with shock, he didn't move. While the clock on the wall loudly counted out the seconds, he stared down at her, silent.

Finally she realized he wasn't going to answer.

Expectation turned to uncertainty, then to pain. Slowly she climbed to her feet, avoiding his gaze, avoiding looking at her entire, silent family. "I understand. My mistake. I thought your offer from Easter still stood. After I doubted you, I can understand why you don't want me now."

"Don't *want* you?" The words appeared to burst from him. "Elena, how could you think such a thing? I love you, I adore you, you're mine. My mate. Of *course* I want to marry you."

She started to smile, freezing when he held up his hand.

"But I need to know you're certain. Absolutely, positively, one hundred percent sure you can accept me as I am."

Only she—and Isobel—knew what he meant. He wanted to know how she felt about his other half, about his wolf.

"More certain than I've ever been about anything." She let her voice convey her wonder. Briefly, she told him about her cousin's death so many years ago, and how she'd devoted her life to trying to make amends. "I found comfort in the familiar, peace in taking no chances. But now, I'm in awe of what you can do." She paused, knowing he would understand. "You're beautiful, Jared. Every aspect of you. And in addition to that, you've been given a great gift. You're a doctor. You have the ability, the compassion, the training to heal."

Unable to resist, she kissed him again. Long and deep and certain. As he kissed her back, she melted into him.

The entire Cabrera clan began clapping. One or two of the nurses even joined in. Even Isobel Gies applauded, the expression on her face welcoming and full of delight.

Pink-cheeked and flushed, Elena turned in Jared's arms and faced them.

Just then, Joy poked her head out of Melissa's room, frowning. "What's going on out here?"

Several Cabreras, including Mom and Pop, rushed over to tell her. "The baby's fine?" she asked, her gaze finding Elena, who smiled and nodded.

As Joy began to weep from happiness, everyone began talking at once. Jared tightened his arms around Elena, kissing the top of her head.

"Welcome to the family," she said, still smiling.

He looked from Elena to his mother, then down the hallway to the door where tiny Nichole slept. "And welcome to the Pack," he told her, low-voiced, so only she could hear. And he kissed her, claiming her for all time as his mate.

* * * * *

The Colton family is back!
Enjoy a sneak preview of
COLTON'S SECRET SERVICE
by Marie Ferrarella, part of
THE COLTONS: FAMILY FIRST *miniseries.*
Available from Silhouette Romantic Suspense
in September 2008.

He cautioned himself to be leery. He was human and he'd been conned before. But never by anyone nearly so attractive. Never by anyone he'd felt so attracted to.

In her defense, Nick supposed that Georgie could actually be telling him the truth. That she was a victim in all this. He had his people back in California checking her out, to make sure she was who she said she was and had, as she claimed, not even been near a computer but on the road these last few months that the threats had been made.

In the meantime, he was doing his own checking out. Up close and exceedingly personal. So personal he could feel his blood stirring.

It had been a long time since he'd thought of himself as anything other than a law enforcement agent of one type or other. But Georgeann Grady made him remember that beneath the oaths he had taken and his devotion to duty, there beat the heart of a man.

A man who'd been far too long without the touch of a woman.

He watched as the light from the fireplace caressed the outline of Georgie's small, trim, jean-clad body as she moved about the rustic living room that could have easily come off the set of a Hollywood Western. Except that it was genuine.

As genuine as she claimed to be?

Something inside of him hoped so.

He wasn't supposed to be taking sides. His only interest in being here was to guarantee Senator Joe Colton's safety as the latter continued to make his bid for the presidency. Everything else was supposed to be secondary, but, Nick had to silently admit, that was just a wee bit hard to remember right now.

Earlier, before she'd put her precocious handful of a daughter to bed, Georgie had fed his appetite by whipping up some kind of a delicious concoction out of the vegetables she'd pulled from her garden. Vegetables that, by all rights, should have been withered and dried. She'd mentioned that a friend came by on occasion to weed and tend it. Still, it surprised him that somehow she'd managed to make something mouthwatering out of it.

Almost as mouthwatering as she looked to him right at this moment.

Again, he was reminded of the appetite that hadn't been fed, hadn't been satisfied.

And wasn't going to be, Nick sternly told himself.

At least not now. Maybe later, when things took on a more definite shape and all the questions in his head were answered to his satisfaction, there would be time to explore this feeling. This woman. But not now.

Damn it.

"Sorry about the lack of light," Georgie said, breaking into his train of thought as she turned around to face him. If she noticed the way he was looking at her, she gave no indication. "But I don't see a point in paying for electricity if I'm not going to be here. Besides, Emmie really enjoys camping out. She likes roughing it."

"And you?" Nick asked, moving closer to her, so close that a whisper would have trouble fitting in. "What do you like?"

The very breath stopped in Georgie's throat as she looked up at him.

"I think you've got a fair shot of guessing that one," she told him softly.

* * * * *

*Be sure to look for COLTON'S SECRET SERVICE
and the other following titles from*
THE COLTONS: FAMILY FIRST *miniseries:*
RANCHER'S REDEMPTION by Beth Cornelison
THE SHERIFF'S AMNESIAC BRIDE
by Linda Conrad
SOLDIER'S SECRET CHILD by Caridad Piñeiro
BABY'S WATCH by Justine Davis
A HERO OF HER OWN by Carla Cassidy

Silhouette®

Romantic
SUSPENSE

**Sparked by Danger,
Fueled by Passion.**

The Coltons Are Back!

Marie Ferrarella
Colton's Secret Service

The Coltons: Family First

On a mission to protect a senator, Secret Service agent
Nick Sheffield tracks down a threatening message only
to discover Georgie Gradie Colton, a rodeo-riding single
mom, who insists on her innocence. Nick is instantly
taken with the feisty redhead, but vows not to let his
feelings interfere with his mission. Now he must figure
out if this woman is conning him or if he can trust her
and the passion they share....

Available September wherever books are sold.

**Look for upcoming Colton titles
from Silhouette Romantic Suspense:**
RANCHER'S REDEMPTION by Beth Cornelison, Available October
THE SHERIFF'S AMNESIAC BRIDE by Linda Conrad, Available November
SOLDIER'S SECRET CHILD by Caridad Piñeiro, Available December
BABY'S WATCH by Justine Davis, Available January 2009
A HERO OF HER OWN by Carla Cassidy, Available February 2009

Visit Silhouette Books at www.eHarlequin.com   SRS27598

REQUEST YOUR
FREE BOOKS!

2 FREE NOVELS PLUS 2 FREE GIFTS!

Silhouette®

nocturne™

Dramatic and Sensual Tales of Paranormal Romance.

YES! Please send me 2 FREE Silhouette® Nocturne™ novels and my 2 FREE gifts (gifts are worth about $10). After receiving them, if I don't wish to receive any more books, I can return the shipping statement marked "cancel." If I don't cancel, I will receive 4 brand-new novels every other month and be billed just $4.47 per book in the U.S. or $4.99 per book in Canada, plus 25¢ shipping and handling per book plus applicable taxes, if any*. That's a savings of about 15% off the cover price! I understand that accepting the 2 free books and gifts places me under no obligation to buy anything. I can always return a shipment and cancel at any time. Even if I never buy another book from Silhouette, the two free books and gifts are mine to keep forever.

238 SDN ELS4   338 SDN ELXG

Name _____ (PLEASE PRINT) _____

Address _____ Apt. # _____

City _____ State/Prov. _____ Zip/Postal Code _____

Signature (if under 18, a parent or guardian must sign)

Mail to the **Silhouette Reader Service:**
IN U.S.A.: P.O. Box 1867, Buffalo, NY 14240-1867
IN CANADA: P.O. Box 609, Fort Erie, Ontario L2A 5X3

Not valid to current subscribers of Silhouette Nocturne books.

Want to try two free books from another line?
Call 1-800-873-8635 or visit www.morefreebooks.com.

* Terms and prices subject to change without notice. N.Y. residents add applicable sales tax. Canadian residents will be charged applicable provincial taxes and GST. Offer not valid in Quebec. This offer is limited to one order per household. All orders subject to approval. Credit or debit balances in a customer's account(s) may be offset by any other outstanding balance owed by or to the customer. Please allow 4 to 6 weeks for delivery. Offer available while quantities last.

Your Privacy: Silhouette is committed to protecting your privacy. Our Privacy Policy is available online at www.eHarlequin.com or upon request from the Reader Service. From time to time we make our lists of customers available to reputable third parties who may have a product or service of interest to you. If you would prefer we not share your name and address, please check here. ☐

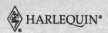

nocturne™

COMING NEXT MONTH

#47 DEADLY REDEMPTION • Kathleen Korbel
Daughters of Myth
War threatens all the faerie clans. To help restore
balance, the queen's daughter, Orla, is sent to the enemy
clan as a hostage bride to Liam the Avenger. Now they
must negotiate their tempestuous marriage as they work
to save their world from destruction....

#48 THE NIGHT SERPENT • Anna Leonard
Lily Malkin is an ordinary woman—or so she thinks. Until
she's caught up in a ritual-murder investigation led by
Special Agent Jon Patrick, and Lily discovers she's been
stalked through her nine lives by the Night Serpent. Will
this life be her last?